THE
MISSING
SISTER

THE MISSING SISTER

ELLE MARR

THOMAS & MERCER

Text copyright © 2020 by Elle Marr
All rights reserved.

Published by Thomas & Mercer, Seattle

www.apub.com

Amazon, the Amazon logo, and Thomas & Mercer are trademarks of Amazon.com, Inc., or its affiliates.

ISBN-13: 9781542006057
ISBN-10: 1542006058

Cover design by Shasti O'Leary Soudant

Printed in the United States of America

For Kevin

I was too young that time to value her,
But now I know her. If she be a traitor,
Why so am I: we still have slept together,
Rose at an instant, learn'd, play'd, eat together;
And wheresoe'er we went, like Juno's swans,
Still we went coupled and inseparable.

—*William Shakespeare*

I smile because you are my sister.
I laugh because you can't do anything about it.

—*Unknown*

Chapter 1

Day 1, Sunday

Come to Paris. Your sister is dead.

The rest of the words from Sebastien's email fade against these opening sentences. The world slams to a halt—again—and I suck in another stupid, shocked breath as though it's the first time I'm reading his email instead of the eighty-second.

"Nous sommes arrivés, mademoiselle." The cab driver speaks to me without turning, wide charcoal eyes peering curiously through the rearview mirror. He yanks the parking brake. Stubby fingers push buttons on a digital console displaying the cost of my trip from the airport in euros. The route to Montmartre passed in a blur despite unrelenting morning traffic. Children run wild on the sidewalk beside us, high on summer vacation, fast food wrappers trailing their bands of twos and threes. The urban doorways of this northern pocket of Paris alternate between adult film rental businesses and glass panes leading to residential apartments. Voices rise above the engine's rumble, words in French carrying through the window; a couple examines an accordion on a collapsible table.

I hesitate before locking my phone, then logic reigns; I count out what I owe. One thing I truly appreciate about Europe: unlike American currency, euros correlate in size to their value; the tiny ten-cent coins are dwarfed by the fifty-cent pieces, which are half the weight of the euro coins. I couldn't care less about the precise artistry of the European continent on each face.

Angela was born a mere two minutes before me, but she took with her the creativity of the womb, leaving me to steep in pragmatism.

Where is she now? Is she in some drawer? Is it cold? Is she alone?

"Merci, monsieur." I place the money in the driver's grooved palm, then exit the cab. Pairs of people move across the open square of the adjacent Pigalle metro stop, as if the buddy system is obligatory—everything better with someone else there to share it. Twin girls with yellow hair skip rope by a fountain, and a breath whooshes out of me as I watch them. Over the fountain's spouts a sculpture of the Greek goddess Persephone hunches. Her carved expression howls with sadness, and tears of pigeon shit frame her mouth.

When Angela first arrived, she sent photos of herself in front of the Eiffel Tower with silk scarves wrapped around her dark hair, sunglasses covering half her face. Her Grace Kelly phase from adolescence never fully expired. It was Angela's sense of poise—the confidence that she could rival a princess—that made her so enthralling to men and women. The only stranger I ever idolized was Marie Curie.

Different scenarios leaped to mind when I read the first email from Sebastien saying Angela was missing—then the second, then the third, announcing her death. I tried to rationalize the irrational: Angela was over their relationship and stopped returning his calls. Angela took an impromptu trip to Turkey (her way of moving on). Angela packed up in the middle of the night and changed apartments without telling him. My sister loved a dramatic exit almost as much as a romantic beginning.

I was wrong. After struggling through French headlines on *Le Monde*'s website about a shooting at the Sorbonne University, where Angela was doing doctoral research, I started the calls. I left ten messages on Angela's voice mail. I called a dozen different numbers associated with the Paris police and spoke with indignant Parisians who could not understand my shitty French. When the American embassy contacted me as Angela's next of kin, the news became real. When Inspector Valentin called to inform me of Angela's probable homicide, it became a nightmare.

"Bracelets, mademoiselle?" A man in a torn T-shirt lurches into my path, waving red and white woven bracelets two inches from my face. He dangles another at my nose, grabs my hand to slip it on my wrist, but I jerk away.

"No!"

He reacts like I slapped him—eyebrows up, open mouth. I add *merci* to my curt rejection, but he's already approaching a young family. *Deep breath. You just got here. Chill the fuck out.* I shake the sudden tension from my fists and look upward to the sky. Clear blue strung with wispy cirrus clouds fills my vision as I wait for the clenching fear to pass.

Angela's apartment building is neighbor to a grocer's stand and faces the sprawling expanse of the city block. Along a narrow street opposite the metro stop, a farmers' market is underway. Friends kiss each other's cheeks as they pause—more shoppers than I've ever seen at a San Diego market—enjoying the atmosphere, probably making lasting, happy memories. The sweeping melody of an accordion intones the charming soundtrack Paris is known for and makes me grind my teeth.

I set down my duffel bag before the austere wooden entrance to Angela's building. Thanks to a trip to France we took as a family, I recall Montmartre was the center of Parisian street art about a century ago. Artists splay in chairs beside colorful tableaus or black-and-white photographs every five feet.

I like art—the kind diagramming nervous systems and the human body, sketches from the eighteenth century. Not the kind delineating hopes and desires. Abstract art and the indefinable have always seemed like a waste of time to me.

Give me reason. Give me finite.

Not Angela. My twin sister's uncanny ability to zero in on whatever bleeding heart was nearest in the room was a running joke in our family. We would say she could hear a fly being swatted two houses down. She loved the emotions and complexity of a moment, whether in art, books, or a chubby child's glance at a passing ice cream truck.

Once I was reading on the back porch and heard her crying. I set down my dinosaur book and found Angela inside our tree house giving a memorial service for a butterfly whose wings she'd accidentally torn off. Not knowing what to do, I hugged her and told her we could bury the insect like a dinosaur. Then someone would find its fossil one day. We used the box from my new microscope as the coffin and a sheet of newspaper for a cushion, not yet understanding the process of fossilization.

The call box of her building displays her name—DARBY ANGELA— and every cell in my body seems to draw another stupid, shocked breath that this is happening. I press her button. In spite of myself, I imagine her light cadence answering: *Good day, Moon.*

Tears well in my eyes, seeing her so clearly I could pull her from my thoughts. I lean into the metal bars—cool on the sudden flush that heats my cheek—while my knees bang against the wrought iron gate of the glass entryway. Sobs climb my throat, clawing to air the pain that balls my fists, when a man, late twenties, appears, standing behind the glass. Startled, I step back as he opens the door; his tall frame barely fits within the shadowy entry.

"Bonjour, mademoiselle." Dark hair is parted meticulously to the side. "Shayna?"

I steel myself in the company of this stranger, who I now realize must be my sister's boyfriend. A man I didn't know existed until his emails arrived. "Yes, that's me."

"I am Sebastien. Call me Seb," he adds. His accent wrestles with consonants in English, making them thick and adding extra syllables. *Call me Seb-uh.*

In the narrow hallway, aquamarine walls emphasize lustrous marble tile. The temperature instantly plummets once I'm inside, the chill jolting my senses. I wipe my chin as the door shuts with a vacant click. What if Angela were the one greeting me instead of this *Seb-uh*? She would have rushed forward, thrown her arms around me—our last words, spoken in anger, forgotten—and squeezed until I heard a vertebra crack. I would have protested, groaned aloud, but inwardly loved it, had I ever visited while she was alive.

Our footsteps ring through the lobby as Seb leads me to a winding iron staircase, past a single door marked CONCIERGE. Beneath, atop a bristly doormat, headlines blaze from a newspaper's front page. Most of the text could be in Russian, for all I recognize it, but the side column's title I know immediately: Traffic. Instead of feeling gratified I'm reading French in Paris, irritation tenses my jaw; the daily commute is what makes the news around here, not my sister's death.

"May I?" Seb takes my duffel bag, then raises both eyebrows at its light weight. Clothing for only three days makes for easy travel. We step onto the stairs, single file, before he abruptly turns back.

"Please forgive me." With a trembling finger, he touches the hair at my shoulder. "You are exactly identical. Except—"

"My eyes, I know." I step back in the confined space. The look on his face disturbs me. Is that longing? Desire? For Angela, obviously. I'm a sad substitute for what has been taken from us both.

Seb leans in closer, and his scent is musty, like a library or a coat retrieved from a winter storage bin. "Forgive me. Is one eye green?"

I nod, pressing against the railing of the staircase. The metal digs in above my kidneys. "Angela's are both brown. It's the only way we differ. Phenotypically." As identical twins, Angela and I have gotten this kind of curious reaction all our lives. The stares, the awed giggles. It's old hat for me and beyond tactless on Seb's part in this situation, regardless of whether he's in mourning, too.

"How unusual for a Chinese woman. Half—of course. Your Scottish side is probably where that green comes from." Seb releases a sigh. "Your mixed heritage was something Angela was very proud of."

Seb dissolves into tears, dropping my bag. His broad shoulders shake as his large hands cradle his face. One moves to his heart. I glance to the second floor for help, then back toward the front door—but we're alone. Part of me wants to sympathize with him and share Angela experiences together, to revel in our memories of her and support each other as best we can. Instead I stand frozen, hoping he remembers who he is and who I am as quickly as he lost his shit.

A sob-hiccup escapes from his fingers.

My hand rises, hesitates at his back, then pats lightly.

I have no idea what the hell to say here. Seriously. I just want to do what I came to do and go home. I'm holding on by a thread myself and can't spare a second of comfort for anyone else. A grimace slides down my face as I recall all the material left to review so I'm up to speed before classes start in a week. It sounds callous, but finally starting medical school is all that's kept me going these last few weeks, last few years. My parents and I have been working toward this since high school, and it's only now within reach. Angela, on the other hand, was never interested in following such a traditional path. She always munched baguettes to her own beat—obsessed with World War II, literature, and cultures since we were kids. *The odd lady out,* she liked to say. Hence why she stayed on as a doctoral candidate in the Sorbonne's history program.

At least, that's what she'd decided three years ago—the last time we talked.

Seb takes a measured breath. "Please excuse me. It has been a very hard time." Deep-blue eyes dart to mine. "I am so sorry, I mean, of course you know that. Angela is your sister. It is—"

"Fine. I'd just like to get up to her apartment. Whenever you're ready," I add, relieved that he's stopped blubbering. Does that make me heartless? No. It makes me pragmatic, efficient, and no doubt mired in some selfish stage of grief.

He sniffles, then continues up the stairs, bag in hand. We move at a melancholy pace. When we reach the landing of Angela's floor, Seb turns to me with a weak smile. I stand awkwardly while he digs in his pockets for the key.

"I'm sorry, I don't know much about you," I begin. "Do you live here? How long have you known . . ." *No.* "How long did you know my sister?"

He pauses, examining the key ring. A pocket flashlight hanging from it catches the light. "She did not share much about me?"

I flounder for the right words. Even I'm aware of how hurtful this could be. "No. Well, we really haven't spoken in three years. Since our parents' funeral."

He nods. "I feared as much—she was always very private. We did not live together, but we were in a relationship for a year before . . . before the shooting."

Hearing the words in person drives reality home in a way that was missing while processing details alone in San Diego. I let down my guard a little. "You know, your emails were pretty confusing at first. You said Angela disappeared in a shooting at the university, then you wrote that she died. I thought she'd been shot, but the police said they found her in the river. Is that right? Did the shooter take her?"

"You did not have an English speaker discuss with you?"

"The inspector spoke English, but the connection was pretty bad each time."

Seb turns an ancient key in a gray door, the only door in this blunted hallway. "I see. I was so distraught when I wrote to you, my English must have translated poorly. She disappeared during the chaos, and the shooter killed himself. Her body was found ten days later in the Seine, unidentifiable but for her tattoo. The police still do not know who is responsible for her death."

"Tattoo?"

"The one on her ankle." He stoops to lift his pant leg, revealing a Gemini astrology symbol on his own ankle. Two vertical pillars are bookended by horizontal curves—a Roman numeral two, bent at the top and bottom. The symbol for twins. "We got them together one day, after she said I was her other half. Her twin. Figuratively, of course," he adds, checking my reaction.

The hurt I feel throbs all over, pierces my jaw. Angela refused to come home for Mom and Dad's memorial service. Then she had the nerve to replace me, her only family left, with this yahoo—even figuratively.

A cold wave of remorse replaces my outrage. I will never have the chance to bicker with her again. To make up and apologize for my own self-absorbed actions years ago. My sister is gone.

Fresh tears prick my eyes. "Are we going inside?"

Seb doesn't move. Instead, he places a hand on my shoulder. "You will identify the remains, then help me clean out her apartment, yes? I would also like to recount her last steps together if you think it is possible. The police do not know how she got from campus to the river. No other student was removed from school property in this sense. We must find out who targeted her and what happened. I could never replace the knowledge of a true twin," he adds, lowering his head.

Long lashes, the kind to make any housewife in Orange County jealous, cling to his skin, still wet. I nod. For the first time since I arrived, a flicker of hope ignites that coming here was the right thing to do. I owe it to Angela to learn more about her last years. To meet the people—the life—she chose as her own.

He opens the door, allowing me to pass through first. On a whiteboard above a desk at the far end of Angela's studio apartment is her familiar scrawl. My heartbeat quickens seeing her writing—maybe one of the last things she ever wrote.

But as Seb closes the door and turns the lock behind us, I realize the words on the whiteboard aren't in English or in French. Instead, I recognize the childhood language Angela and I invented, the one we used whenever we didn't want our parents to know something. As we got older and grew apart, the language became a throwback to more innocent times.

I inch closer to the whiteboard, while Seb moves to the bachelor-size refrigerator in the corner.

Greek letters written in Angela's slant cover most of the whiteboard. Your average kid from San Diego would probably consider Greek an alien language—especially with the letters written backward and upside down, as they are here—but not us. The dots and swishes that decorate the flat tops of the symbols form a pattern that feels like home. I absorb the words as casually as if it had been weeks instead of years since my sister and I last exchanged notes.

Too casually. Too fast to really grasp their meaning. I read a second time. A third. I blink, and the symbols pulse through my eyelids and set fire to the brief reprieve of calm I felt a moment earlier.

"Are you thirsty? Hungry? How are you feeling?" Seb rummages in the kitchenette cabinets, then stops when I don't answer.

Every exposed hair on my legs, arms, and neck stands on end. Angela's message to me reads:

ALIVE. TRUST NO ONE.

"Shayna?" Sebastien's voice is at my ear. "How are you feeling?"

No one. Not even her boyfriend? The man with a key to her apartment and hands the size of waffle irons.

I turn to face his barrel chest and raise my eyes to his.

"Parched."

Chapter 2

When we were kids, a clear dirt path still existed from our home straight to the beach, to a sandy inlet only a handful of intrepid surfers claimed as theirs. Nowadays, most paths in the area, and in San Diego as a whole, are laid in concrete, brick, or wooden boards. *Filters,* Angela would say as we got older, *standing between us and what is real.*

The cool dust that covered our feet and crept up our ankles and told us we were alive back then led us to a cove, an earthy chute that spit us out from encroaching suburbia and into a world of magic. Seagulls and hidden crabs waited along the water's edge and beneath the sand, sometimes under stubborn rocks that would relent only to four tiny hands. Seagulls were part dog, in our mind, the way they followed us around, and we named them—*No, that one's Rory, not Fred.* We expected a message to be hidden in every bottle we came across and that at any moment a mermaid would surface near the horizon and flip high in the air. The dirt path was a gateway to discovery; it was there we first started babbling in our own made-up language. We drew tentative scribbles in the sand until they became consistent shapes with meaning, opening a new dimension of possibility.

Moon, Angela would say to me as I frowned in concentration, *let's make our own magic.*

We stuffed napkins with our words into soda cans and set them adrift, certain a reply would come.

Turns out, I only had to wait twenty years for one to turn up in France.

✤

Seb busies himself getting me water from the kitchen while I cross to a sweeping window with open shutters. The square below boils with life. I turn away. The outdoor warmth cloaks my back, making the apartment frigid by contrast.

Angela's studio is utilitarian, a perfect square, with wooden beams protruding from the ceiling. The largest furniture item is the twin bed tucked against a wall, a simple white comforter draping its frame. The kitchen nook is squeezed in the left corner, beside a closet-size bathroom and a set of drawers.

I look anywhere except the whiteboard.

"I'm really tired," I announce. "Would you mind if we start cleaning later today? Jet lag is catching up, and it's three in the morning for me."

Seb regards me, not speaking. A breeze flicks a dark strand of hair across my face, but I don't move. Holding his eye contact feels important for some reason, like if I don't, he'll see right through me—that I'm not actually tired, but rather that potent adrenaline is flooding my veins.

He nods. "I will return this evening. I live on the Left Bank, so I will be here by seven o'clock, if that is okay."

"Sounds good."

He turns to leave, casting another sorrowful glance upon Angela's personal items and the tiny bed they probably shared.

"Sebastien?"

"Seb. Yes, Shayna?" His voice brightens, as though I might put off my nap.

"The key?" I hold out my hand, wondering whether it's his only copy. The floorboards moan as he crosses to me. Two keys dangle next to the pocket flashlight of the key ring—one, a regular aluminum kind similar to my own house key in my suitcase; the other, three inches of metal, almost an inch wide at the base, that looks like it was forged in a blacksmith's shed circa 1562. Like it once belonged to a jailer.

He hesitates above my open palm, then steps back. "Do you know what this note reads?"

I flinch. "Note?"

He shrugs toward the whiteboard beside me. "I have never seen her draw that way before. It was here when I came looking after she disappeared. I have been trying to figure it out for weeks. There seems to be some kind of pattern."

My teeth catch my lip. "She used to doodle a lot as a kid."

"Doodle?"

"Draw, I mean. Since we haven't spoken in a few years, you might have a better guess than me." I turn and close the shutters halfway, my attempt at subtlety—*Goodbye, Seb.* I turn back. "When were you here last, before she disappeared?"

His gaze shifts to over my shoulder. A child screams laughter somewhere beneath us, the sound fading into high-pitched giggles. After another beat, he places the keys in my hand. "Maybe a few days prior. The note could have been there then, only I did not notice it. Enjoy your nap, Shayna. Welcome to—" He stops himself with an abrupt noise. "Well, I am glad we met."

I lean against the windowsill, watching him leave. The door closes. My breathing stutters to a gasp.

ALIVE. TRUST NO ONE.

As kids on the beach, we made up our own language by inserting a nonsense syllable after each vowel. In the third grade, we took the idea one step further and started writing it down, inserting the symbol for pi—two vertical bars with a squiggly line on top—as the nonsense syllable. When both of us became interested in mythology in the fifth grade, we translated the letters into Greek and wrote them backward and upside down. Accents and semicolons were added to each top horizontal line to confuse the casual viewer, a form of insurance. No one else knew our secret code. No one else could've duplicated it.

She is alive. My twin is alive.

My chest buckles, punching the air from my lungs. Faltering, half-formed breaths struggle for depth.

Single births always wonder at us, the multiple births. News outlets feature stories about one twin getting into a car accident and the other twin feeling a jolt of pain and fear on the other side of the city. I didn't feel anything three weeks ago. No terrible ache, no spasm of fright. When Seb emailed me, I wondered if my lack of premonition was somehow because I had stopped being a good twin, if I had forsaken our supposed ethereal bonds and now we were like any other siblings. If I was to blame because I didn't feel and share in her pain, left her to shoulder the suffering of her death alone.

Angela is alive.

My head falls forward, and hot tears spill down my cheeks and onto the mess of discarded papers beneath her desk. Key words pop from the titles of the books piled at my feet. *History. Paris. Ancient. Twelfth century. Famine. War.* An encyclopedia in French rests on top of a small inkjet printer. As much as she enjoyed a good story, Angela never read the fluff that decorated supermarket checkout stands. We're alike in that way.

The note could have been there then. Seb's words rebound in my head as I stare at the whiteboard message. Half of the final symbol is missing, partially erased. What if this message was written a month ago in a bout of nostalgia? What if this is a cruel inside joke or a note to self? Dates occupy the lower-left-hand corner of the whiteboard, also partially erased—4/7, 4/1, 4/. Ghosts of other notes that were wiped away to make space remain—*hrough*, and *ave bewitched me*—and a list of words in French I don't have the context to guess. I press my cheek against the wall beside the whiteboard and squint. Is the marker residue uneven? If our language was written more recently, the marker might be fresher somehow. Thicker. But is that marker residue or dust? I push back from the wall with a grunt and look around the studio.

In adolescence, Angela always went off the deep end in decorating, emphasizing color and decor over utility—adding a fuzzy rug on top of the carpet to provide stylistic layers. But this space is spartan. There's no television, no electronic gadgets aside from her laptop and printer. No books for pleasure, and nothing decorating the walls apart from the whiteboard and a corkboard hanging opposite that holds random leaflets, coupons, and a medal from the Paris half marathon. I wonder how long Angela's lived here. The only framed photo in the room, near buried behind a tin cylinder of pens on the desk, is of our grandparents before they left China and immigrated to San Francisco on a steamer ship. A large beer stein from Berlin has the place of honor on the kitchen counter. Our aunt Judy, a loud, assertive craft brewer in Idaho, would be proud.

I step away from the whiteboard, feeling it burn at my back, and cross to the small counter of the kitchen nook. Seb had retrieved a mini water bottle from the fridge; I pound it. The coolness of the water is a shock to my insides, like the flood of cortisol to my system.

My eyes flit to the twin hieroglyphics on the whiteboard. Part of me wants to run with this rejuvenated squeak of hope, and part of me knows Angela's gone. The note is just an eerie coincidence. I can't lose sight of why I'm here: to answer some questions for Inspector Valentin, confirm that the body they have is Angela's, pack up her apartment, donate clothing and textbooks I don't want, and ship her home to San Diego on Tuesday.

I step out into the hall, dimly lit by the skylight, and assess the landing—empty. Angela's is the only apartment on this floor in the narrow building, as though its architect was in a hurry to reach the top and forgot to create a neighbor. I try to lock up, but the dead bolt is resistant. The key moves millimeter by millimeter counterclockwise, and I alternate pushing and pulling on the door to try to line up the bolt and the hole, until I begin swearing.

"May I help you?"

I scream and whirl to face a man standing at the stairwell. Thick blond hair falls across his alarmed expression. Flat palms snap to his chest.

"Sorry! Didn't mean to startle you."

"No," I gasp. "I'm fine."

The man frowns, takes a step backward. "Did you need help closing up?" A French accent billows his words, the vowels taking on a rounded sound. High cheekbones make him appear underfed.

"Thank you, I got it." I push against the door and confirm the lock is secure.

He straightens a purple dress shirt, then holds out a hand. "Shayna Darby? My name is Jean-Luc Fillion. I'm your embassy liaison."

"My what?"

"I'm from the American embassy." He lowers his hand when I don't move. "I'm terribly sorry for your loss, Miss Darby. The embassy would like to be of service to you, whatever you need, while you're in Paris. I don't know if you saw me, but I was at Charles de Gaulle waiting for you, after the digital fingerprint stations." He pauses. "With a sign."

The wheels slowly begin turning in my overloaded brain. Yesterday, before I left for the airport, a member of the embassy called to say he would meet me at baggage claim, to help me handle anything that might arise while I'm here. Apparently I promptly forgot about it. "Yes. I mean, thanks for driving out here to catch me."

Jean-Luc shifts his weight. He looks up to the fourth floor, then back to me. "My pleasure, miss. I actually live above your sister's apartment, so it wasn't any trouble."

Both eyebrows shoot into my hairline. "You live here? That's . . . convenient." My tone is playful, but my stomach immediately pinches. Angela's note flashes to mind before I brush it away. I can't start off by rejecting government officials; they're the handful of connections I have abroad.

"Can I see a badge?"

He fishes a black leather square with a clip from his back pocket. "Of course."

When he flips it forward, a generic office mug shot stares back at me. Not a hint of a smile against the white background—at once bureaucratic and legitimate looking. I catch his name across the top and a few numbers before I feel sheepish and return it. "That's fine, thank you. I should get going. I'm actually meeting the detective on my sister's case."

He waves me forward with a tight smile. He must have sat in two hours of traffic to the airport and back. "Of course. I'll walk you down."

We descend in silence, excepting each creak of the warped steps. At the bottom, beside the open door marked CONCIERGE, a woman digs in a large army-style backpack with a fold-over top. An empty reusable grocery bag dangles from a thin arm. Coke-bottle glasses and gray-streaked black hair would give her the appearance of a regular grand-mother, were it not for the items she withdraws from her backpack: a retractable measuring tape, a boxing glove, and a book with Cyrillic script on the cover.

Unable to find whatever she's looking for, she throws up her hands, swears in Chinese, then kicks the door back open and disappears inside.

If Angela really is gone, what will happen to her apartment? Has she paid rent? Does she owe any?

"That's Madame Chang." Jean-Luc lifts his chin, already acting the tour guide. "And the last you'll probably see of her during the day. She's a night owl."

I nod. "So you know . . . knew . . . Angela, too? Since you live here." The past tense feels garbled in my mouth, uncomfortable. Less than an hour earlier, I felt an endless void of panic and loss. Now there's only a bizarre hollow emotion, sucked dry and stuffed with queasy uncertainty.

"I moved in recently, but I saw her once or twice, yes. It's why the brass at work thought I would be the most available of all the repatriation employees. I'm actually one of the foreign interns."

"Ah. So you do all the bitch work." I can't help admiring—testing—his level of English.

Jean-Luc clears his throat. "That is correct." He hands me a business card from his pants pocket. A phone number and his name are printed on one side. "If you need anything, you know where I live."

I slip the card in my bag and thank him, already turning toward the main entry. Although the last thing I want to do is leave the whiteboard unattended, to part ways with this—possible—proof that my sister is alive, I step outside. Its invisible tether trails behind me, as I hail a cab and wonder whether Inspector Valentin knows more than his muffled calls suggested.

Chapter 3

Montmartre bustles in the afternoon with a deep humidity that moistens every back. Street vendors hawk items around me as I climb into the cab in a daze. The driver takes me down a hill, through what appears to be the tourist section—the Champs-Élysées, he announces—awash in dazzling verandas and brightly colored flags swaying overhead in the breeze.

We pass over the Seine River from the Right Bank to the Left. Couples sitting outside cafés sip wine and tiny coffees while observing the crowds. At a stoplight, a man juggles a soccer ball from knee to knee on the base of a weatherworn statue, drawing curious onlookers and a few alert policemen.

This city is Angela's home, her permanent address for the last three years. Instead of finishing up at UC San Diego, as I had done, mere footsteps from where we grew up in La Jolla, Angela stayed in Paris after spending a semester abroad. I got her reasons why. She discovered ancient urban planning studies during her sophomore year of college, and the Sorbonne is world renowned for its program in that field. While I was happy for her, I didn't understand why she would choose to be so far away from our family. From me. Why she would move to the land of *Da Vinci Code* mysteries, baguettes—when she's been gluten-free since we were twenty—and Serge Gainsbourg, a cultural hero of fetishists and machismo. And especially why she stayed after our parents' deaths.

Outside the police station, pollution mingles with the thick summer air to insulate the street like a blanket. I head for the metal doors. Menacing gargoyles clutch the corners of a stone portico, glaring as I pass beneath. Inside, I pass through the door in the one-way glass to where two metal detectors and a guard armed with an AK-47 flank a second set of doors. I try not to stare as I continue inside—my first sighting of the French military. Individuals wait along the walls on cushioned benches, one man sleeping, mouth agape. Framed black-and-white photographs decorate the walls, and a sprawling mural of a Napoleonic battlefield hangs above the reception desk, like a warning that history often repeats itself.

Behind the sweeping wooden desk, a middle-aged woman with Shirley Temple curls clacks out a thundering rhythm on a keyboard. "Mademoiselle, bonjour," she says as I approach.

"Bonjour, madame. Inspecteur Valentin? J'ai rendez-vous avec."

The receptionist smirks at my five-year-old's French but picks up a telephone and speaks quietly into the receiver. With a sharp nod to me, she replies, "Take a seat," in English.

Most people in the lobby this Sunday afternoon are drunk, high, or talking to themselves, except for an older woman knitting pink yarn that barely hangs past her wrists. I pick the corner bench nearest the desk just before another one-way glass door swings open. A small man in slacks and a tie breezes through, barely breaking stride as he zeros in on me. A cloud of mint moves with him, cutting through the smell of stale booze and body odor.

"Mademoiselle Darby, bonjour. Je suis l'inspecteur Valentin." He extends a firm handshake, drawing himself up to meet my height. A bulbous nose is his leading feature, countering a heavy brow. Thinning hair dusts the crown of his head and gathers into a ring of curls, monk-style.

Brilliant green eyes seem to extract information without speech, assessing and searching my face. "Suivez-moi."

I follow him down a brightly lit hall and pass an office clearing stuffed with cubicles. He pauses beside a glass wall that separates his office from the peons but still gives the visual illusion that he remains a part of the team. The door bears the outline of a predecessor's name.

"Alors, Mademoiselle Darby." Valentin closes the door behind me, cutting the noise of chatter and phone calls in half.

"Excusez-moi, mais . . . Can we speak in English, please?" Speaking to him over the phone was a damned travesty. Although he did switch from French to English when I asked, between the faint transatlantic communication and his accent, I only understood every other word.

Valentin's eyes narrow. Slender fingers tug on a black necktie, loosening the knot without shifting his gaze. "Of course."

He steps behind a desk to sit in a leather swivel armchair, surveying the folders and envelopes that cover the surface. "Sit down, please."

I move a series of clipped papers from a chair to the floor and do as I'm told.

"Firstly, I am so sorry for your loss, Miss Darby. I cannot imagine the pain you must be experiencing in this moment." The words are well rehearsed, probably used far too often, but I struggle for footing all the same. Relief at knowing Angela is alive battles with the intense grief stomping my heart, shaking me certain my sister is dead.

Seb's words reverberate in my head: *The note could have been there then.*

A cardboard box with no lid sits on a filing cart next to Valentin's desk. Scrawled across the side are my sister's name and a word I recognize from clicking through articles on *Le Monde*'s website: *Preuves.* Evidence. The blue sleeve of Angela's favorite college sweatshirt drapes over the edge, and the sight of it ignites a round of goose bumps on my skin. She wore that everywhere junior year.

"Would you like a tissue? Miss Darby?"

A tear splashes the pocket of my shorts. "Shayna. What happened, exactly? I know you explained everything over the phone, but I want to hear it again to make sure I understand."

The desk phone rings, interrupting my agony. The mundane, everyday sound feels like an affront—the world continuing to go about its business. Valentin silences the noise, but a red, insistent light continues to flash. "Of course. I understand it is confusing. Information has come in slowly and bit by bit."

He clasps his hands together. "Here is what we know: Angela was on the Sorbonne campus June 29. She entered the library at 1:05 p.m., according to surveillance cameras. A shooter entered the campus at 2:13 p.m., opening fire on the international relations hall, the foreign language hall, and the library. Conflicting witness statements insist Angela ran into the courtyard with the other students—out of view of security cameras. Others suggest Angela was taken from the library, kidnapped."

"By whom? The shooter killed himself, right?"

He nods. "Yes. We do not believe the shooter was involved. Ten days later, a body was recovered from the Seine, with a bullet wound to the head; we have not yet confirmed this was the cause of death. As the body was submerged in water for almost that length of time, the only identifying factor that police could use without proper medical records was the tattoo dressing her ankle, based on Sebastien Bronn's declaration. Rumors have leaked to the media that an American has been missing since the shooting, and we are trying to contain this information before releasing a statement. Identifying your sister's remains will not take long," he adds. "Until when do you plan to stay?"

I stare at him until my eyes burn and I'm forced to blink. "I'm leaving Tuesday. Angela didn't have any tattoos when I last saw her. How am I supposed to ID her?"

Valentin purses his lips. "Many times, family members recognize things they don't remember until they are faced with their loved one. Perhaps that will be the case for you tomorrow."

"Wait. Can't we go now? I thought I was coming to see you, then we would go straight to the morgue." I crack my pinkie knuckle, a burst of anxiety resurfacing the bad habit.

Valentin's eyebrows draw up and together. "The morgue is only open Monday through Friday for nonemergencies. If I may ask, why schedule your visit for so short a duration?"

"Shit."

"Miss Darby?"

Why did I assume we would go immediately? The last few days, I've been distracted trying to wrap my head around Angela's death. In contrast, when my parents died, I asked so many questions that I was given a copy of their incident file to ensure I had the same information the police had. Granted, their case wasn't shrouded in ambiguity—it was a car crash, plain and simple. Except it wasn't. Not to me, anyway.

"Miss Darby?"

I shake my head, snapping back to the present. "I wanted to stay longer. My trip is brief because classes start next week and I have tons of work to do before then . . ." My voice trails off as I hear my own idiocy. *Your sister is dead.* Valentin doesn't blink, but I get the sense he's mentally recording everything I say, each sniff I make.

"All right, so what can I do today? Have there been signs posted— *Last seen with*—or some tip line set up? Have the police cross-referenced phone numbers from her cell phone with new acquaintances? I could go through her old emails and try to find any red flags. I can be extremely meticulous, and I'd like to help—"

Valentin lifts a hand before I finish speaking. "There is nothing for you to do, Miss Darby. We are pursuing this investigation in every way possible. Even if your sister were alive, I would not ask you to hold a press conference and plead for information regarding her whereabouts. That is not the French way. You will have to content yourself with waiting and avoiding strangers while the police continue their efforts."

A shiver climbs my spine. All the better. Public speaking is Angela's forte; I can't imagine a million people watching my panic attack.

Valentin reaches across a stack of folders and hands me a business card. He clears his throat. "You have my office phone and now my mobile phone. Please call if you have any questions before tomorrow morning."

I stare at his card a moment before registering that he thinks the conversation is over. "But what about her killer?" I can't leave without something—anything that says progress is being made, that I'm not in this all alone. Leaning forward, I grip the edge of his desk. "Don't you have any suspects? What are you doing to find this guy?"

Valentin sits back in his chair, thumbs twiddling in infuriating nonchalance. "It might be a woman, Shayna. We're pursuing several leads."

I have half a mind to scream at him, to slam my fist against the desk like the fucking Hulk, but I measure my tone. "Like what? What if someone tries to contact me since I'm Angela's sister? Shouldn't I know whom to avoid? If I were a killer and I saw me and thought my job wasn't done, I would—" But the words *finish the task* won't go past my teeth; I'm fully realizing for the first time, in Angela's city, wearing a mirror of her face, how close I am to that reality. The only worst-case scenario left: me going missing, too.

His thumbs reverse direction. "We have been carefully monitoring developments in an adjacent investigation, believing it might be linked to your sister's death. I cannot release specific information at this time. Have you been following the news?"

"No, I've been busy mourning," I snap.

"French news. *Le Monde, Le Figaro.* There have been multiple murders recently, all bearing similar marks to those found on your sister. Clément Gress?"

"I don't know who that is."

"Gress was the first of these. He was found in a dumpster behind a frozen foods store. He had been dead for hours, yet missing for days."

"And how is he similar to Angela?"

He shakes his head. "He is not, overtly. None of them are. Their commonalities are restricted to the cranial bullet wound and one or more tattoos of some kind. Therein lies the problem."

"So you think someone took Angela from campus, during the shooting, during all the chaos. And that person may have killed already before that?"

"Possibly. We don't know whether the abductor is a series murderer or whether they acted uniquely. We are still determining what happened in the ten days between Angela's disappearance and the body's discovery in the river. That is why we need to confirm the identity of the corpse tomorrow, to search for additional commonalities with the others. A family member's identification will push the American government to provide dental and medical records more quickly."

I nod, but my mind locks on two words, barely hearing the rest. My heart pounds against the thin cotton of my tank top. "A series murderer. Like . . . a serial killer? You think Angela was murdered by a serial killer?"

Bright-green eyes fix on mine as Valentin inhales a minty breath. "Good day, Miss Darby."

He escorts me back down the hall, into the lobby. In a trance, I thank him. The woman's pink knitting now reaches her lap, her needles continuing to clickclickclick. Several individuals seated along the benches lift their heads as I pass, their gazes following me through the one-way glass. When the sunlight hits my skin, I don dark glasses on autopilot and retrieve an elastic from my bag to wrap my short hair in a messy bun. A trio of men on the sidewalk stops their conversation to watch, and my body stiffens instinctively.

I take off down the steps, around the corner, at a speed I hope is assertive and not intriguing, not even caring when my hair tumbles to my shoulders once more.

Valentin's words ring in my head. *Series murderer.* If someone out there is aiming to finish with me what they started with Angela—to finish the task—it's going to take a lot more than a change of hairstyle to stop them.

Chapter 4

from: Angela Darby <ange.d.paris@smail.com>
to: "Darby, Shayna" <shayna.darby93@smail.com>
date: Jan 12, 2015 7:32 a.m.
subject: Greetings from France (Adventures Abroad)

Dearest Shayna—

Holy stinky cheese, Batman, I'm in PARIS! Yaaaassss! This first week has been filled with pastries, poor directions, an abundance of body language (*wink wink*), and my French roommate seems pretty cool *en plus*. There's this crazy-hot guy downstairs, and we haven't talked yet, but I think he's in my International Conflict class. I'm hoping he needs a study buddy this semester. Naw'm sayin'?

Okay, I'm getting ahead of myself: I miss you so much! Seriously, Shay, I'm sorry for the tiff we had at New Year's. I know you were part annoyed at Teddy's flirting with me (he's not worth your time, honestly), and part worried that I was leaving, but

I feel really, really good about this move. And it's only for a semester. Here, in the Sorbonne's massive international student residence hall, in the middle of Paris, with random French Army guards who walk around with automatic weapons (seriously. Democratic socialism is intense), I feel completely safe. Ever since the first day of orientation at UCSD, when we visited the Education Abroad booth, I've had visions of crêpes raining powdered sugar, and it's so lovely being here now.

Being so far from you does feel weird, though. You never said it, but I'm well aware it's the first time you and I have been more than one hundred miles apart. I hope you'll come visit. Paris would *freak* over our American, sassy-pants twinning. (I'll have the pants ready; you bring the sass.) Single births surround me, and while life is incredible here, it would be great to experience it with you.

Also, it's cold. Like stick-your-tongue-to-a-flagpole cold. So when you visit, ask Mom to pack more long johns, please. A dozen. And something with extra warmth, like a fur coat (the non-animal-harming kind)?

Moving away for a semester isn't going to change the fact that you are my sister, my twin, and we are connected by something even your science can't explain. All the calculations in the world can't define why I know exactly when you're sad or feeling awkward or embarrassed. Even without being side by side, you know when I'm out of sorts. Remember the night the end of freshman year when you couldn't sleep, and I called you the next day to tell you about my breakup with Mike? No one can explain that, not even you.

I don't know when I'm going to email this off just yet, because I know how upset you were when I left. Maybe give it a few days? It is true I've been in my own little world the last three years with Alpha Delta Beta while you've been knee-deep in pre-med, but I think we've also had the chance to grow up and find our own identities (*she said, with a furtive glance. "Right?"*). If you ever want me to come home, just say the word. I mean it.

This email account will be used to document my adventures abroad. Reply here with any tips you have for me in Paris from that big ole brain of yours. Snail mail or messages in Coke cans plucked from the Atlantic are also cool. I love you. Please don't be mad anymore.

Bisous ("kisses" in French),
Angela

Edit: I'm sending this to you. Twin for the win.

Chapter 5

Just before I opened the email from Seb declaring my sister was missing, my hands had been clutching the silver frame of my smartphone case. I was laughing. Doubled over, wishing for a glass of red wine. A state grant I applied for was set to be announced that week, and I was checking my inbox every hour; any and all money was needed to pay for the next four years of medical school, even though half the tuition was covered thanks to my parents' estate.

The smart tweed dress I had chosen for UC San Diego's medical school social hour was itching the tops of my knees, but I didn't care. Everyone was friendly, excited to begin this next chapter in our journey toward becoming doctors, and I was tossing educated quips right and left. *Rare, like AB negative, am I right?* A circle had formed around me—young men and women, and Tiberius, the token salt-and-pepper student. I felt alive, awake where I had been asleep for the last three years mourning the loss of my parents. I felt like Angela.

Social hour turned into two with me leading the charge, Diet Coke in hand. I suggested Abuela's Tavern down the block. The Sea Breeze Lounge was closing soon, and we needed a place to keep the party going. Some genius wanted to walk along the water instead, but I vetoed the idea; the trauma of a childhood jellyfish sting had never really faded, and neither had my repulsion for the shoreline—I could never separate my earlier happy memories of the beach from the slick taste of fear that coated my mouth after that day. When June humidity blanketed La Jolla Cove, as it did then, translucent mushroom tops could be seen floating on the choppy waves, the jellies' migratory bloom in full swing.

Kelsey, from Minnesota, volunteered that she'd recently moved to Pacific Beach, and *wasn't Garnet Avenue crazy congested?* The three native San Diegans (myself, Clarisse, and Tiberius) corrected her in unison: Gar-*net*! A peal of laughter bubbled from my throat and made me forget for a second that life was hard.

Then I dragged a finger down the screen of my smartphone to refresh my inbox.

Angela's bathroom mirror reflects dark shadows ringing my eyes. I'd give all my state grant money back to return to that moment at the Sea Breeze, refreshing incessantly, before Seb's email arrived. To the bliss of not knowing my sister might be gone forever.

I step out from the bathroom and find Seb crawling under the bed. "What are you doing?" I ask.

He inches backward like a garbage truck, slow going, then gestures beneath the bed with a hooked thumb. Gelled black hair sticks out in a dozen directions, dust bunnies hugging the tips. "I found some boxes behind the cookware container. Can you reach them?"

Seb arrived at seven o'clock on the dot, ready to try and piece together Angela's disappearance. After leaving the police station, craning behind the entire drive back for a glimpse of anyone following me, I returned to the apartment and began sorting through her wardrobe. Then I gave up; I couldn't box up my sister. For the last two hours, we've been reading old essays and leafing through books, separating them into piles of Maybe, Irrelevant, and Potential Clues. Hunching over anything Seb thinks might lead us to the root of Angela's demise.

Logic and sanity insist I believe my sister dead until I visit the morgue. If it is true she's still breathing, I'll have different decisions to make—there's no way I can leave this city, abandon her in this country, on this continent, if she's in so much danger that she's gone into hiding.

From where I sit, the whiteboard's writing is messy. It was written hurriedly, slanting up the side of the board as though Angela ran out of room. A word I hadn't noticed before remains beneath the partially erased numbers: *Code*. Nausea serrates my stomach. Did Angela simply use our language as an example of a code, or a demonstration to someone? The edge of another word is smeared—*ée*. Was her cry for help nothing more than a practice session to keep up her skills?

Shit shit shit. I keep my head down and focus on slowing my breathing. My cheeks flush in the cool interior of the apartment. Yellow sunbeams heat my bare calves through the open window; the sun is finally setting at nine o'clock. The longest day of my life.

"Shayna?" Seb speaks loudly, like he's repeating himself. "The boxes?"

I slide underneath the bed, feeling queasy. Why am I consenting to this exercise in prolonging the pain, the debilitating squeak of hope that's pierced the emotional armor I donned when I stepped off the plane? Out of courtesy? Politeness? That doesn't sound like me. Grabbing the closest storage box, I inch it backward, corner by corner. It clears a path through discarded socks.

Sebastien wipes the top as I sit back on my heels. "I wonder how I missed this last week." He smooths back his hair, dislodging a few dust bunnies. With careful movements, he untucks each flap until the box's contents are revealed.

This man was so intimate with my sister he had a key or knew where she hid her spare.

"Did you really look through all of Angela's personal stuff?" My tone lands flat, accusatory, maybe more in line with how I should be interacting in the shadow of the whiteboard message. Although I was aiming for conversational, I also don't care. I don't know this guy, regardless of how well Angela did. In some twisted, petty part of my brain, I am mad he was here by himself, in this sacred space.

In the filing box beside me, a layer of tampons covers a photo of Angela's smiling face, pressed to the cheek of a model, from the looks of her companion. He's tan, with the right amount of stubble and deep, indented dimples. A Taser peeks out from beneath the picture, surprising me. Had she felt threatened even before the shooting at the Sorbonne?

Seb looks at me, an innocent pinch in his forehead. "Angela passed away. I am trying to follow her last steps and find out why she died, who took her. If I must dig in old crates to determine who, I will."

We each remove a file, then thumb through the papers within. My thoughts zigzag despite my calm expression. What else do I think I know about Angela, but don't? What other strange photos of ex-boyfriends am I going to find with her current beau beside me?

Focus. Everything in this space is contradictory. Be logical. Find the through line just like you would with a patient profile in school.

Seb pores over an undergrad multiple-choice test from the Sorbonne—Angela got an A in English—*go, girl*. Slanted sunlight highlights his square features and a patch of chest hair peeking from the white V-neck shirt he wears.

If Seb is good enough for my flighty sister to date for a year, I need to learn more about him. I need his insider knowledge of my sister's recent activities, likes, dislikes, how she spent her days. I've got to go deep to decipher any coded clues that might be hiding here and get some context. Starting with this weeping willow of a boyfriend.

"Seb?"

"Oui? I mean, yes?"

"Where did you learn to speak English?" I fan through a folder of papers. A moment passes in silence, and I wonder what Seb is seeing in my face, shadowed beneath the window. How many times has he sat in this exact spot with my sister? What will he do without her?

"At school, mostly. I was a biological sciences major, and many academic journals are in English." He breaks into a smile, baring pearly whites. "Languages come easy to me."

I nod, absorbing his cheeky raise of one eyebrow. "I was a science major, too. Human biology, premed."

"Bio-sci and history double major. Although history did not serve me very well, studying neurology."

"Wow. So you finished medical school already? How old are you? You look too young to be a doctor."

Seb leans back on his palms. "I have thirty. I have been done with my residency program for a year but have been working in the medical field much longer."

"Interesting." *I have thirty.* Thirty years old? I resume searching for clues (cryptexes, ciphers, coded letters, cave drawings, etc.) and try to catalog this information. Seb appears devoted to Angela, willing to do whatever it takes to learn what happened to her. It's impressive. Angela's type was traditionally the homecoming king, an ideal partner to her queen. Now it seems she prefers the arrogant nerds that always appealed to me.

Typical—they invariably preferred her. When we were fifteen, I asked my honors biology classmate, Ashton Wheelan, out to a movie, having read in a magazine that confidence was attractive to boys. He said yes—until he realized I wasn't Angela. He said he wanted someone more *on his level.* Considering I had just beaten him for the highest grade on our final exam, I knew what he meant: Nonsciencey. Miss Congeniality. The *fun* twin.

Even the last New Year's Eve Angela and I spent together, we were competing for a guy. Teddy Nguyen, a genetics major who lived in the dorm room below me, had asked me out several times; I just couldn't meet up while studying for first-semester senior-year finals. After helping Angela prep for her Medieval Medicine class, I invited him to a party she was throwing, and the two of them flirted over the spiked punch all night. She swore she was only playing the welcoming host. But I knew she enjoyed taking something I wanted. It had been that way between us since we were children.

"Listen, Seb. All these are just old tests and papers from her undergraduate studies. I found her agenda book earlier but haven't looked at it yet. Should we read that?"

"You do not want to look at the rest of these folders? There are also many more that rest under the bed."

I withdraw a file from the box, entitled SORBONNE RECORDS. Small, rectangular receipts are flattened within, some stapled to larger papers, most just lying free. Swirling drawings trace the backs of two receipts.

"No, I don't," I say abruptly. "Let's move on. I still have to pack all her stuff and donate what I can't ship." My extreme need to organize becomes amplified in stressful situations. Surveying the room littered with papers, clothing, and boxes, I feel like I might break out into hives.

Seb drops the folder back in the carton; it lands with a dramatic slap. "All right. I will defer to your twin powers."

"Excuse me?"

"Your twin powers. Angela mentioned them. You were psychically connected? Studies have shown infant twins are able to sense the other's discomfort without seeing or hearing the other."

"You're joking. Right?"

He smiles like I just asked him to explain gravity. "This power resides somewhere in the cerebral cortex, the area that controls our empathy, and the basal ganglia, the area of our brains that houses intuition. There are many mysteries associated with twins. Although I do not know if it pains you to discuss them."

"Um. No, I'm not . . . pained."

"Science is at its limit," he continues, absentmindedly stroking the tattoo on his ankle. "Science is always at its limit until it surpasses itself.

The earth is flat until it is not, gravity pulls greater on a fat man until it does not, and there are only sixty elements in the periodic table until there are not." He pauses, inviting me to disagree with him. "We're only a few steps short of understanding the final mysteries this world has to offer. Until we learn there are more."

I nod slowly. "Let's check out her planner."

Seb stands while I busy myself with an essay on globalization. He certainly *seemed* intelligent. Opinions about science aside, I guess he would have to share some of Angela's hippie-dippie beliefs in order to date her for so long. *Twin powers?*

Flipping backward through the eighteen-month planner, I get a snapshot of Angela's life. The more recent days in late June are empty except for one containing a circle with the number fifty-eight inside it and a few notes that repeat on a weekly basis. Names and drawings begin around January; flipping back to December, every other day is scribbled with deadlines and bar outings. One square is decorated in candles and stars.

"Who is Nour?" I ask. "Angela went to her birthday party last August."

Seb shakes his head. "No idea. But we should contact him or her. Nour can be the name of a man or a woman."

I release a deep sigh. My understanding of everything feels so limited. "Well, where is Angela's stuff? Cell phone, passport, purse."

"Gone. I assume she had them when she disappeared. Perhaps the police have them. You could ask your inspector." Seb stacks loose papers on the desk.

"What do you do again?" It makes sense that the police wouldn't tell Seb any of the details. It's an open investigation, and he's not family. So is he plying me for information?

He returns my expectant gaze, then scoffs, reading my subtext perfectly. "I do research and work for the Paris Historical Archives. I apply neurological theories to remains found at archaeology sites. That's how Angela and I came to meet, when she visited one of my projects."

I turn back to the agenda and the near-empty month of June. Some people meet in coffee shops or through online dating. Never my sister, Angela, the romantic twin. She'd have to fall in love in a cold cave, where huddling together for warmth is synonymous with first base.

The green leather cover rubs soft against my dry fingers. A thick border is drawn around Thursday, June 28, in permanent marker, the day before Angela went missing during the shooting at the Sorbonne. I consult May and find the same thick border around each Thursday of the month. From April, extending back to the previous August, the Thursdays of each month are decorated with a square of black ink; the early squares contain the phrase BARRIÈRE D'ENFER.

"What does this mean?" I crouch beside Seb where he sifts through articles on the floor.

"It is the entrance to the catacombs of Paris."

"And what does 'Barrière d'Enfer' mean?"

Sebastien grins a row of pointy teeth. "The Gate to Hell."

Gooseflesh covers my skin as I scan his face for a laugh, a flinch, a tell. Is he kidding? I search my meager store of French history and what I remember from the handful of French films I watched with Angela. Is such a macabre name common here? More importantly, Seb seems to be enjoying my discomfort, his grin widening. Is he messing with me?

"Are you okay, Shayna?"

"I'm not sure. Is that really the translation of 'Barrière d'Enfer'?"

Seb rises, straightening to his full height. His outline blocks the desk lamp. "Shayna, that is the literal translation. Otherwise it is referred to as the Portal. Would you like to see it?"

My upper lip curls. "Why?"

"Because it was the subject of Angela's doctoral dissertation. She was studying urban planning of the twelfth century and the catacombs' role in World War II."

He maintains a blank face, but I hear his irritation. Perhaps frustration that I don't fully believe him. "Let me guess," I say, "the Nazis named it the Gate to Hell during the Occupation?"

"No, they did other things down there." He cracks a smile. "How about tomorrow?"

Courtesy might suggest I laugh off my initial suspicion and change the subject to persuade him everything is fine. Instead I continue analyzing the thick border drawn around each Thursday. If he's offering up a tour of Angela's thesis subject, who am I to refuse? "Sure," I finally say. The better I understand this Paris version of my sister, the better chance I have of solving her dry-erase Rubik's cube. Even as the hope that she simply ditched Seb and went to Florence lingers.

When I look up, Seb has pressed his lips into a straight line. He folds his arms across his chest. "Angela did not tell you anything about me, did she?"

I look to the safety of the window behind him. "Not a thing."

"Shayna, I am not perfect." He sighs and lowers his gaze, like it's some big revelation. "But I loved your sister, and I am trying to help. I have already spoken to Inspector Valentin and his department multiple times. Angela was my only family, too."

My hackles rise—I am annoyed he would compare our family situation to his. He's probably estranged from his father or in a fight with a cousin. "Oh really?"

"Yes. My older brother and I were raised by my grandparents, who died when I had twenty. Baptiste died in Afghanistan four years ago, fighting with the French armed forces. Baptiste was my sanity, then Angela became my world."

I stare at him, at his earnest expression and the pain drawing his mouth, trying to reconcile my willingness to believe him with the whiteboard's message beside him. *Trust no one.* His eyes become glassy, fixating on the floor. A large finger reaches up to dab away tears while I struggle to choose a side.

I don't trust him—I can't, not with Angela's warning. But I need him to help me learn what happened to my sister. There's no way I can navigate the city or my sister's French life for the next two days without someone who knew her, but why doesn't he shut up and make this easier? Why does he need to feel explicitly accepted?

In the eighth grade, Angela impersonated me when I had to give a presentation required to graduate middle school. I've never felt the comfort she always did in front of a camera or a crowd of people, and I also suck at asking for help. Rather than let me puke on my shoes, she stepped into them without my asking and helped us both progress to the next level. Seb, on the other hand, won't volunteer without me making the first move.

Be nice, I tell myself. *Be like Angela.*

I clear my throat to speak. "I'm sure she felt the same way about you. She always chose good people to be around."

The bunched frown releases slightly. "Thank you, Shayna. Losing a sibling is a terrible loss I have known. I am only here to help."

Heat climbs my neck. For the first time in years, the pain of my estranged relationship with Angela fully throbs in my heart. It becomes clearer with each awkward pause that Seb knows my sister in all the ways I didn't bother to learn. Talking about her like this, seeing her emotional effect on someone else, reminds me of how wonderful our relationship could be when we weren't fighting. Before all the bad words, hard to take back and even harder to forget, were uttered in the wake of our parents' deaths.

Angela always took after our auntie Meredith, our father's sister, notorious for turning any afternoon into an emotional hurricane. When we were nine, Angela kicked a hole in her closet when she wasn't allowed to ride her bike; at fourteen, she cried so hard she gave herself a bloody nose when she didn't get the lead in the school play; at seventeen, she sat in our childhood tree house wailing, in protest of our parents missing her performance at a theater festival because they would be on vacation. It was during a premed psych class that I started to wonder if Angela and Aunt Meredith were both somewhere on the spectrum of emotional imbalance—maybe bipolar—though they were never formally diagnosed.

What if she hadn't died? Could our relationship have been repaired? I was far from a model sister myself. I flaunted the red envelopes—lucky money from our grandparents—I received for my straight As, and sometimes I pushed Angela when I knew she was at her breaking point, as only siblings can. If she were alive, could we regain at least some sense of the family that we lost three years ago when our parents died?

For so long, I blamed myself for their deaths.

It's only recently I've begun to move past that.

Seb pulls out his cell phone. "It is late. I will meet you tomorrow morning after you finish at the morgue. Then we will go to the catacombs and continue our search for information." He nods to our tiny clue pile: a few receipts from June, found on her desk, that the police thought were useless and hadn't confiscated; a research paper about the catacombs bearing edits in red pen; and now her agenda.

I stand and follow him to the door. "See you tomorrow." I lock the dead bolt behind him, my words more a promise to myself that I'm ready. His footsteps groan down the stairwell into the marble foyer.

My stomach growls. Considering I haven't eaten anything since a sandwich this afternoon, I open Angela's laptop to search for supermarkets nearby. I could use something to drink. Only one of them is open at this hour, a place around the corner from here. I'm about to close the window when a bookmark at the top of the screen catches my eye. *Moon.*

Hope floods my chest. I stop breathing.

Everyone, including our parents for a while, called Angela *Sunshine*, while I was the shadowy contrast to my sister's effusive personality. Complicated, painful emotions rise as I recall her name for me—*Moonshine*—before either of us knew that typically meant bathtub gin. *Moon.*

My trigger finger hovers over the link, then clicks. A public post from a blog she hasn't touched in years opens, displaying a single phrase followed by numbers:

Divine Research

48535.75 2201

A scream cuts through the square outside the apartment. *What the hell?* I rise and peer through the open shutters; the fountain is deserted, the sidewalks empty in the lamplit dark. Was that a person? A chill skips along my arms. The sound was feral in its sharp appeal, then abruptly silent.

Valentin's accented English echoes in the quiet: *Series murderer. Divine Research.*

Moon.

The lifetime of intensity I've experienced today alone threatens to pour from every cell of my body in snotty tears, but I don't let the sobs begin. My sister's final communication to me could be staring me in the face, possibly containing the answer to why she disappeared, why she died. There's no time to fall apart.

Grabbing the apartment keys and my wallet, I head downstairs. Outside the building door, a look in each direction reveals a sleeping homeless man, no one else. Around the corner, the convenience store is empty at nine thirty on a Sunday. The young cashier points to my liter of Coke Light and smirks. "Party big?" He eyes the Bank of America debit card I offer, putting the proverbial two and two together on my nationality.

I pay without replying, not knowing where to begin. (Yes, a debilitating party of one.)

Dark green imprints the light skin of his inner elbow—a tattoo. He catches my glance, then pushes his sleeves higher so I can see the faded right angles of a swastika. A proud smile spreads his thin lips as he hands me my receipt.

I hurriedly exit the store. Emotions jumble in my chest as I reach Angela's building and jam the jailer's key in the door—disgust, confusion, anger. Why would anyone be proud of a Nazi tattoo in this modern era? Upstairs, inside her apartment, I slam the door as if someone were on my heels. I pause, my heart pounding against my ribs, and suck down a gulp of air. Faint streetlight filters through Angela's shutters. Shadow hands stretch across her bed and seem to grow longer with each second I stand still.

In the dark of night, and with far more important tasks ahead, I don't have the bandwidth to mull the implications of that cashier's grin or wonder whether he was silently judging me as something unclean. Whether he was viewing me as some mixed-race disgrace.

Whether the neighborhood convenience store clerk, or anyone else, mistook me for my sister.

Chapter 6

The morgue sits on a small island between the Left and Right Banks of Paris, as if neither one wanted that much death on their side. Sounds of traffic carry from behind a row of perfectly square hedges lining the sidewalk where I stand. From a tour boat on the Seine River below, a disembodied voice speaks in French.

I pause before a commanding archway to soak in the morning sunlight, to feel connected to something I recognize all the way over on this continent. While Angela was nocturnal, I've always been a morning person. It's strange to be here without her. Part of me envisioned finally visiting her in a few years, after medical school, with a husband, maybe a baby—when I could be fully armed against any anger she might lob my way, when I had everything I'd set out to achieve, despite the cost to us both. My husband would take care of the baby while I worked in oncology research. He'd keep the home tidy and have a cheese plate ready when I arrived home, followed by dinner at seven o'clock. The perfect househusband to make me believe I might deserve our little corner of happiness.

Carved designs decorate the bronze door nestled within the arch. A simple cross, couched in an alcove above, sits atop a Latin inscription that probably reads, tongue in cheek, *Dead men tell no tales*. I stare at the great brick building that is the Paris morgue, wondering whether the answers to my questions about Angela lie inside.

Last night I searched through every desktop folder and bookmarked website on her laptop a second time in the event I'd missed another message. I clicked through all of her torrent files and haphazardly explored a code-source editor program I didn't understand. I gave packing another go but only got as far as one box of clothing and beer steins. I couldn't do more. Not before seeing for myself that Angela is the body pulled from the river.

Divine Research. What did she mean? Divine as in *guess*? Guess her research? Guess the meaning of her research? Or are they two separate words, bearing two separate instructions? The possible combinations— together or separate—as nouns, verbs, or adjectives, are endless.

Divine: Guess, determine. Holy, transcendent.

Research: Investigate, probe. Analysis, inquiry.

The time stamp on Angela's blog post read June 1, 2014, the end of our junior year of college. However, the author can choose the date that displays on the post; just because it said *Published on June 1* doesn't mean it was. Those eleven digits might not mean anything at all.

Around three in the morning, I fell asleep imagining what my world would be like six hours later. What kind of truth I would learn only fourteen steps away from where I stand now.

She must be inside this building.

She can't be inside this building.

My phone buzzes, interrupting my exercise in the Schrödinger's cat paradox. Inspector Valentin's name scrolls across my screen, a bad sign. He should already be here.

"Good morning, Miss Darby. I must apologize, but I cannot attend you at the morgue."

"What? Why not?"

He clears his throat. "There has been a break in a case. The morgue director will be quite helpful and will answer any questions you may have. Again, I apologize to leave you to this task, but it must be done before you fly home tomorrow."

"Of course. Thanks." I hang up, already reaching toward the brass handles of the door. Interesting that he said *a case* and not *our* or *your* case—bad sign number two, and it's not even 9:00 a.m.

"Bonjour," a raspy voice rings out. A middle-aged security guard stands to greet me in the empty lobby. Crumbs tumble down the straining buttons of his shirt; a pastry wrapper peeks from the trash bin beside him. I search among the limited French phrases I know by heart.

"Bonjour, monsieur," I reply. "Parlez-vous anglais?"

The security guard breaks into a goofy grin. "Leetle bit."

Another try. "I need . . . directeur de la morgue."

He straightens, shoulders back, chin up. "Suivez-moi." With an open palm, he motions for me to pass through the security gate. A large, leafy plant I can't identify decorates one corner of the lobby, and a wide billboard lists the building's office numbers beside names. High-vaulted stone ceilings give the appearance of a courthouse or an old manor, but for the antiseptic smell carrying from the air ducts. Uncomfortable memories of being treated for lice by the school nurse pop into my head.

The security guard leads me down a narrow hallway lit by dim panels above. We pass more than one corridor, and I resist imagining where they go, what secrets they hold, what procedures are performed farther in.

We come to a door with a plaque fixed beside it: Directeur de morgue. My escort opens the door without knocking. An older man, around what would have been my dad's age—late fifties—sits behind a broad cherrywood desk, papers stacked in bunches before him. Rows of filing cabinets line one side of the office and remind me of a game I played with my dad as a kid—*Where does the virus hide?* He would label his filing cabinets (*hands, feet, nose, eyes, mouth*), and I'd have to locate the virus—a travel pack of tissues—before it infected the rest of the body. Angela always wanted to play, too, but my seven-year-old self, jealous of the attention she got showing off what she'd learned in dance class, would never allow it.

The room stretches wide, with no windows to provide a sense of the time of day. The security guard rattles off something in French, then leaves us with a smile.

The director nods to me. "Asseyez-vous."

I slide onto an aluminum folding chair. Though the temperature crept up an extra five degrees today, a sweater would be handy in the sudden winter of this building.

"How can I help you?" the morgue director asks in French, peering at me from above square-rimmed spectacles. A blazer hangs on a coat hook in the corner, and his white button-up shirt is fastened to the neck. He regards me clinically.

"My name is Shayna Darby. Can we speak in English? My French isn't great."

Slate-gray eyes widen. He stands. "Ah, yes. I have waiting you since weeks. Inspector Valentin apprised me . . . expect you. My condolences. Angela, correct?"

I nod, choosing to ignore the lack of conjunctions and prepositions and instead feel grateful he's willing to speak on my terms. He grabs a set of keys from the wall.

"My name is Julien Park. We see her now."

A slick, bitter taste fills my mouth as I follow him down the narrow, dimly lit hallway. Fear courses through my body at finally being here, living out my nightmares of the last three weeks. I focus on the pleats in Park's trousers to stay calm. The width of the hall forces us to walk single file, with Park's head inches from scraping the paneled ceiling as he barrels forward. The bounce to his gait seems better suited to a jaunt at Six Flags than an institution of death. We pass through double doors to a bright hospital wing, where the space opens and I can breathe easier.

Refrigerated air gusts from vents on either side—refreshing against the nausea gripping my stomach.

He halts at a door marked CONSERVATION. I search for the nearest exit in case the unthinkable—my sister's body—is in fact inside this room, and find the hallway extends another fifty feet, then forks into a right and left turn. The only sure way out appears to be the way we came.

Park uses a key to open the door. Metal drawers line each wall of the room in floor-to-ceiling squares. Each bears a label identifying its contents, except for one. The air smells sickly sweet, perfumed and covering odors, masking decay. I cross to where Park waits beside the unmarked stainless steel box. He raises his chin a fraction.

"Your sister passed a week underwater. She changed. This, not your sister." The full gaze he fixes me with seems defiant, challenging. Choosing to believe the director means Angela has changed state, from my sister to a putrid, soggy remnant of a person, is the only option I have. If he meant otherwise, that this is literally not my sister, could that mean . . . ? What could that mean?

A burst of vanilla-scented air claps me in the face, and I dissolve into abrupt coughing. The director remains grim. "Believe me, this smell is not worst you encounter today."

He pulls hard on the drawer beside us, bending with his knees, until it extends fully. A white cotton sheet covers the cadaver that slides out. Cold temperatures have kept decomposition at bay, but an underlying smell pricks my nostrils, standing the hairs of my neck on end. When I identified my parents, it was from behind glass and in the presence of a police officer—nothing remotely this intimate. Questions I haven't allowed myself to consider since stepping into Angela's apartment resurface. Is she cold? Is she happy? Is she at peace?

The director turns to me, tilting his head to the side. "I give you a moment."

A click of the door seals me in alone with a room full of death. I stare at the slopes and valleys of this woman's shell. A metallic taste tickles the back of my mouth.

It could be Angela. It could be anyone. Angela and I are above average in height, five foot six, with medium builds. I'm heavier in the hips, and she's always been busty, but no one would notice this except for us. *Is there a unique detail to Angela's body that marks her as different from anyone else?* Valentin's question rang in my ears for days after our phone conversation, along with my stuttering lie: *I—I don't know.*

We share a birthmark. In the most unobtrusive of places—only a select number of people would see it.

I lift the sheet to peek underneath and hesitate, struggling between total revulsion at being so close to a cadaver and the terror of discovering that it's Angela. The steady thrum of the ventilation system shuts off; silence engulfs the space. A smell like waterlogged bread left to rot at the foot of a restaurant pier rises, mingling with the vanilla. I clear the sheet from the body, ripping the bandage off in one swift motion.

Ash-colored flesh fills my vision, mottled from long-term submersion in water and exposure to the appetites of fish—chunks of skin missing sporadically throughout; a nipple chewed halfway off. Dark hair rests in tangled clumps that reach the elbows. The face is almost nonexistent. An ear that was once pierced multiple times from cartilage to lobe hangs by a single flap of skin. The lips are gone, straight teeth laid bare. The eyes, mercifully, are closed. I won't bother verifying they are brown. A hole marks the forehead above dark eyebrows. The gunshot wound.

A heave racks my shoulders as I move down the body to examine the most important place. Deep ligature marks show on the wrists, and a tertiary glance shows more of the same at the ankles; she was tied up before death. I pause at the cadaver's hips. The pubic hair appears oddly normal, and out of respect for the person this once was—and because

I cannot believe that I'm here—I mentally block it out for what I'm about to do next.

Slipping two shaking fingers between the knees, I apply pressure until the thighs part just barely. Discolored, spongy skin stares at me, like a zombie's. But the puckered flesh at the top of the inner right thigh is unblemished and without any trace of the semicolon-shaped birthmark that dots both my and Angela's skin.

I take two giant steps back and slide, dumbfounded, to the ground. Shock pulls my eyes wide before something works its way up my throat. Inappropriate noises bubble, gurgling like a carbonated drink. I cover my mouth as best I can against the shaking of my ribs, but it's no use— giggles spill from my lips, and pressing my hand tighter only makes me laugh more.

Growing up, Angela always worried we would be mistaken for the other, even as she wanted us to be the *twinliest* of twins. She dressed in flowing earth-mother vibes in college to contrast my jeans and sleeveless button-ups but chose complementary colors to mine. Wore her hair down when she knew I liked mine up. She went to such lengths to set us apart and make our individuality known while still definitively linking us. Now she's been mistaken for a stranger without nipples.

A sob interrupts my laughter and then I'm crying, bawling into my hands. Pools of wetness seep onto my tank top. My body quivers against the wall, digesting this final truth: she's alive.

"Mademoiselle?" The director cracks the door.

"One second," I reply, standing up. The body now seems a stranger, where seconds ago it could have been my own severed arm. I whip the sheet like I'm making a bed. It billows across the corpse. Who is this person? Remembering how Seb already identified this swollen stunt double as Angela, I check the left then right ankle and find the tattoo he mentioned. The symbol for Gemini. A Roman numeral two, curved at the top and bottom—the astrological sign for twins, although it, too, took a beating underwater; the skin is wrinkled, distorting the image.

Could our birthmark have been removed? Could Angela have gotten it lasered off? Is the Gemini symbol a common tattoo here?

Details. These are all details I can't process yet. Angela is *alive*. The only thing that matters is my sister is not anywhere near this morgue.

Angela's whiteboard message flashes to mind. She's alive and on the run from someone.

I pause, my hand on the doorknob. Once, in high school, I borrowed Angela's red skirt to wear to an interview—to pop among the applicants—despite her texting, Do not borrow it. Sibling relationship be damned, when she discovered this, she was livid I'd *disrespected her boundaries*. She'd explicitly told me not to do something, and I did it even so. She was always insistent that when she said something, she meant it.

Knowing this, I wonder if I need to take her words on the whiteboard at their most literal sense—to trust no one. Not even figures of authority or morgue directors.

Park uncrosses his arms when I emerge with a sniffle. I fix him with a grieving stare, then spit out the words before I can falter. "This is my sister. It's Angela."

His eyes reduce to slits. "How you are sure?" His tone is cold, detached.

My hands fidget at my sides. I cast about for the right words, not sure of the answer in any language. Angela would have known that one of the first things on my list would be to come and see for myself she was dead—after identifying our parents' bodies, there's no way I would have swept aside this moment for closure.

And she left two notes meant only for me; she wouldn't want me to divulge anything I learned here, especially on official paper. Right?

I draw another finger below my lashes. "I'm sure. Can I sign now?"

Park remains unmoved. His mouth purses. The hallway's sterile lighting magnifies the throbbing in my head. "Monsieur?" I say.

"Miss Darby, this body is like balloon. The body . . . was shot after death. The tattoo was . . . *appliqué* . . . after death. How you are sure?"

I stare at him, my fake confidence rattled. Valentin never suggested the tattoo or the gunshot were made postmortem. Why would someone tattoo and shoot a body after it's already dead? And why didn't Valentin tell me? Was he trying to trap me in a lie?

The certainty I felt minutes ago is gone, sucked up into the ventilation system, but I can't see any way to deviate from the course I've chosen. For whatever reason, Angela hasn't revealed to the police that she's alive. I need to know why. "I'm sure. It's Angela."

The director throws his hands up and bounce-walks away. We pass through the double doors, back into the cool lighting and into his office. With quick strides, he rounds the desk to grasp a folder, then thrusts it into my hands. I open it. *Identification du corps* is written across the top of the first sheet. Several paragraphs of French precede a space for witnesses to confirm or refute the identification of a body. Sebastien Bronn signed his declaration July 9, two weeks ago.

"You understand what you are sign?" Hooded eyes twitch at each corner.

Out of all the text, there is only one sentence I understand completely:

Ce cadavre est celui de MADEMOISELLE ANGELA DARBY.

This is Miss Angela Darby's body.

Silence reverberates in the small space of Park's office. The magnitude of what I'm about to do weighs on me like a sweaty woolen blanket. My signature will essentially close the book on my sister's disappearance. Why would she want me to sign away her investigation? What could make her so scared or feel this trapped that she wants to remain "dead"? Her two notes to me boomerang in my head:

Alive. Trust no one.

Divine Research.

This moment may come back to haunt me, yet I can't escape the conviction that I'm doing what Angela needs me to do. "Yes. I sign now. Pen, please." I reach across Park's desk and pluck one from a plain ceramic coffee mug. He implores me again in French to reconsider— he's given up persuading me in English—but I tune him out. I can still go to Valentin and try to extract information from him, to make sense of this, without admitting what I know.

With a flourish, I sign my name below Seb's, then place Angela's file on the desk. For whatever reason, my sister doesn't want to be found by just anybody, and especially not by the police.

She's waiting for me.

Chapter 7

from: Angela Darby <ange.d.paris@smail.com>
to: "Darby, Shayna" <shayna.darby93@smail.com>
date: May 3, 2015, 3:37 p.m.
subject: Outstanding news

Dear sister—

I hope this finds you well and enjoying the consistent vitamin D (sunrays) I traded in for fresh pastries. Skies are on the cloudy side here today, but
you know what?

I'm walkin' on sunshine! Whooooaa!

Such is the constant ballad of joy ricocheting in my
head, as I type this from a café on the Champs-
Élysées—no big deal (*hair flip*)—because I just
confirmed: I'm staying! The Sorbonne dubbed me a
real-life graduate student, and I'll be able to enjoy
the summer before school starts in September,
tracking down spots where famous authors died
while enjoying cheap wine, pinkie finger poised in

the air. The Sorbonne has an amazing doctoral history program that can be completed in four years, and it provides research internships for hands-on experience. How crazy would it be to study European history in Europe? It would be so nuts it's ALMONDS, and exactly in line with my theme of choosing more.

Life is so rarely what we expect, dear sister. I feel like our generation has been told by everyone—our parents, our grandparents, by society—to settle. Settle for whatever you can grab on to, and don't let go once it's yours. *No, no, no!* Our generation has to do better, to choose more, to settle for *more*—when the world is offering less. Instead of waiting until I'm retired, I choose to live now. To enjoy the world, my youth, my ambitions and my dreams now, now. Because tomorrow is not promised, little (by two minutes) sister, and we have to do the best with what we've got. *Let it be known!* said the preachy twin.

I hope you can be happy for me, Shay. A doctorate in four years for pennies is beyond anything I thought possible for myself. (Democratic socialism for the win!) The problem is I can't leave France without finding an apartment, setting up a bank account, and receiving my student visa—I can't come home before school starts again this fall. (Democratic socialism fail.)

My agenda has been a Rorschach test of scribbling notes and broken pen stains lately, nailing down all the dates and documents I have to provide. I'm sorry I've been so MIA and we haven't Skyped— I've only been to the Louvre once this month (*hair flip*), I'm that busy. Part of me wants to throw a giant fit each time I argue with the immigration office, but I don't. You really have to go along to get along here. I can't help thinking how we would own this city, were we here together.

I hope you can support my decision, though it may come as a shock. You've always known what you wanted to do and followed in Mom and Dad's footsteps, no restless wings necessary. You were all so single-minded about school and medicine, and I've never been. About anything. For the first time, it feels right here.

But I know you're lonely, because I feel it, too. In my bones, in my tiny residence hall dorm for semester-abroad students, when I'm not experimenting with mystery foods, I feel your sadness and longing. You'll say it's the hippie-dippie in me that worries salad leaves feel pain being torn from their mother roots, but it's the twinning. Remember how once you woke up early from your nap and asked Mom to make dumplings because you knew I wanted them? We could always sense what the other desired without her having to articulate it.

If ever you feel like talking, dear sister, just close your eyes and reach out for me (cue hippie-dippie)—emotionally, mentally, spiritually extend to me, and I will be there. The ancient religions called it "divining with God on a higher plane." We've been doing that with one another since diapers, and there's no reason to stop now.

I'll keep writing to you even if you don't respond for a while. You'll probably go to your quiet place and digest all of this info, per usual. I'm grabbing a drink with Hans, but later I'll be around if you want to Skype.

Also, def let me know how your exam went. I know that class was a bitch last quarter.

Twin for the win,
Angela Sophia

Chapter 8

My feet take me outside, down the morgue steps, on autopilot. My mind is in a thousand places. I'll go to the police station now and hope Valentin isn't already in the field, ask him questions, pose them in a way so he doesn't suspect anything. Then go home and tear Angela's place apart.

"Shayna? Hello?" Seb, standing off to the side of the building, waves a hand. In his short-sleeved blue shirt and dark-wash jeans, he blends in with the crowds making their way to work or the dozen museums nearby; I walked right past him.

"Oh, hey. What are you doing here?" There are no cabs on this side street. Weren't there a dozen an hour ago? I scan the next road over, visible through the row of manicured trees.

Seb lifts his eyebrows. "I am here to meet you. We are going to the catacombs still, yes?"

"Yeah. Yes. Listen, now isn't a good time."

He observes me, registering the shadows on my face, as if he knows I've lost five pounds in the last week and failed to rest well my first night in Paris. As if he knows something surprised me inside the building behind us.

"You do remember, yes?" His forehead creases. "I did not want you to be alone after identifying . . . the body." His eyes drop, and we both look away—him because he still believes Angela's dead, and me because if I look him in the eye one second longer, he will know the truth.

Should I tell him? Wouldn't I want to know? "I remember, yes. It's . . . That was an experience inside. I'm still processing what I saw."

He nods. "I understand. I am here because when I had to see her . . . I was alone afterward, and it was very hard. I did not want that for you." The pain in his voice makes me look up again. The knowing sympathy he wears knocks against the internal walls I built inside that Conservation room.

Men and women in business suits walk by in a hurry. How long will it take to reach the police station in rush-hour traffic? Without knowing the city, I have no way of estimating drive time. The sooner I leave Seb, the sooner I can ply Valentin for information.

With a sharp cough, I resume staring at the ground. A purple *Space Invaders* alien is spray-painted on a concrete square. "Thank you for making the trip here. But I think being alone would be the best thing for me now. I'll see you later." I turn to leave, but he grabs my arm.

"Please." Anguish lines his face, around his mouth, beneath his eyes. "Going to the catacombs will be good for us both. You may learn more about what made Angela happy here, and I can finally learn more about my almost sister-in-law."

His words catch me off guard; all I can do is nod. A tentative smile lessens the tension in his skin. He releases me, and we walk toward the main boulevard. A patina-layered archway, long turned green by the elements, presents a stairwell into the underground transit system. Empty beer cans line the ground twenty feet below, while candy wrappers swirl in a passageway breeze. Seeing the catacombs is a high priority— they're what Angela devoted herself to here. I can go see Valentin this afternoon, and a visit to Angela's favorite place will provide more time to figure out what to say to an officer trained in detecting deception.

Almost sister-in-law. The phrase seems to whisper in my ears. Was Angela that deeply in love with Seb? I pause at the railing, bewildered by so much of the last hour.

"Are you coming?" Seb asks. Both his feet are already two steps down.

Crowds of people jostle to their destinations below, their bodies pushing up against each other in the narrow, subterranean hall. There is no metro system in San Diego. There's the trolley that acts as a quaint subway system aboveground, but this underground network teems with life unknown, harboring blind corners and few exits hundreds of feet beneath fresh air. What if there's a stampede? What if there's a fire? Anxiety I didn't know I carried cuts my breathing short.

Seb watches my face and steps closer. "A taxi might be best," he murmurs. He heads up the stairs past me and hails one. We climb inside as I try to recall when I began hating tight places. As we merge onto the freeway, two cars collide in a fender-bender, and I flinch; Seb notices.

"How did you sleep?" he asks. The miniature screen on the back of the passenger seat displays a stern woman on a news segment. The ticker along the bottom says something about traffic hurting the city. *Deep breath, Shayna.* "Briefly. But I did find something."

I withdraw my cell phone from my handbag, then click through my notes to find the one where I wrote down the information from Angela's blog. Maybe Seb can cast some light on my discovery while I practice extracting info. "A number with the words *divine* and *research* above it. Does this mean anything to you?"

Seb examines my phone screen, zooming in and out with his fingers. "There are eleven digits—ten, if the zero is not relevant." He whips out his own phone and dials, placing it on speaker.

"Bonjour, Maison de Kebab," says someone on the other end. Rock music with French lyrics blasts from the small device. From the front compartment, our cab driver turns his radio up.

"Hmm. Why do you think a kebab restaurant is significant?" Seb ends the call, looking to me for an answer.

Angela leading me to a Turkish sandwich shop makes about as much sense as if I told her to go to the butcher—we haven't eaten meat in years. I shake my head, trying to recover the certainty I had last night—that this message must be something real and useful.

"I don't know. It just seemed like . . . the message was meant for me, or something. I found it on her computer."

Seb lifts an eyebrow. "And Angela said *she* was the spiritual sister."

I place my phone back in my bag, next to Angela's agenda. He leans in. "You brought your passport? If someone steals it, you will be delayed in returning home. The American embassy will take days to issue a new one."

"And lose it in the madness of Angela's apartment?" The place was a sea of upturned boxes and crates when Seb left last night. He doesn't even know I kept going. "No way. Better to have it on me."

Seb shrugs. "As you wish."

Small boutique shops and restaurants line the roundabout of the Denfert Rochereau metro stop. Trees extend to claim their territory from sidewalk plots, while baby strollers group together beneath chatty mothers.

We step from the car to the curb, and Seb faces a small house. "Welcome to the catacombs." Reverence fills his voice, making it breathy. Not a house—a toolshed painted dark green. Attached to it is an imposing stone building, which in my California frame of reference I had assumed was the tourist attraction—not some rickety structure that looks like a gust of wind might take it down.

"Oh" is all I manage.

Seb gives a wistful sigh. "The catacombs are five stories deep and eleven thousand square meters in surface area. There are six million Parisians buried below, spanning seven centuries and two hundred miles." His eyes shimmer in the morning sun. "Shall we?"

"Five stories?" Gauche laughter catches in my throat. If I couldn't handle the metro, how will I handle centuries of crypt tunnels? I place my weight on my back heel. "I'd love for you to tell me about them here."

Seb looks at me. "This is why we came. You did not realize they were so deep?"

His tone is flat, but it couldn't carry more judgment than what I already feel; he's right. I should go down—to glean even a second of communion with my spiritually minded sister, to see whether she left another clue behind. With a little more than a day to find her before my flight home, this is the best next step I have. A way to understand the person my sister became, knowing she isn't lying on a steel slab. I take a deep breath. "Okay. Let's go."

"You are sure?"

"Yes. Before I change my mind."

Past the ticket kiosk and inside its slim corridor, framed illustrations tell the history of rock quarries turned catacombs. While the quarries were leveraged for raw materials, the time came when the Black Plague accelerated the need for new burial ground. Several bouts of the disease struck the city, and existing cemeteries in the center of Paris dating back to the first millennium couldn't handle the strain—the underground walls of adjacent buildings ruptured, and bodies fell into neighboring basements. Seeing an opportunity, city leaders decided certain areas of the tunnels would serve as new burial sites for old bones, and the larger cemeteries' remains were relocated. From mining pits that evolved into structured tunnels, the Black Plague turned the underground matrix into mass graves.

As we begin the descent on a narrow spiral staircase, Seb recounts political details from the seventeenth to the nineteenth centuries. He speaks with more vigor than I've heard from him yet.

I nod through clenched teeth as he moves on to the prehistoric lakes of Paris and how they created the dank smell invading my nostrils now. With no sunlight or source of heat here, the chill is arresting. Placing my feet on each slender, spiraling step becomes a lesson in endurance and balance, when I just want to hunch over and shiver. The thin fabric of my hoodie provides all the insulation of tissue paper.

Once I make the mistake of looking up and see men and women clambering on our trail, the light from the lobby long gone from view, and the realization that we're essentially trapped underground slams into me—that I can't push through those bodies to get up and out, that I must pass through the catacombs, all the way to the other side, to exit. That, according to Valentin, there may be a serial killer out there, hunting down Angela and maybe me by mistake, and I've cornered myself five stories below the surface. Panic claws at my chest, as if it were a literal zombie risen from its marshy tomb below. What the hell was I thinking, agreeing to visit this place when I can barely stand the claustrophobia of the subway and someone could follow me down here and attack at close quarters? When Seb taps me from above and asks if I'm okay, I realize I've been muttering *shit shit shit* on a loop.

Finally, when we reach the bottom of the staircase, the vertical chute opens into a tall antechamber (thank you, God) with a concrete floor. The pinch between my shoulders lessens a little. *The best way out is always through*—one of Angela's favorite quotes, and I don't have a choice now.

Above a diagram of sediment layers displayed on the wall, large black arrows direct visitors into the next room. With each step forward, the arrangements of skulls lining the path become more frequent as the concrete gives way to dirt and the occasional puddle, but they're oddly reassuring—they remind me of photos I found in

Angela's dissertation folders. If she can spend afternoons and evenings here, I should be able to.

Sibling rivalry propels me slightly faster down another tunnel with a stunted ceiling, like a string of dwarves once pickaxed their way through. Seb chatters on behind me, his voice a warm thrum.

"You were close to the truth earlier when you asked whether the Nazis named the catacombs. In fact, both the Nazis and the French Resistance used these tunnels to get around Paris during the Occupation. Angela found the matrix compelling for these reasons, and more."

Hearing mention of the Nazis recalls the store clerk's tattoo and the discomfort I felt last night. Another shot of unease stabs my belly. "Of course she did," I reply.

The dull, flat scent of mold lies beneath the pervasive damp, like centuries of rot have taken hold deep within the catacombs, unaffected by the fresh air brought in by foot traffic from above. I retch when I get too close to a slimy wall. A shelf has been carved out of the rock and filled with sticks. When the light shifts, I realize they are femurs.

"Did you come here with Angela often?" I ask, averting my face, not wanting to see one more bone.

Lips tremble like he's holding back another sob-hiccup. "Our time together here was very short. Too short." Seb is the only person who might understand my pit of loss right now, even as I struggle to understand what her absence at the morgue means. She could be out there—injured, alone, scared—waiting for me at this very second, hoping I find her before someone else does. Or she could simply be gone; she could be dead, just not lying in the morgue, but buried somewhere else.

A German couple passes, gesturing to the engraved rock beside us, breaking through my panic. *Deep breath.* Angela wants me here. Divining her research was a clue. The catacombs are her research subject. This is the right next step.

I step into a new gallery of bones. *Breathe.* "Did you help with Angela's work? I don't know if neurology really applies to urban planning."

Seb sniffles. "Not exactly. But I enjoyed hearing about her learnings. A geologist I know conducts archaeological research in the catacombs, and Angela applied for his internship so she could spend more time in the ossuary after the tour office closed."

"Naturally." I shudder, imagining these passages empty of visitors and even creepier. "Anything else hidden here besides skeletons?"

"Oh yes." He perks up. "It is a labyrinth. Full of secrets and surprises around every corner. In the late eighteen hundreds, the caretaker of the catacombs went missing." He gestures with his hands—*poof!* *Gone.* "Ten years later, his body was found in an obscure area, not usually frequented. A man so intimately acquainted with the ossuaries, the caretaker himself, became lost to his death." Seb leans in, then wiggles his eyebrows. "*Naturally*—anything can happen down here."

I squint at him, then walk a few steps ahead. Disturbing anecdote aside, he thinks we're friendly enough to tease me. Cute.

Several paths lead in the same direction, according to a mounted plaque. Beneath the plaque, a security guard reaches into a knapsack at his feet and takes out a baguette sandwich. My belly growls at the crisp scent of lettuce and ham in this dusty, dirty setting. The normalcy of it unlocks something in my brain. "Has anyone ever lived down here? I mean, have these—" I motion to the well-crafted walkways, smooth roofs, and pillars holding up seventy-five feet of earth. "Were these always used as quarries?"

Angela disappeared from campus in the chaos of a school shooting. A tiny voice inside me has been wondering since I saw her thesis draft: *Could she have escaped to the catacombs? Was she then followed by her ultimate attacker?* Fully allowing the notion to form, then giving life to the question, is liberating. I step forward, the better to catch Seb's answer.

He rubs the back of his neck. "Speaking as a scientist, and having worked with several archaeology teams here, no. No one has ever lived down here. Only died."

I stare at the V-neck of his blue cotton shirt. Through it. The dirt walls seem to absorb his words before I can grasp them, latch on to them, and refute them somehow. Then all I have left is the echo of an argument I almost made, a would-be hidden fact I read in Angela's work last night, a *gotcha!* theory that might have held water, were reality not so painfully apparent and true.

I needed to come down here. To gain some insight into my sister's world and also some clarity at her options. This is not one of them.

❧

Cabs await tourists at the exit of the catacombs, eager for fares. I tell Seb I need to go back to Angela's apartment to finish packing, but in truth I'm dying to find Valentin and ransack the apartment for more notes. Then my stomach rumbles, and he insists on buying lunch.

I have to eat eventually.

"All right, let's make this quick. Where do you want to go?" I ask.

He smiles. "It's a surprise."

I return a deadpan expression.

"It's only fifteen minutes away from here, and on the way back to Montmartre," he says.

"That'll do."

We grab a cab and arrive at Seb's secret destination, along a public park. When I go to pay the taxi driver, Seb huffs and insists that he'll buy the fare. We exit the cab, and the trees spread wide and thick above our heads, olive colors mixing with beige in the arid summer. As the branches thin out toward a clearing, the Eiffel Tower looms like the icon it is, erect and imposing over the hundreds of people taking pictures beneath.

We walk along the paved path toward the center of the park, and the smell of pot rises to mix with cigarette smoke. I look up—

—and pause midstep. The circle with the fifty-eight inside it, the one in Angela's planner, is the restaurant Seb means to take us to now. The 58.

We take an elevator to the middle base of the tower. Inside the restaurant, glasses of wine are already waiting on the white tablecloth when we arrive, which explains the phone call Seb made in the cab. I shoot him a glance, and he grins. "They know me here."

The wine is tempting—it would relax me, loosen me up—but I say, "I'm good with water. Thanks."

"You sure?"

Sunrays pass through the window and seem to make the wine glow. The memory of its crisp flavor, the delicious bite of aftertaste, returns to my mind unbidden. "Not a fan of wine," I say.

"Suit yourself." He asks the waiter for a bottle of sparkling water. "Let us recommence. What about this agenda? This Nour friend whose birthday Angela celebrated?"

I nibble on a hard crostini from the woven bowl on the table. The one clue I managed to find that seemed plausible—the numbers in the blog entry—led to a fast food joint. The mysterious number fifty-eight? Just a restaurant she probably visited with Seb. The catacombs visit was helpful in seeing what Angela devoted herself to, but there were no hints as to her traumatic last steps. Still, visiting Nour seems like a reach. Does one party with Angela a year ago make Nour a high-priority lead, especially with time running out before my flight? I open my mouth to dismiss Seb's suggestion, then remember his devastated expression in the catacombs and check the urge. He just wants to know what happened to the woman he loved.

Be nice. Be open. Be more like Angela, I tell myself. Pragmatic can still be nice.

Seb peruses the menu, oblivious to my mental tug-of-war. "Are you hungry?"

My stomach gurgles. "Starved."

"Angela always liked the salads here. Maybe you should try one."

Heat spreads across my cheeks. "Are you entertaining the idea that I'm my sister right now?" I aim for matter-of-fact, but my words sound flirtatious. He thinks she's gone. How can he not want to believe I'm Angela?

This is crazy. And messed up on so many levels. I should have suggested McDonald's.

Seb pauses to reflect. "Words cannot express how I miss her. When I first met you, I thought your resemblance was incredible. Now I'm beginning to believe two women could not be more different. Where one is analytical, the other breathes artistry. Monsieur?" He stops the nearest waiter. "Deux Calvados, s'il vous plaît."

"Calvados?" I ask.

"A regional brandy from up north. Normandy. Angela loved it—it's an aperitif. Traditional before the main course." He speaks with energy, sounding almost Italian in the way his words string together. Round ears stick out against the close cut of his hair, like a little boy who hasn't grown into them yet.

The server sets down two miniature vases of liquid before I can reply. "I'm good, really."

Seb shrugs. "I understand. I hope you don't feel I am pressuring you. This is merely a French lunch." He offers a small smile.

Raising my glass of water, I say, "To thinking like Angela. And finding her attacker."

"Santé." Seb clinks my glass with his. We discuss our only thing in common: Angela. Her time in Paris has been productive—earning honors at the Sorbonne, making friends, taking up half marathons, discovering new restaurants. Each time Seb volunteers some detail about my sister I'm unaware of, a pang of guilt then regret stabs my ribs.

We move on to discussing travel and places we'd like to visit. Seb says something that doesn't translate well.

"Now, what is caboodle? I don't think we think it means the same thing." I toss back the rest of my water. Seb sips his second Calvados. A shift change has occurred, and new faces in uniform populate the floor.

"Not caboodle, *Kabul.*" Seb clears his throat. "My brother. He was stationed there in Afghanistan when he died. Chemical warfare was being used, both as a physical and moral tactic." Seb turns his gaze to the window. "Worse . . . if it can get worse . . . I fear I disappointed him while he was abroad." His shoulders hunch forward.

Conversations seem to hush around us, as though in response to Seb's confession. Emotion tightens my throat at the image he paints with his words: two brothers, separated by some of the most heinous, appalling acts this world can offer—not twins, but the closeness Seb seems to still feel for his brother could be a mirror to the love I have for my sister. Seeing him so heartbroken, years after his loss, jars loose some of the wall I'd built between us back in Angela's apartment.

Angela, where are you?

"This is none of my business," I say. "But whatever happened between you two, you have to forgive yourself. You know that, right? Your brother's death is a tragedy. Not your fault."

"No, I know. Perhaps. I just would hate to have disappointed him in the end. My family's opinion is very important to me. When I became a neurologist instead of a surgeon like my uncle, it did not go well. My uncle has never stopped telling me how disappointed he is." Seb gives a clipped laugh. "So maybe I should care less about family."

"Maybe."

My thoughts are lingering on Seb's morose expression, him staring out the window, recalling his brother's death, when he raises his glass. "Then let us toast. To not seeking happiness in others' opinions. To finding stability from within."

We exchange cheers. Sunlight shifts toward the tall buildings and museum along this side of the tower.

"Shall we?" Seb rises, offering his arm to me.

"Did we pay the bill?"

A smile stops at his mouth. "Have you ever done a *restau-baskets*?"

"Restaurant . . . basketball shoes. Dine and dash? Are you serious?"

He doesn't blink from my stare. I can't tell whether he's messing with me again. Shock pierces the relaxation I felt.

Seb cracks into a grin. "Come, come. It was a joke. Here comes the server now. The look on your face!" He bursts into laughter, then pokes my side until I start to laugh, too.

We descend in the elevator to the ground level after paying (he insists again), then he stumbles into the park, with me following. A pair of costumed sailors, the kind you take photos with along Hollywood Boulevard or Times Square, amble toward the river. Couples lie flat on their blankets, staring at the clear sky.

"Man," I groan.

Seb plants himself on the wooden boards of a park bench. He pulls me into his lap. "Who?"

"Whoa, hey—" Up close, creases mark the corners of his eyes—dark-blue spheres, rich in color. I'm suddenly more aware than I was even in the restaurant that he's the kind of guy—scientific, serious—that I would usually fall for, not Angela. And is there a part of me—a small part—that would feel satisfaction if he chose me over Angela, or at least his memories of her?

I stand, almost as if to distance myself from my thoughts, but he pulls me back. Seb says something in French that sounds amused, and the sweet scent of Calvados reaches my nose. The fabric of his cargo shorts is bumpy against my thin leggings.

"We didn't find anything this morning," I whisper, conscious of how close our faces are. His palms are warm on my arms. "We're no closer to discovering how or why she disappeared or . . ." Tears fill my eyes, betraying the careful stoicism I've been wearing in public.

Large thumbs caress my cheeks. Seb whispers in a soothing tone, "Je suis là, ma belle."

The poetic sound distracts me as he pulls me to his lips. What starts out as a soft kiss deepens, becomes a passionate embrace; in the background, a street performer with an accordion plays a haunting song, and I lose myself for a moment. How long has it been since I've connected with someone? After my parents died, I collapsed, isolating myself in my childhood home, unable, until recently, to muster the enthusiasm to continue pursuing medical school, set adrift even from my own sister, who'd lashed out at me. I've been craving connection with someone even if my practical side has never acknowledged it.

His tongue forces my mouth open and explores me, one palm gripping my neck, the other clutching my hip. Greedy kisses penetrate my skin, sending a tremor to my thighs. My back arches, and he moans into my neck, "Mon Angèle."

I gasp. All of a sudden his taste is sharp, cloying. I pull away, registering only that Seb's wide eyes mirror my horror.

Down the street I run, faster, like the thief I am. Running like I just kissed my dead sister's boyfriend. At the river's edge, I slow to a walk, and the noise of Parisian rush hour drowns my sobs along the boulevard. I force myself to travel a mile on foot before grabbing a cab, to drown my thoughts in honking horns, loud radios, and the conversations of people meandering past.

Despite my effort to forget them—to pretend they were something less devastating—Sebastien's mumbled words in French remain clear.

My Angela.

Chapter 9

Each year, the June gloom sweeps into San Diego with lugubrious clouds taking up residence, refusing to leave until July. The June my parents died was unseasonably hot. The clouds entered early, an ominous warning of the dark period to follow, and the gloom made my late-May graduation ceremony a dreary, humid affair, the months that followed downright interminable. It was an endless overcast sky that mirrored my grief exactly. Later that summer, I deferred med school entry, citing a death in the family—two of them. I moved into my parents' home, because it held all my happy memories left; Angela wanted me to sell it, but I didn't want to say goodbye to the memory of our parents and our foursome, too. Surfing, gardening, and self-defense classes dominated my days.

My newfound pursuits distracted me, all right—until five o'clock. Dusk was the first hint loneliness was inbound; the absence of traditions that began during my childhood and lasted well into college was deafening. My mom and dad used to put on Frank Sinatra or Billie Holiday—something jazzy—when they came home from their offices after work, and on Fridays my mother always bought peonies, whose fragrant scent lasted through the entire weekend.

I missed Angela most during those times, when grief would weigh the heaviest. She was the only one who knew the pain I felt. Siblings, for better or for worse, are the only people in the world with whom you share so many experiences, who outlast friends and lovers, who understand you because they witnessed your formative years firsthand. Once, through blurry eyes, I caught a glimpse of myself in a window's reflection, and for a second—a bittersweet second—I thought it was Angela, come home to surprise me. To cry with me. So we could hold each other. That night was one of the hardest.

The second year I deferred my medical school admission, I began interning at the local veterans' hospital on UCSD's campus. The emptiness lingered. Yet interacting with the world again reinforced the desire to be a part of it—not simply slink along in the shadows. My parents had been killed on impact, their car slamming into the valley below the freeway; modern medicine could not have saved them, even if they'd slammed into a hospital. Watching people benefit from established treatments—casts for broken bones, dialysis, radiation—was reassuring. Consistent. Dependable. The whole experience restored in me a sense of trust and control in life again. This predictability felt like the polar opposite of the emotional chaos I'd been living, losing my parents suddenly.

Studying oncology this fall was the cornerstone of my plan to move forward. Treating cancer would be fulfillment enough, I was hoping, to ease the perpetual ache I still felt. I wanted to help revive trust and control in the lives of cancer patients and their families, wherever I could, to share with others this newfound sense of balance.

Sweet idea, thinking I could restore someone else's family, if not my own. That was before I knew what lay ahead in Paris.

Warm, buttery flakes of croissant flutter to the ground like dragonfly wings as I inhale another bite. To think, this is the first time I'm eating one, and there's a bakery right down the street.

It's the first time, and my flight leaves in twelve hours.

A homeless man with pink-rimmed eyes mutters to himself beside Angela's building's doorway. It's the same man as the first night when I went out for soda. In the light of day, he seems even more isolated against the midweek hustle of people hurrying by.

A woman in athletic gear pauses to watch me from across the street. We lock eyes. She doesn't bother to check right or left for cars as she steps into the road and heads straight toward me. Valentin's warning to be on guard—each stranger a potential serial killer—surges in my thoughts, and I drop my croissant in a panic. The woman runs at me—and then a man leaps past me straight into her arms. The couple embraces. A car honks for them to get out of the road, and they stroll away arm in arm. I draw a hand down my face, willing myself to laugh, knowing there's nothing funny about it.

My phone buzzes, causing me to jump. I cringe, digging in my messenger bag, already certain it's another of Seb's calls. He phoned twice yesterday but didn't leave a message. When I returned to Angela's apartment after wandering the city in a daze, a note with an apology was wedged under her door. The scent of his musky cologne lingered in my hair, on my tank top where he rubbed his face against my neck, until I took the hottest shower Angela's pipes would permit.

Roaming along, unchaperoned, I came to a few conclusions. The first was that Inspector Valentin was probably not my best source of help. If he'd known the body in the morgue might not be Angela's—and how could he not?—he'd purposely concealed it from me. The second: Seb is too emotional, and too available. Remembering his suggestion that we go down inside the catacombs, then spend an hour and a half at one of his and Angela's favorite lunch spots, only proves that he's treating this like a nostalgia tour—a trip down memory lane with the world's best substitute for his girlfriend.

I retrieve my phone and swipe, already dreading his words.

Shayna, please. I am sorry. Let us continue our search this afternoon. I still have ideas before you leave. It was a mistake induced by alcohol. Completely my fault.

A hard laugh bursts out of me. No shit. Did Seb really think he was kissing Angela? Who did I think I was kissing? How much of the day's idiocy was rooted in the Calvados he drank, and how much was me being starved for companionship these last three years? I press a palm to my forehead. Instead of divining with Angela and reaching out for her, I reached for her boyfriend. Emotion chokes my throat, and I take deep breaths through my mouth.

Two cabs have passed by. Three SUV taxis idle within a block, and I walk down until I find one empty. My phone buzzes again. Sebastien Bronn scrolls across the screen, but I silence it as I climb into a car.

After my shower, I dived into a folder on Angela's laptop that I'd only glanced through before. One document within it listed articles to read, followed by books and encyclopedias, with half the titles already crossed out. Another spreadsheet logged the time she spent in the catacombs over the last year, with increasing visits over the last six months. There was a folder of images relating to the ossuaries, some in sepia tone, some clearly modern, presenting dapper-looking officials and fatigued workers. Another, entitled To Be Used, contained her own photographs shot within the tunnels. In one photo, tibia bones formed a deep-set shelf blending into a wall of ribs. Angela was always territorial; despite having access to images online, she would have wanted the photos in her thesis to be her own.

When we were kids, Angela had this exquisite designer doll, the kind that goes for hundreds of dollars, and which I secretly loved. Our mother had it customized to match our features, half Asian, half white, fairly assuming I wouldn't want my own doll since I'd shunned the usual Barbies Angela played with. But this one looked like me, like us, and so I loved her.

One day, Angela caught me playing with it. *What do you think you're doing?*

I had looked up from my bed, where I was giving the doll her one-year checkup, imitating what I thought our parents did for work. *Playing doctor. Want to?* I wasn't far off—my dad was a family practitioner and my mom was an obstetrician.

That's not what doctors do, dummy. Nurses do that stuff. And she's mine. Angela had yanked the doll away, and the foot had smacked me hard in the chin in the process. We each waited for me to cry, but I didn't. *Don't take my stuff again,* she hissed and left my room.

I'd gotten off easy, in retrospect. Her retribution would come later, when I was most vulnerable, but in that moment I was only pleased I could spend more time with the doll.

I let my head relax against the cracked leather seat of the taxi and drum an aimless rhythm on the middle armrest. A mini television mounted on the back of the passenger seat blares a human-interest piece on smugglers tattooing their victims.

Rummaging through Angela's files turned up only what I'd noticed before—class essays, notes, bills, and e-receipts. Her agenda seems to be the only useful clue to her whereabouts. I withdraw it from my bag and flip to last August. Nour's address is clearly written in my sister's cursive, the last letter ending in a curlicue. I unlock my phone to text a reply to Seb.

Headache. Talk later.

As soon as I click my phone to black, it begins ringing. Really? "Yes?"

Pause. "Miss Darby, this is Jean-Luc Fillion. Is this a bad time?"

The embassy liaison. "Oh. I mean, no, now is fine. What can I do for you? I don't have any bitch work today." I'm smiling, but I don't think it's audible.

Jean-Luc gives a polite laugh. Ha-ha. Not enthusiastic but not offended. "Just wanted to follow up and see how your visit was going," he says. "You're flying out this evening, right? I'm still happy to help in any way until then."

"If I need something, I'll reach out. Thank you." I hang up, dismissing the urge to beg him to come with me to Nour's. Although Seb is suddenly a world of confusion—revulsion—for me, I shouldn't dismiss his idea to visit her/him. There's no time left for wavering. To borrow from one of Angela's favorite figures in history, Winston Churchill—if you're going through hell, keep going.

I don't have another option.

A six-story yellow apartment building rises from the suburbs of Saint Denis, on the outskirts of Paris's sports stadium. A trio of garbage cans lines the street, stuffed to the brim with plastic bags and cardboard. Something deep-fried wafts from a kitchen nearby, and saliva pools in my mouth. A deflated soccer ball lies in the gutter, covered in grime. I glance at Angela's planner again.

Nour. Apartment 23, Rue de Mignon, Saint Denis.

White tile peeks through the building's open doorway, the door handle dangling loose by a single screw. I hesitate, noting the empty street parking, make sure no one has followed me, then step inside.

Plaster, metal, and concrete flooring decorate the scene. Eggshell paint adds to the vacuumed, prototypic atmosphere.

French rap carries from farther within as I climb the stained, carpeted steps to the fifth floor. The darkness of the stairwell gives me pause on the landing, but I press on.

"Who's there?" a woman calls in French from behind a thick metal door with no peephole.

"It's Shayna. Angela's sister." Footsteps approach. The chain is lifted, and the dead bolt slides back. Frizzy black curls with pink tips emerge from the apartment, creating a pastel halo framing a round face. Slanted sunlight penetrates the gauzy curtain of a window behind, dilating my pupils from the dark hallway.

"Nour?" My vision adjusts, and the young woman inhales a sharp breath.

"Angèle." She grabs me by the shoulders. "Holy fuck, you're alive!" She yanks me into an embrace. Her sharp chin quivers against my collarbone. "Oh my God, I was so worried."

"No, I'm not . . . ," I mumble. "I'm . . . Shayna, Angela's twin."

The young woman's grip lessens. She pulls back to examine me with wide brown eyes. Understanding melts the happiness from her face. "Merde."

A man steps out from the kitchen to give a low whistle. Is *he* Nour? The apartment is dim—a television shows a paused movie— but they could be cousins, for all their shared traits: wavy black hair, dark eyes, and lean builds. There's a large mole on the man's cheek, and, when he smiles, a front tooth is chipped like he once lost a fight. He says something in French that makes the woman shoot him a dagger glare.

Please, God, let one of them be Nour.

She rubs her eyes. Her accented English lingers between us, and I relax a little knowing we can communicate. Fuchsia hair dye contrasts and embellishes the brightness of an emerald stud piercing her left nostril. A spandex leotard dips low on her chest while pockets of skin at her hips peek from sagging jeans. Her bright-red lips pucker to the side. "You are the sister of Angela. Is that Angela's . . . hoodie?"

I smile. She knows my sister well enough to know her wardrobe and probably a few of her habits. Jackpot. "I'm sorry I didn't call first. I only had an address."

We stand awkwardly, digesting my anticlimactic entrance.

"Pas de problème, chérie." The man steps forward. "I am Hugo, a friend of Nour." He lifts his hand in hello. His head tilts to the side, appraising me with charcoal-rimmed eyes.

Nour remains rooted to the spot. "How can I help you?" She crosses her arms beneath her chest, though her voice softens. "I imagine you're looking for her."

"Actually, I'm . . ." Nour's face drops, and I recall the feeling of expecting the earth to crack open and swallow you whole, of standing on the anxious precipice, waiting for the terrible blow. Not knowing whether Angela is alive. Valentin's throaty voice edges forward from my memory: *Rumors have leaked to the media that an American has been missing since the shooting, and we are trying to contain this information before releasing a statement. A family member's identification will push the American government to provide dental and medical records more quickly.*

I don't blame Nour for holding out hope. Even as there's no way I can let on the true levels of batshit crazy reality has become. Taking a cue from the police, until I'm certain Angela is dead or alive, I'll have to maintain the status quo. Adopting a tense expression appropriate to discussing a missing sister, I resume. "I'm trying to learn more about her time here in Paris. Can you help me with that?"

Nour stares at me, her brows stitched tight. Where seconds ago she exuded a fierce strength beyond her small frame, now she appears childlike, full of questions and also deep sadness. "What was your name again?"

"Shayna."

She releases a breath. "Happy to help, Shayna. Anything to drink?"

"A glass of water, please. Paris is hotter than I expected."

Away from the confined quarters of the city center, Nour's studio apartment is spacious, if cluttered with yellow bags and clothing. Twice the size of Angela's, the layout extends like a suite, with three massive windows overlooking the modest neighborhood below. A pair of boys throws a rugby ball in the street.

"Please excuse the mess. I wasn't expecting . . . well, anyone apart from Hugo." Nour grabs me a mini water bottle from the fridge and opens one herself. She leans against the counter and resumes her assessment of me in between swigs. "Has there been any progress on Angela's case? She's been missing since late June."

"Not much. Has she been talked about in the news?"

"The media says she's the only person still unaccounted for from the day of the shooting. We've all just been waiting and praying." Nour hugs herself. Hugo wraps an arm around her.

"Did you know Angela, too?"

"No. Never met her." He offers a tight-lipped smile.

I take a sip of water. "I found your name, Nour, in Angela's old agenda. I was wondering if you could tell me what her life was like the last few years. Did you spend a lot of time with her?"

Nour hesitates before replying. She gazes at me. "C'est bizarre . . . The only way I know you're not Angela is she would have tried to flirt with Hugo already."

Hugo scrunches his nose.

She smiles. "Angela and I were in Imperial World Literature class together, my third year of college, her senior year. We did some group projects at a time when her French was not so good. We helped each other. Her patience is responsible for my level of English today." Nour pauses. She struggles to say something, leaning against the counter that encircles the kitchen.

"We hadn't been close for a while, me and Angela. Life does that. Takes you to other things that seem important, instead of people you care for," she whispers. "You really look so much alike." She drops her head. Pink curls shudder, a neon crown.

I don't know what to say. What should I say? "We are . . . identical." *Stellar, Shayna.* I crack my pinkie. "It seems like you two were very close. I missed so much of her life these last three years she was in Paris."

"Everything has been crazy. First the shooting, then Angela disappearing—two students died, did you know?"

Some pocket of memory registers. "I think I read that. Did you know them?"

She lifts her head, tears on her face. "Does it matter? This is a rarity here. This is not like in the United States, a school shooting every month. It is almost impossible to obtain a gun in France if you're not military. You have to go on the European black market."

I open my mouth to defend my country, but the verity of her words, the anguish of her voice stops me. It's true; I read about the students, then glossed over the shooting's details that didn't directly relate to Angela's disappearance. Traumatic headlines don't faze me like they used to. I don't have enough bandwidth to care as much as I would like. Maybe that does make me callous. Shame coats me all over, and I examine the calendar on her wall to avoid meeting her gaze. Notes, arrows, and circled dates cover the page. Just like Angela's.

"You're right," I whisper.

"She missed you. She talked about you all the time, about the missing sister from her life back home. Things you would have said and done. Locations she wished you were here to see. And now I'm having the exact same conversation, only with her twin about her. Putain, c'est bizarre." Nour steps back from the counter to lean against the sofa, where Hugo now sits.

Did she tell you she abandoned me after our parents died?

What did she tell you, exactly? That I never came to visit her?

Conflicting emotions batter me on all sides as I think about the times I needed Angela while she was eating cheese in Paris, hanging out with Nour. Another shot of jealousy and frustration pokes at my insides.

"What was her life like these last few months?" I try again. "It seems she was knee-deep in doctoral studies."

Nour wipes her lashes with orange nails. "Angela is a good friend, but she's . . . how do you say? Ambitious? She knew what she wanted. We did not see each other so much over the last year. The last time we hung out was my fucking birthday last August. I only learned about her disappearance from friends."

A twinge of pride registers. My flighty sister, Angela, was focused. "I wonder if Seb knows any of them. Do you have their numbers? I'd love to speak to them."

Nour stops picking at a cuticle. "Who is Seb?"

"Angela's boyfriend. They were dating for a year before the shooting. Angela never told you about him?"

She shakes her head. "No. I don't think so. A year? My party was almost a year ago, but we haven't really caught up on campus in ages. I'm in the master's program for costume design."

"Okay. Well, what about those friends? Do you think I could ask them a few questions?"

"Sorry, love. Most people at the Sorbonne are on summer holiday right now. People leave the city and go home to the countryside or holiday somewhere in Europe."

Must be nice. No wonder the police have made almost no progress in solving Angela's case.

"Do you have any idea who might want to hurt Angela?"

Nour's face hardens, but her reply is instant. "Manu. I don't know if she's capable of attacking Angela, or orchestrating anything against her, but she didn't like her. They were friends at first, then they had some kind of conflict. She actually stole Angela's bike six months ago."

"Did Angela report it?"

Nour shakes her head. "Not that I know of. Manu kept harassing her in these ways. Angela would go to the toilets, and Manu would go into her purse and take her metro tickets. Pressure Angela to allow Manu to drive her home."

"How do you know all this if you didn't see Angela over the last year?"

Nour shrugs. "Everyone knew—other people saw it. I ran into Angela one time at the campus store, and she looked exhausted. I asked her what was wrong, and she nodded behind her. Manu was staring at us from a table."

I nod myself, imagining the scene. How difficult must it have been for Angela to navigate harassment in her second language? Someone should have helped her.

Hugo begins to play with Nour's hair, but she doesn't react. She leans forward, as if to tell a secret. "Manu is also rumored to have connections to a few . . . how do you say . . . gangs? And she is Roma."

Hugo throws up his hands, speaking in French at a mile-a-minute pace, frowning at her words. Nour shouts him down, then points to me, and they both quiet.

"Um, what is Roma? Italian?" I offer.

"Gypsy." Nour side-eyes Hugo, daring him to object, and he lifts his hands with a huff. "They move around a lot."

"Well, where is she now?"

"No one has seen Manu since before the shooting."

"So she's missing, too? Is there anyone else who could talk to me about Manu? Someone who knew both her and Angela, and who is not on holiday?"

"You should go see Delphine Rousseau, Angela's dissertation director. I think she's teaching the summer school session. She would have more information about Angela's studies and whether Manu is still enrolled at the Sorbonne or skipped out to Belgium." Corkscrew curls tilt to the side, emphasizing the last possibility. "Manu's full name is Emmanuelle Wood."

My mind is spinning. It's not crazy Nour never heard of Seb if she and Angela didn't see each other most of last year. Even if they were good friends in the two years prior. But that, coupled with learning more about this *frenemy* Angela had, is unnerving. What other variables to this equation am I missing? I thought Nour might shed more light on Paris Angela and my sister's routines, but these insights only leave me anxious and feeling like I know even less than I did before. "Thanks. And thanks for the water." I turn to leave when Nour moves to my side.

"I wish I could show you around, but I'm under deadline with the Paris Opera this week. I hope you find what it is you're looking for. Just be careful. France is not very friendly to foreigners at the moment. It's actually giving us Muslims a break." Her laugh stops short, relaxing into a smile. "Let me know if I can help more. Good luck, love."

Nour kisses me on both cheeks, and Hugo does the same. Despite the rough start to our introductions, I shut the door feeling a little less alone.

Outside the police station, I pay my cab driver in a bleary-eyed trance, then step to the curb. Collecting my thoughts the best I can, I jog into the police station and sail through the metal detector to pause before the same receptionist from Sunday.

"Inspector Valentin, please?" I ask in French.

An annoyed sigh shakes the woman's jowls as she looks up. A crossword puzzle on her cell phone is illuminated in her palm. Eyeing my frazzled expression, she turns to her computer and makes a few clicks. Thick, hair-sprayed curls protect her face like a helmet. "The inspector is out of the office."

Crap. "When will he return?"

"No idea, miss. Do you want to leave a message for him? He can call you tomorrow." She lifts a few notepads, moves a stack of papers.

A cold chill snakes through my chest. Tomorrow. My flight home to San Diego leaves at nine tonight. And what have I accomplished? I kissed Angela's boyfriend, ruining my relationship with my guide to this city. I met with Nour and Hugo and learned Angela might have a stalker. I think Angela is alive, but I signed away any suspicion that she may still be breathing somewhere, confirming her dead. Have I accomplished anything? More likely I've left things worse than when I arrived.

That body in the morgue wearing Angela's toe tag is not my sister. Whose sister is it?

"You are American." I jump at the slurred English hissed into my ear. "You should not be so proud to be an American." A man with wiry, white-streaked hair, who'd been sleeping on one of the wall benches, teeters two inches from my face. Something brown stains his T-shirt, and he smells of whiskey. Sweat covers the deep wrinkles of his forehead.

"I'm sorry?"

He sneers. "Your country thinks it can do whatever it wants whenever it wants." Angry English dissolves into angry French, alerting everyone else in the lobby that we are not friends, that I don't know who the hell this person is or why he grabs me by the shoulders. "You are all damned! Americans, you are damned by God himself!"

"Olivier, au secours! Monsieur, arrêtez!" The receptionist waves frantically for the security guard.

A man launches toward us and rips the guy off me, wrestling him to the ground. Expletives in French howl from the drunk's mouth as he struggles against the full nelson laid on him. Olivier, the security guard, handcuffs my assailant, then drags him away by the scruffy collar.

I straighten my shirt and massage my skin where I couldn't shake him loose. The receptionist asks me whether I'm okay. I nod. She smiles reassuringly, then turns back to her crossword game. I peer around the lobby. Everyone resumes their conversations, my brush with violence forgotten. Did that just happen?

Lunatics: a normal part of police life.

How quickly are other events, cases, and missing persons forgotten? I hate to think what will happen to Angela's case in a week, or a month from now. Will her file gather dust in Valentin's office until he tosses it somewhere in the basement? The idea of actually leaving, knowing my sister's body isn't on a metal tray, but lying—dead or alive—somewhere else, causes me to shudder. Our secret language on the whiteboard is a warning.

I can't fly out tonight.

I thank the receptionist, then duck off to the side. My cell phone's search browser shows a flight departing Paris on Sunday, landing me at San Diego International late Sunday night, with time zone differences. Just in time for the first day of UCSD's med school orientation. Moving forward, I have to buckle down. Cut out all distractions to find Angela. No more Seb. No more fake-trusting nature.

My sister is alive. The idea is enough to make me light-headed when my arm starts to pulse; a bruise takes shape where the drunk attacked me. Remaining in Paris will require more than simply intentional choices and being alert. I need someone who can walk me through this city and all of its hidden pitfalls and interactions in another language. I still need a guide.

I scroll through my phone to this morning's call log, then press down.

"Allo?"

Heavy breathing carries through the receiver, and I have to wonder whether looping in another Frenchman is wise. Whether there's any wisdom to staying here. Or whether I'm about to ask another witness to document this week's slow implosion of my life.

Chapter 10

from: Angela Darby <ange.d.paris@smail.com>
to: "Darby, Shayna" <shayna.darby93@smail.com>
date: Jun 23, 2015 3:04 a.m.
subject: (no subject)

Dear Shayna,

Tell me it's not true. Tell me this is a terrible nightmare. Tell me Mom and Dad are still breathing.

I've gone through eight tissue boxes. Three rolls of toilet paper when I ran out of tissue. I don't know where the tears keep coming from.

No words can express the depth of the black hole in my stomach, eating a pit where my organs once were. I picture it like something out of *Star Trek*, consuming all of my happiness, my spirit, my will to do anything, and leaving only blackness behind. It won't stop. When I close my eyes, I see Mom's long dark hair and Dad's thinning, russet tufts falling into the abyss. So I try not to close my eyes. I try to memorize photos of them, replay the sounds of their voices in my head and Dad's shrill finger whistle—but the second I close my eyes, the images of them falling return. I didn't even see them, as you did. When you identified the bodies.

Mom and Dad are gone.

I'm so angry at myself for leaving, for being here and not spending the last few months of their lives with them. All because I felt lost at home. Confused. Scared at the quarter-life crisis bearing down on me. *We are orphans.* My heart physically aches at the thought of you alone in our parents' home, to the point where I looked at the medications I'm taking to see if they created palpitations.

Do you remember when I locked you in the hope chest in Mom's closet? We were six. You made me so mad because you wouldn't let me in to play with her shoes, though there was more than enough room, so I locked you in. Mom and Dad were having dinner with Aunt Meredith and Aunt Judy downstairs— Aunt Meredith had just broken up with another boyfriend—and they didn't hear you screaming. I said I didn't hear you, either, and I didn't really—it was mostly stifled. But I felt it. I felt it in the way my own stomach seized and my heart almost tore through my ribs. I broke into a sweat all over and thought I was going to puke. I know it felt longer to you, but I lifted the latch after maybe a minute.

Your panic, your fear, your terror were all mine in that moment, which is why it hurts so badly now. We carry more than our own pain—we shoulder the other's buried, center-of-gravity suffering. As my sister, my identical twin, our connection spans distance and time. Even now, my stomach knots at three in the morning, because on the other side of the world it is six in the evening and you are wide-awake and grieving. It's why I've decided to muffle this ache here in Paris. I'm not coming home. I can't.

You have always been the stronger of us. I doubt I would last in the same room with you, with so much agony in one space, one chest, one breaking heart. Your courage differentiates us, whether I want to admit it or not. Going from place to place trying to ignore my issues, avoid them, always searching for something more, has gotten me little headway until now. I'm constantly in self-preservation mode, ready to fly away at the drop of a dime, while you are steadfast. But I'm different here. It feels different this time. Going home would destroy that on so many levels.

It is a hot poker shoved into my eye, the thought of leaving you to manage the grisly details of their service alone, and you don't have to. Let Aunt Judy and Aunt Meredith handle most of the details. We're twenty-one years old. No one should have to lose her parents like this, both at the same time, right after college finishes. This is bullshit.

You should not have to deal with this. I should not have to deal with this. So I'm not going to. I'm sorry. Please understand. I know you won't, though, and that's okay.

I am so sorry.

I love you.

TFTW
Angela

Chapter 11

A breeze slides along my bare skin and momentarily clears the air. Then the cigarette smoke snaking from the trio of fourteen-year-olds beside me resumes permeating my T-shirt, my hair, my shorts, my skin. Barf. An aggressive red palm has been preventing me from entering the crosswalk for, I swear, five minutes—all the more frustrating when I've finally found my embassy liaison. Watching him across the street as he runs his hand through thick blond hair makes me feel like a voyeur. In a burst of paranoia, I glance around to see whether someone is watching me.

The café Jean-Luc suggested would stand out anywhere else. But, situated next to the Sorbonne, Café des Étudiants was only one of a dozen with a "colorful canopy and chairs and tables out front. You can't miss it." Seems I strive to prove people wrong wherever I go, because I looped the block twice.

As I finally make it across the street and sit down in a steel bistro chair, Jean-Luc finishes an espresso. In his green skinny jeans and purple T-shirt, he looks strikingly casual for a workday.

"Mademoiselle, bonjour." A portly man with dusky skin and more hair on his jaw than his head greets me with an uninterested smile. "Vous désirez?"

I point to Jean-Luc's tiny cup, then spread my hands. "Like that but bigger, please."

"Un café allongé, s'il vous plaît," Jean-Luc translates with a crooked grin that reaches his ears. The waiter returns with my coffee, and we both lean in over our drinks. The familiar scent of roasted beans is a small comfort in an otherwise foreign environment; I allow myself a moment to breathe deep with eyes closed, let the clicking of heels along the sidewalk and the acceleration of car engines in the street fully swell in my ears. An infant cries somewhere around the corner. When I look up, Jean-Luc is staring at me.

"Miss Darby. What can I do for you?"

"Shayna." He's four, maybe five years older than me. I place my cup on the table and smooth back a flyaway hair. "And I'm in need of a guide around the city through this Sunday. I'm not sure what your week is like, but I can ask someone else at the embassy if you're busy."

Jean-Luc's dark caterpillar eyebrows lift. He rests knobby elbows on the table. "Sunday? I thought you were leaving tonight."

"No one knows the circumstances of my sister's death, and I have to learn more. I need help retracing her steps. I'm happy to pay you."

Jean-Luc waves a hand. "Of course not. Helping you is part of my job. But don't you think the police have it handled? I'm not sure attempting to double their work is how you should spend your days here in . . ." His voice trails off at my stony expression. "Okay. If you're set on this, the embassy wants to help. Just let me know what you need."

"Thanks."

The waiter drops the check, and Jean-Luc says something in French to him. Jean-Luc nods a chin in my direction. "Anything to go? Straight coffee grinds to sniff later?"

I laugh in spite of myself, in spite of everything. "I guess I was really excited about that café allongé thing."

He smiles, then pays in cash.

Jean-Luc's knowledge of the Sorbonne cuts my search among its seven dispersed campuses in half. It would have taken me hours to determine Delphine Rousseau's office is on the central campus, across the river on the Left Bank. We walk the four blocks to the Sorbonne, the oldest and most revered university in France. Divining Angela's research myself is leading nowhere—assuming that was her intention when she wrote her blog post to me: *divine research*, or guess/discover/analyze her studies here. Hopefully, her dissertation director is clued in to Angela the Academic.

From outside, the university appears like many buildings in Paris: severe, regal, probably levying skyrocket rent for the interior apartments. Its architecture could be from the 1800s or earlier (dates were always Angela's forte), with high windows over ornate sills and carved stone shaped as drooping fabric, a frieze above each panel of glass. The perimeter of buildings spans an area of several blocks, staking its claim on the sidewalk real estate. From where we stand, a broad iron gate is the only way in.

Across the threshold, we head for a brick structure with sculpted vines curving along a rigid archway. Modern glass doors contrast the deep-set, chiseled words above—SCIENCES HUMAINES ET SOCIALES. In the lobby, locked cases display grades from the most recent semester alongside a large directory listing rooms. We climb to the second floor, ignoring the curious stares of the afternoon custodial staff, and arrive at the office marked BUREAU D'AMÉNAGEMENT—the urban planning office. A man with a towel approaches us and asks a question.

"He wants to see a student ID," Jean-Luc translates, "and says we can't be here without one."

When Jean-Luc explains we're not students, the man raises his voice—an angry bark—and he holds out a hooked thumb. He motions for us to leave—"Allez!"

On the first floor below, people look up from their books or phones. Jean-Luc replies in a low tone as a woman marches over to us from the stairwell.

"What is the issue? The exchange program office is downstairs." She glares at us. Graying brown hair kinks into a natural sphere and is the only indication of her age. Red-framed glasses drape from a chain around her neck and contrast with the black silk blouse she wears. A white coffee mug trembles in her hand. I nod at Jean-Luc. If he's here, he can take point.

"Bonjour, madame." Jean-Luc says something, then mentions Delphine Rousseau.

"That's me." She fumbles putting glasses to her face. Slanted eyes widen as she takes me in. "Oh merde, Angela." She jerks backward, and coffee splashes the wall.

"No, I'm Shayna—Angela's sister?"

She clutches her chest. "Goodness. I had no idea Angela had a twin. Hello . . . Shayna."

My heart deadens, just an ounce, hearing Delphine's response. *Past tense.* The phrasing I'll never get used to. "Would you be willing to speak to us? I'd like to learn more about my sister's academics."

Delphine unlocks the door of a small office. She says something to the janitor that appeases the angry expression on his face. He mumbles something else, then wipes up the dripping coffee.

"Let's step inside." Delphine leads us into a stunted room, dominated by a window the length of the wall. A modest metal desk is covered in stacks of papers, accordion-style folders, foam stress balls, and framed photos. Lush greenery of the courtyard below and a bakery beyond the campus perimeter are visible from our location on the second floor. Students lounge at the base of a stone stage connected to a building, some reading books and most engrossed in their phones. Delphine hangs a leather satchel on one of the brass hooks lining the wall. She sits down in an ergonomically correct mesh chair, then folds her hands on the desk.

"I must apologize for Gérard. He thought that you were reporters."

"The shooting was three weeks ago. I would think the reporters would be on to other events by now." I sit opposite Delphine in a cushioned folding chair.

Delphine exchanges a look with Jean-Luc, beside me. Nour's scolding voice returns to mind. *This is not like in the United States, a school shooting every month.*

"What can I do for you two? I'm very sorry Angela remains missing." She allows her sight line to fall to the stress balls, as though giving me the space to fall apart or collect myself. (As if I had the time to do either.)

"Thank you. I've been reading Angela's dissertation notes and was hoping you could provide more insight. How did she come to the catacombs as her subject? Did you see her the day she disappeared?"

Delphine nods. "As I told the police, Angela first came to me a year ago. She read an article I wrote on the Roman catacombs and their significance to the urban development of the gladiator culture. She wanted to do the same research for Paris, from an outsider's perspective." A Parisian accent barely rounds her *r*'s, and instead she sounds borderline English, her *t*'s pronounced with clarity. "Angela's vanishing is a tragedy."

I suppress a shiver. *Vanishing*—as in gone completely. Forever? "Can you tell me where she was in her research when she disappeared?" Jean-Luc is motionless in the corner of my eye.

"I'm not entirely sure," Delphine begins. "But I do think there is a correlation between her studies and . . . Perhaps if she were less ambitious in her work, Angela would still be here."

Her words fall heavy in the otherwise silent room. When I inhale it feels unpracticed, unusual, like I haven't taken a full breath since entering the building. "What do you mean?"

Delphine rounds the desk to sit on its edge. Her arms hug her small frame while long legs extend for balance. "Let me preface this by saying my words are rank speculation. And I hope what I am about to say is not too disturbing."

The hair on my neck bristles. "Please."

Delphine clasps her hands together. "We still do not know who is responsible for Angela's disappearance, nor how the shooting is related, if at all, yes? We only know that the shooter was a young man. Disgruntled and dissatisfied with the world. He was a student here, so he knew summer school classes would be in session that day. He targeted anyone associated with the departments where he felt mistreated. He did not plan this with anyone who was a student or a member of our faculty and said so in the note he left in his apartment. Shame that he killed himself when the police arrived."

"It is."

"I've been teaching doctoral students for a while. Twenty years at the Sorbonne's division of Urban Planning and Social Sciences. I have never seen a student come to this program and excel so quickly as Angela did. Her work was excellent, and her French was okay, but she was—what's the word?—eye-catching from the start."

"As a foreign student, it was even more impressive." She shakes her head. "It's very American to come in and dominate a room—you all are quite loud, you know—and I think that earned Angela a few enemies. She didn't simply dominate with the volume of her voice but also the content of her work."

Every muscle in my body stiffens in anticipation of Delphine's next words. I hesitate to interrupt, but I have to know. "Would someone want to harm her? A classmate?"

Her features crinkle. "The students here are quite competitive. After Angela obtained her internship, she was quieter, less present at events, and I'm not sure if that changed things."

"Less present? When was that? Could you explain, please?"

Delphine casts about for the proper words. "Do you speak French?"

"Not well. But Jean-Luc does." I turn to my companion and wave him into the ring.

He slides forward to the edge of his armchair. "Oui, Madame Rousseau."

They launch into conversation at a speed too fast for me to comprehend. As Jean-Luc asks a question and Delphine elaborates, gratitude mingles with a sense of practicality. I needed someone—anyone, since Seb is no longer an option—for exactly this reason.

"Okay." Jean-Luc turns to me. "After Angela began her internship with the Archaeology Society—"

"Wait, I barely know about that," I begin, remembering Seb's quick explanation. "She wasn't studying archaeology."

"No, she was doing research on urban planning in the catacombs. The Archaeology Society manages a team of people doing maintenance work in the tunnels. Dr. Leroux chose Angela to join them on projects after visiting hours, about a year ago."

"Has anyone spoken to Leroux? Could I?" We both look at Delphine.

"I suppose. I don't know him personally, but you might try contacting him via the university online portal."

"I'll do that. What else?" I turn back to Jean-Luc.

"Angela became more involved with the society," he resumes. "Spending virtually all her free time there, and when she did manage to come to seminars, Angela was distracted. She wasn't participating like before."

Delphine wears a weak smile. "That is correct. Angela was obsessed with her subject. She started taking mapping classes to deepen her understanding of the city's tunnels."

"Why would people hate her for that?"

Delphine hugs herself tighter. "They did not hate her. They envied her. A terrorist group claimed responsibility for the shooting—did you know? The shooter, the young man, joined the Red Brothers only the year prior. There has been a rise in nationalism here in France, like all of Europe at the moment. The United States, too. Many immigrant demographics here feel disenfranchised as a result of that rise, and the Red Brothers capitalized on that."

She pauses, likely inviting me to comment on the recent *us-first* mentality at home, but all I can picture is the swastika tattoo on the checkout clerk I encountered my first night here. Does what she's saying mean there are more nationalists, Nazi sympathizers, or neo-Nazis in Paris? A new wave of extremists under fifty years old, like my cashier?

"In any case—" She sighs. "Internal conflict boils as a result. Angela exuded the kind of social ease and grace that epitomizes equality, the freedom to move between cities and countries that many citizens of France still do not enjoy."

Jean-Luc clears his throat. "Do you think someone targeted Angela because of this envy, or because of her research?"

"Like Emmanuelle Wood," I add, remembering Nour's pinched expression.

Delphine shakes her head. "Emmanuelle was a student in the history department, if I am not wrong. I have not seen her in weeks, but our paths rarely crossed."

Jean-Luc sits at the edge of his chair. "Is there a way to get Angela's school schedule? The classes she chose for this next semester could offer some insight."

As Delphine escorts us to the registrar's office to request a printout, I wonder whether this Manu might be the best authority on Angela's life the last year, given her light stalking.

Valentin's words return from days ago in his office. *It might be a woman.*

We thank Delphine, then exit the building into the courtyard. Topiaries line the walkway out to the street, our very own farewell committee. The words Delphine spoke about Angela continue to resonate: *Less present. Impressive. Obsessed. Distracted.* There was a drastic change in Angela's persona over the last several years—that much is apparent. Before she moved an ocean away from me, her behavior was erratic and emotional but never withdrawn or obvious in public. Was she distracted because she was being harassed or because, like Delphine thinks, Angela was research obsessed? The more I learn, the clearer it is Paris changed my sister in ways I didn't expect. She was better here. It pains me to say it, but away from us, from family, she seems to have been happier, overall. Balanced in a way that she never was at home.

"Where to next?" Jean-Luc pauses beside me at the campus's edge. Only a few bouquets of flowers remain of the piles of cellophane and ribbon I saw when I first searched for images of the Sorbonne—memorial offerings left by mourners. Square pieces of orange paper mingle with the small collection and advertise discounted sandwiches for students.

I raise an arm and hail a black SUV cab coming toward us. "Are you going to keep asking questions?"

Jean-Luc snorts, then follows me into the back seat. We head home to Montmartre, fighting traffic the whole way. Jean-Luc asks about Emmanuelle, about her relationship with Angela, but I sidestep answering each time. Rule abider that I am—finally—I'm following Angela's instructions not to trust anyone.

When Jean-Luc turns to the window, I whip my phone out to text Valentin. It feels weird texting a detective, but each minute counts this week, and I can't go see him with my guide in tow.

> Staying till Sunday, need time to pack up the apartment. What do you know about Emmanuelle Wood? She may have had a grudge against Angela—E was stalking A.

Valentin texts back almost immediately:

> Leave police work to me. Wood is missing and not a suspect. I learned you signed the corpse identification form. Many thanks. If anything new arises, I shall contact you.

"What's wrong?" Jean-Luc asks. He leans in to look at my screen, but I shift it away.

"Nothing. My web access stinks, is all."

Jean-Luc opens his phone to his news app and frowns. "Well, you're not missing anything heartwarming. There was another shooting, in Toulon. South of France."

"That's terrible. Was anyone hurt?"

"Not sure yet. Information is hazy."

"It seems like shootings are becoming more common here, too," I observe. "Any reason why?"

Jean-Luc drops his hand to look at me. "Hard to say. France's long history of colonialism doesn't help when ex-subjects immigrate here for better lives. It's not an easy transition, generally—there is pressure on them to assimilate and little tolerance for those who don't. The system has to do better by them, and not everyone agrees how." We're each silent in our own thoughts as the cab drives onto the Pont Alexandre.

The drunkard's assault on me in the police station might have been more than an old Frenchman hating American politics—he could have been riled by me simply speaking English and not French. There's a vast difference between the experiences of a mixed-race, upper-middle-class American like Angela and those of refugees seeking safety in France, but how much of a role might this socially, historically complex opinion of transients—of anyone who's *other*—have played in Angela's disappearance?

We arrive at Angela's apartment building, and Jean-Luc pulls out his wallet.

"No, I got it," I say and pay with a card.

Jean-Luc puckers his lips—a mannerism I'm learning is incredibly French. "Suit yourself, but I rode in the cab, too. Dinner, my treat?"

I laugh, a nervous tic I can't help, as we exit to stand on the sidewalk. "I've got a date with Angela's stocked cabinets. But thanks."

Jean-Luc smiles, then waves me forward. We climb the stairs of the building together, walking single file just like I did with Seb. Jean-Luc pauses at Angela's landing. "Well, I hope I was of some help today. Let me know if you need anything tomorrow. I could search for the coordinates of another café if you feel like huffing coffee beans."

No matter how good Delphine's, Seb's, or Nour's English is, there are still linguistic hints that show they're not native speakers. *I have thirty. You are the sister of Angela.* I smile at the first I've heard from Jean-Luc: *coordinates*, like some seafaring captain, instead of *directions* or *location*.

"Thanks. I'll keep that in mind." I wave goodbye and dash into the dark apartment. His shy grin stays with me until my eyes adjust to the falling night. The place is a mess. Boxes opened with Seb, the tiny pile of clues, my clothing mixed with Angela's, and shoes splayed about the room. Flicking on the light switch, I toss my bag on the bed, then freeze.

Coordinates.

Angela's mapping class.

I hurry to the laptop, click the bookmark for her blog, and find the message as I left it:

Divine Research

48535.75 2201

A cut and paste in the browser reveals these digits are not a phone number but latitude and longitude. I text a quick message to Jean-Luc:

Meet at 11:00 a.m. tomorrow. We're grabbing an early lunch.

The ping of his cell phone is audible one floor above. Within seconds, I receive his reply:

Wouldn't miss it.

Chapter 12

Famine. Urban planning. Plague.

An orchestral call and response pierces my thoughts. Three notes trill in repetitive sequence outside Angela's third-floor window, and they tear me from reviewing highlights I made in Angela's notes.

The birds' song would be beautiful had I not passed out around two in the morning and woken six hours later with my face sticking to a handout on cities that developed on top of marshland. I fiddle with the shutters, trying to open them to shoo away my avian band, but the damn metal clasp sticks. They're quiet for a moment. Then resume chirping with fervor. Between the shutter clasp and the sticky dead bolt on the door, it's a miracle I can get in and out as often as I do.

My smartphone vibrates against Angela's writing desk, and Seb's name rolls across my screen.

What are your plans today? We need to work together. This is not about you and me.

"Exactly," I grumble. "Get lost, Seb." I lock my phone to black and wonder whether it was wise to share with him that I'd extended my trip.

"Shayna? It's Jean-Luc." His voice carries through the door, right on time. I straighten my dress and scan the room for my messenger bag. After sending an email to the address I found for Dr. Charles Leroux, requesting to speak to him, I fell down a rabbit hole of Angela's browser history; zero progress was made on packing or organizing, again. All of Angela's research papers, including the rough draft of her dissertation that she was working on when she disappeared, line the floor. The different rooms discovered in the catacombs seem to have fascinated her. She mentions a room filled with fibulae, a room devoted to soldiers, judging from the many bone fractures, and—creepiest of all—a room full of twins, if modern DNA tests are to be trusted. She even cataloged the twin skulls, noting fifteen pairs and five skulls without a match. I grab my notes and a bottle of water, then step out into the hall.

"Bonjour," Jean-Luc says. French pop plays from the apartment below us, blaring on a Wednesday morning. Jean-Luc mouths the lyrics along to the music. *Serons-nous détestables?* The distressed jeans and graphic tee that reads in English RANGE FREE (I don't know whether the irony is intended) could be an outfit from the album cover of a brooding band—Parisian hipster chic. For once, he's not wearing purple.

"You seem very French today." He points to my crisscrossed sandals. "Or Roman."

"Yeah, with this heat wave, I started wearing Angela's clothing. All mine is doused in sweat."

Jean-Luc offers a slow nod in response. I pass him and head down the stairs, Angela's sundress billowing with each step. He follows, keeping a few feet more between us than yesterday. While being *too open* in thinking like Angela has had its downfalls—and I do want to quell any idea of flirtation before it begins—the need for clean clothing is real during these extra days abroad.

We cross the street, scattering a horde of pigeons into flight. Jean-Luc watches me from the corner of his eye. "What's our destination?" he asks.

"A restaurant I found: Les Deux Moulins." Last night I punched the Divine Research coordinates into a search engine. It took a few tries, but I found a combination that made sense: 48° 53' 5.75" N, 2° 20' 1" E—global coordinates to a restaurant that served as the chief location for one of Angela's favorite movies. She was obsessed with *Amélie* in high school, and by the end of senior year, she no longer used the subtitles; she understood it perfectly in French.

Jean-Luc's elbow brushes mine as we walk. His knapsack grazes my hip, and I take a conscious step out and away.

A waitress greets us inside the cozy building, almost the same as I remember it from the movie. In place of the cigarette counter seen in the film lie extra tables and banquettes, with a dozen more tables squeezed throughout the room. We follow her jeans and crew-neck T-shirt to a corner booth beside the window. Sunlight filters through the burgundy curtains, casting a seductive ambience. Angela must have loved this.

"Something to drink?" Jean-Luc opens the wine menu.

"A coffee. Please."

Our waitress brings a tiny espresso I manage to down in one gulp.

"You all right?" Jean-Luc's mouth freezes in a taut smile. His eyes dart to my hands, picking at a sugar packet. "Do you need me to interpret the menu for you? Or is this a trick to get me to recite lines from *Amélie Poulain*?"

When I don't answer, he says, "Shayna, you don't have to tell me specifics." Jean-Luc plucks the sugar packet from my fingers. "I understand you're being guarded. I just want to help. To make this easier on you."

Red wallpaper and framed lime-green posters from the movie cover the walls. Movie poster, movie poster, framed set of gnomes, movie poster. What is it that I'm supposed to find here? I finally figure out my sister's second clue after days of wasting time in locations that don't matter, and the words *divine* and *research* aren't suggested anywhere.

There are no posters of gods or Sherlock Holmes—not even a cross or a pair of glasses. Why lead me here?

"Honestly, I'm not sure what I need," I say, finally. "The food is supposed to be good."

A thoughtful line marks the space between his eyes. "Maybe we should ask someone if they know Angela. She could have been a regular since we only live a few blocks away."

His choice of words—*we*—causes me to suck in a breath. I keep forgetting he used to be Angela's neighbor versus simply my embassy liaison.

He waves over the waitress, then asks if she's seen my twin sister before. She peers at me like she's trying to memorize my pores but doesn't recall. Our meal arrives, putting the mini interrogation to an end. We consume our lunch with pensive chewing. My summer vegetable galette—essentially a buckwheat crêpe with vegetables, Jean-Luc tells me—forms a bridge of stringy cheese to my plate, its steam rising then bursting against my lips with each bite. A lot has been accomplished in the past few days. But not enough. Never enough to find her.

Jean-Luc sets down his burger. "This is a nice change for me from the office," he muses. "I wasn't sure you'd be into me helping, at first. You couldn't have known how knowledgeable I might be about the city, whether I was a psycho or sociopath. I mean, I'm not—"

"You just like to freak out women by talking about them?" I offer a half smile, then stab a square of thin pancake. His eyes are a light green up close, less hazel than flecked with gold.

Jean-Luc smirks. "What I meant was I wasn't sure whether you'd allow me to do my job, whether you would trust me. To be fair, sociopaths are pretty easy to spot, but psychopaths—those are the ones that sneak up on you."

The *Amélie* soundtrack loops back on the speaker system, the whine of the accordion mingling with surrounding conversations. I pick at my exotic food while eyeing the dozen fries untouched on Jean-Luc's plate. My mouth waters at the thick sea salt, visible from my chair.

I shrug. "I had my serial killer phase and learned a lot. They like to take things from the crime scene or leave something of themselves, keep trophies, all that stuff. I know about Bundy. You're no Bundy."

Jean-Luc laughs. "No, I'm not. Then again, sociopaths are marked by their turbulent upbringing, some kind of trauma. Maybe an erratic nature, repeated law breaking. Clearly not me—I had a stable home, if with overly critical parents. Psychopaths, though—they lack empathy, unlike sociopaths. They're charismatic, manipulative, great planners. That's Bundy. That's your Manson. And our Ogre des Ardennes. You can't tell with them until it's too late."

"You have an ogre?"

Jean-Luc dips a fry in a ketchup-sriracha mixture. "Michel Fourniret? You haven't heard of him? He's not someone you wanted to meet in the late eighties."

"Got it. Well, I'll be wary of you being too charming."

Jean-Luc turns a shade of red. Chewing his last bite takes forever before he swallows. "Actually, Shayna, I've got something to show you. Something I hope you'll like. Nothing too charming, I swear." A shy smile turns up the corners of his mouth. He peers at me from beneath thick, dark lashes, gauging my reaction.

"Bathroom." Warmth climbs my neck, and I slide from my chair before he notices. The weight of his gaze follows me until I bolt down a narrow hall in the back, through a door marked TOILETTES.

I enter a shrine as the restroom door swings shut. Celebrity photos plaster the toilet stalls. Signatures from the film's cast are scrawled across their headshots. The rest have been graffitied by fans and restaurant patrons.

None contain any divine element I can identify—although I would accept a piece of burned toast with a dubious face of Buddha at this point.

"Everything okay?" Jean-Luc asks when I return. "You look pale."

"Just tired." Emotionally. Physically. I remain standing by the cleared table. "Ready?"

The elation I felt at discovering Angela's blog post, her note to me—*Divine Research*—has all but disappeared. The momentary confidence that buoyed my hopes when I realized those numbers were latitude and longitude has dissipated like a gray curl from a teenager's cigarette here.

"Not yet." Jean-Luc gestures for me to sit. He pulls a sheaf of clipped papers from his knapsack, then lays it on the laminate table-top. "For you."

He slides it across to me like a Bond operative. The cover sheet's heading reads:

Bureau des Nations Unies, Conseil de Sécurité.

Office of the United Nations, Security Council.

"What is this?"

"I came home last night and did some research of my own." Jean-Luc pats the space beside him. He scoots a foot over to show there's no funny business. On his cell phone, he shows me a website with the title *Les Archives de Paris 1*. In the History section for 2015 is Angela's name along with the title of her Sorbonne research paper—in English, given her bilingual undergrad degrees.

"Wow," I breathe. "I've never seen this. Are all undergrad papers published online?"

Jean-Luc shakes his head. "This must have been one of the handful chosen by the department to represent that year's work. You have to be a student at the Sorbonne to access the archives, or be granted permission like the embassy. This"—he taps the file with his index finger—"contains hard copies of her graded and published essays."

Hope blazes in my chest, renewed by Jean-Luc's ingenuity. The papers seem to tingle in my hands, a new treasure trove of Angela's work. A stupid grin tightens my cheeks, squinting my eyes. "I never would have found this."

"Happy to help." He waves a hand.

I shake my head in disbelief and turn back to the cell phone screen. "I wonder why Angela wrote about the homeless."

Jean-Luc relaxes into the booth. "Well, that was the summer of the record heat wave. It killed around seventy people who had no shelter and no air-conditioning. A lot of elderly died."

Despite this revelation not being the burned toast I was expecting, tears fill my eyes. "Of course she would devote her thesis to the forgotten."

"Your parents must be proud of you both—a Sorbonne doctoral candidate and a med school student."

A clumsy sound issues from my throat. "Ah, they were. Our parents died. About three years ago now. The embassy didn't tell you that?"

Jean-Luc's mouth drops. He straightens to face me. "No, I had no idea. They only provide us with information they consider relevant to your visit. I'm so sorry."

I shrug, then reach for my bag. "Thank you. Drunk driver in San Diego. An accident, and sudden, when he careened into them on a narrow juncture."

Jean-Luc stops my hand. His eyes are glassy. "You know. Just in case no one has ever said this to you out loud: it's not your fault. That they died."

"Excuse me?"

He ignores my amused expression and, instead, he waits. Watching me. Attempting to force a response from the heavy silence that falls like a morose curtain between us. Amusement shifts to irritation; what kind of response is that, to a confession like mine? I'm split between anger and a desire to believe his words.

The former wins out. "I'm aware, thanks. Is this a part of your bitch duties now, psychoanalyzing me?" I lower my gaze and stare at the gift he gave me seconds before. Whereas the action seemed so thoughtful and generous then, providing my sister's essays now comes off as presumptuous, boundary crossing, and inappropriately intimate. He doesn't even try to argue.

"I've never lost anyone, not like a sibling," he says, slowly. "My relationship with my parents isn't great, but I can go visit them an hour away in Rouen if I want. However, guilt, I know. Growing up in a small town in Normandy, I got into some . . . trouble. My friend and I, Benoît, were pretty aimless. We were classic bourgeois kids—bored, with money we stole from our parents." He pauses. I look up, and he's staring at the table's checkered design.

"We started experimenting with hard drugs. Pot turned to cocaine, which for a split second turned to heroin. Benoît overdosed. The hospital was able to reverse the effects, and he pulled through the longest night of my life, but with consequences. He lost some cognitive ability while he was unconscious, before the paramedics came. Now he lives at home, going from one dead-end job to the next. While I play tour guide to attractive foreigners in Paris." Jean-Luc exhales the words slowly, like they might detonate in his mouth.

"That's terrible. I'm so sorry," I murmur, wishing I had something more meaningful to add.

He turns to me, angling his body in the tight space. The bustle of the restaurant resumes with a roar, breaking my focus on the tremor of his voice, the rise and fall of his chest. He musters a smile that stops at the apples of his cheeks. "It took me years to really understand that it wasn't my fault. Even though I'm complicit because Benoît and I did that together—I'll always be part of that story—sometimes, awful things happen. What we do with that knowledge is what counts. You know?"

Sunshine peeks through the thin fabric of the curtain, turning his hair golden brown. A hopeful mien replaces the pained expression of seconds before. So optimistic, so sure I'll agree and understand. The words *Yes, I know* lodge in my throat, tucked away and frozen because I can't say them out loud. Even if Jean-Luc has come to terms with his role, I know he's wrong—I am to blame, indefinitely, without reprieve. He doesn't know the whole truth. Not even Angela does, and yet she shunned me after their deaths anyway.

A rogue tear slips down my cheek as Jean-Luc wraps his hand around mine.

"You know, my sister was no picnic," I begin.

Jean-Luc lifts his eyebrows. "Everyone here seems to think so."

"Yeah, exactly. She was wonderful in so many ways. Kind, enthusiastic, supportive of others, and smart. But she had another side that only the family saw. Once, when our parents went to a conference in Orange County and didn't tell us, she went home and found the house empty; she was furious. She broke a super-expensive designer doll that our mother specially commissioned for her when we were ten, that looked like us. Like our mom."

Jean-Luc hesitates. "I . . . Ah, is that so bad for a kid?"

"We were sophomores in college, living in our own apartments. I was with her when she called them, demanded they tell her when they were leaving town next time; her anger was so intense, almost irrational. Like she didn't trust them not to up and leave one of these days." I pause as the irony hits me. "Which, in hindsight, was correct."

"What did your parents do?"

"What they always did. They talked her down and reassured her they were coming home the next day. They promised they would tell her their travel plans in advance next time, and she calmed down. My mom was really hurt Angela broke the doll, but she never said anything, not wanting to upset Angela again."

Jean-Luc gives a sympathetic nod. "Everyone's got skeletons, Shayna. And a few loopy relations."

"Sure." I sigh, saying things I've only said to my therapist. "And that example might not seem all that shocking. But it was typical of the Angela we lived with—her ups and downs, a tendency to fly off the handle suddenly and unpredictably. There was one time when we were kids on the beach, when my parents had to separate us for a while because she tried to . . ." I trail off, shaking my head. "It doesn't matter. Here it seems she'd put those issues behind her. Like Paris, or getting space from me, from all of us, was what she needed." The thought jabs me just below the ribs, a self-inflicted wound.

The waitress returns with our check, and Jean-Luc pays in cash.

Outside, the streets are full of hungry white-collar workers shuffling by in a hurry to grab a bite. We navigate the crowds without words or looking at each other. Against our brick apartment building, the same homeless man rises with the help of a cane I hadn't noticed before. He stretches, joints audibly cracking. His tuft of graying black hair seems freshly showered. Pale skin appears ruddy in the shadows.

We climb the stairwell to Angela's apartment. Thick beige carpet muffles our steps on her landing. There are wooden beams, sound and heating insulation in between Angela's apartment and Jean-Luc's, but I remember how I heard the chime of his cell phone yesterday. I wonder whether he's heard me crying at some point.

Jean-Luc follows me to the door. "So did you find what you were looking for at the restaurant?"

I pat the sheaf of papers he gave me, tears well behind me now. I'm not sure how I allowed them to make it as far as my eyelashes. "Not really. But this is a great alternative."

He steps closer. "I'm around for whatever you need this week. I hope you know that, Shayna. Even if it's just to talk."

I nod, feeling more like my normal self with each noncommittal shrug. Embarrassment at being so emotional in public, with a virtual stranger, is peeking around the corner and tiptoeing closer to my flushed cheeks. "I know, thanks. I'll be sure to—"

His arms draw me in, tightening around my frame, the action so unexpected I stop midsentence and don't struggle. He hesitates, then presses his cheek against my head. The urge to shove him away rises—to scoff and insist I'm not so needy that after only hours together I would open wide all my wounds and stand them on a crate for him to ogle. Instead, I close my eyes. The anxious fluttering of my stomach moves upward to my chest.

He pulls back, eyebrows linked in one bushy strip. "I'll see you later."

I step into the apartment, a mass of contradictions: energy, fatigue; relief, despair; clarity, confusion. When his door clicks shut one floor above, I collapse onto the bed and curl into an exhausted ball.

Chapter 13

Ambassade (embassy)

    Comment dit-on? (How do you say?)

    Combien? (How much?)

A nasal buzz rips through the air, jarring my barely legible scrawl. The list I've been making—vocabulary, names, notes, and descriptions of people I've met so far and their relationships to Angela—extends a page long. Pain shoots across my sleeping foot as I stand and stumble to the square box next to the door.

"Hello?" I call, pressing first one button then another. It buzzes again beneath my finger. "Hello?"

"Miss Darby, it's Inspector Valentin. May I come up?"

I press the large button, which allows entry, then I survey the studio apartment. It's trashed, overrun with papers and empty boxes. Valentin's tight, deliberate gait announces his location in the foyer, up the stairs, rounding the corner to the third floor. I stash a bra in my duffel bag, then fluff the blanket as the footsteps end outside.

Valentin greets me with a curt smile. He pats down the curly sides of his hair and then shakes my hand. "Mademoiselle." The scent of mint carries with him despite a heavy perfume of curry that was cloaking the hall earlier. Seeing him again in person reminds me how much I've learned and how much I've lived since we met four days ago.

Valentin stares at the mess I've made. He steps over a crate of binders and a cardboard box to the desk chair covered in papers. He moves the pile onto the closed laptop, then he gestures to the bed. "Miss Darby."

"I prefer to stand."

Valentin sits at the desk. "As you wish."

"How is Angela's case going? Are you making any progress?"

He allows himself a smile. A reddish stubble glows along his jawline, as though he hasn't slept much, either. Good. "It is . . . progressing. I hoped to ask additional questions, if you are amenable."

I slouch along the kitchen counter. "Let's have it."

"Miss Darby, I hear you have been sightseeing much of our beautiful city. Do you consider that wise?"

"I'm sorry?"

"Forgive me, Miss Darby." Valentin crosses thin legs. "You have come to Paris, presumably to gather your sister's belongings and say goodbye. Instead, you were seen gallivanting about with someone you just met, while this continues to be an open investigation. Do you think this is wise?" He taps his forefingers together like a disciplinarian actually expecting a response.

My mouth splits open. "You were following me?"

"You are an interesting-looking woman. Someone memorable, as your sister was. It is possible that her beauty and friendly nature may have contributed to her demise. The intelligence we gathered on your sister makes it clear how visible she was at the Sorbonne. It would be unwise to imitate the foundations of her death."

"I'm not *imitating* anything. I'm getting by."

Valentin stands. "In France, we do not take this tone with inspectors. You are vulnerable. Especially as a woman who does not speak the language fluently, and in need of trustworthy companions. Angela's killer is still at large, along with a potential series murderer."

As if I'd forgotten. There's a constant knot in my neck from looking over my shoulder. My instinct when I step into a room now is to scan the space and locate a second exit.

"Right. And they may be one and the same? Have you made any headway there? Are any of her classmates suspects?" Delphine's words in her office ring clearly in my head. *The shooter did not plan this with anyone who was a student or a member of our faculty and said so in the note he left in his apartment.*

Valentin stiffens. "The investigation is ongoing."

"But why would anyone target Angela?"

"I assure you, the police are working on it."

"But as a foreigner, maybe someone felt she was a threat, or something. There's been a lot of hostility toward outsiders. Maybe—"

"Miss Darby, thank you for your efforts," he interrupts. "I know finding Angela's killer is important to your feelings of closure. I do, really," he adds when I raise an eyebrow. "However, your priority now is to get home safely. And to avoid spending time with unknowns. Are we agreed?"

I cock my head to the side. "Inspector Valentin. Would you be questioning my actions if I were a man alone in Paris?"

Valentin's affable air of concern falls like a drape. His upper lip curls. "You are grieving, Miss Darby. Perhaps we should discuss your sister's case."

I huff and turn toward the window.

"What do you know of Les Deux Moulins?"

"It's a restaurant."

He nods. "Yes. And it is where Angela went to dinner with Sebastien Bronn the night before she disappeared."

I slowly turn back around. "What?"

It's not some great surprise Angela went there with Seb; it's in the neighborhood and of special meaning for her—it's compelling she left me its coordinates. My eyes flit to the ceiling; I wonder if Jean-Luc can hear us now.

Valentin stares at me with confidence, like we're in an interrogation room at the station. "What do you think of Bronn?"

"I think Angela meant a lot to him. Why?"

He pauses just long enough for a cold sliver of unease to creep into my throat.

"Did you know he did a tour of Afghanistan?"

"No. I . . . I thought his brother fought there."

"He did. Baptiste Bronn died from sulfur mustard. A rather antiquated form of chemical warfare you might be familiar with as mustard gas. Both Baptiste and Sebastien were deployed in separate medical units."

Valentin observes me like a lab rat, tallying every muscle spasm. My head is spinning. Why didn't Seb share he had his own experience at war? We spent a full day together and discussed his brother's military stint over Calvados. "Why is that significant?"

He whips out a journal and starts making notes with a stubby pencil. "He was dishonorably discharged from service. I was hoping you could shed some light on that period."

Dishonorably discharged? "I . . . I can't. Did you ask for his alibi for the time of the shooting?"

Valentin dots the paper with a jab, then flips the cover closed and secures the elastic strap. "Believe it or not, Miss Darby, I have done this before. Mr. Bronn was working at the Paris Saint-Germain hospital that afternoon. He is on video purchasing cigarettes from a tabac at the time Angela disappeared."

I rack my memory trying to recall whether he's ever smelled of smoke. We only spent a few hours together each day.

"There is something else," he continues. "There have been new developments—"

"Oh thank God. I knew you didn't come here with only bad news."

Valentin exhales. He takes a long, slow look at the ceiling. The certainty I'm wrong punts my snide optimism.

"There have been new developments in an adjacent case. As part of your sister's investigation, we traced Angela's activities to several days before her disappearance. On Friday the twenty-ninth, she was at the Sorbonne. On Thursday she only left her apartment to perform dissertation work and to go to dinner at Les Deux Moulins with Bronn. On Wednesday she visited Emmanuelle Wood, and Tuesday she was seen on the Champs-Élysées. What do you know of Emmanuelle? You texted me about her."

Manu. Angela's frenemy. The blood leaches from my face. "Angela never mentioned her to me, but we didn't speak for a long time. I don't know much," I hedge, wanting him to confirm before dishing Nour's hearsay. "Why?"

Valentin whips out his pad again and makes a check mark on the first page. "I am sorry to add to the discomfort you must be feeling, Miss Darby, but I must confirm your text: Miss Wood and your sister were known to be hostile to one another. Now Miss Wood is a missing person; she has not been seen in several weeks. Angela may be implicated in her disappearance."

I stare at him, through him, struggling to understand. "How is that possible? Angela has been declared missing or dead for weeks, too. My sister had some tension with this Wood woman, and now you're investigating *her* as a suspect?"

"Wood went missing just two days before Angela did. The day Angela visited her apartment." Valentin returns my glare with steady eye contact. Not a flinch from him, while I feel myself begin to shake.

It's an ugly thing to think, let alone say out loud, but a tiny, cowardly part of me was anticipating this information, waiting for some example of it to crop up—Angela was capable of violence. My stomach clenches the way it always does when I stop to think of my last day on the beach with my sister. The phantom smell of the ocean hits my nostrils, and my mouth waters at the sudden taste of salty air.

Delphine's portrait of Angela seemed to indicate she had changed for the better. But what if Angela's composed Grace Kelly imitation had, in fact, cracked?

"Are you all right, Miss Darby?"

"She didn't . . . Angela would never hurt anyone. What about her killer, Inspector? Is this slowing the investigation into Angela's death?"

Valentin reaches into his pocket, unwraps a candy mint, then pops it into his mouth. "We are doing everything we can. A suggestion, if I may?"

I nod.

"Finish packing your sister's belongings this week, then go home to California. What will reveal itself will occur with or without your presence in Paris. I will update you as we verify more information. Again, I am sorry to convey this news." He crosses to me, then places a hand on my shoulder. "Please. Paris is a large city for a young woman, regardless of your independent nature. Call me, should you have the need."

He leaves. I stay rooted to the spot, listening, until the front entry slams shut below.

I stare across the thin carpet of papers to the open shutters overlooking the square. If I crane my head to the left, the white basilica, the Sacré Coeur, is visible on the hill in the corner.

When I landed in Paris, I knew I was at a disadvantage. Angela and I hadn't spoken in years; I didn't have a clue about her life here or the person she had become. I didn't know what was waiting for me or what painful and surprising things I would find in her apartment. Valentin's words ricochet in my head like a studded boomerang, ready to wound: *Angela may be implicated.* I sink to the ground and wrap my arms tight around my knees against her bed. We had our issues. We had moments that we could never bring ourselves to mention again. But what could have happened in those three years that my sister could be linked to the abduction of another person? Just forming the thought is absurd.

Another glance at the basilica and I cross to the door, nudging a box containing the stun gun Angela owned. The dead bolt slides shut with ease this time, but its eerie whine underlines my growing fear.

I step into the sunlight at the window and find a reprieve from the cold doubts of Valentin's visit. *She didn't . . . Angela would never hurt anyone.*

My own words reverberate in my mind, echoing with their lie.

Chapter 14

from: Angela Darby <ange.d.paris@smail.com>
to: "Darby, Shayna" <shayna.darby93@smail.com>
date: Jul 12, 2015, 7:17 p.m.
subject: James and Claire's estate

My dear sister—
Twin of my heart and blood—
Onetime roommate—
First friend, and first enemy—

It's been a little over a month since our parents met their fate. Even now the words don't come willingly, but I type and erase and type again to force the keys in place. To form the words my fingers were never meant to write.

None of this is fair. Certainly not Auntie Meredith taking off to Puerto Rico because "the damage was done" and she couldn't bear the waiting, or normally stoic Auntie Judy being a pitiful, weeping mess. And least of all, you being forced to deal with plans for the memorial service this weekend, less than a month since the accident. No. We have been thrust into adulthood way faster than is fair.

I know it's been hard for you. Christ on a cracker, it's been awful, period. It's harder for me, though, when I learn—not from my sister, but from the family lawyer—you are the executor of Mom and Dad's estate. Of course! (Of course.) To the very end, it is the three of you, cozy and warm in your solidarity against me. The outsider. Perpetually in the cold of La Jolla Shores.

Details on my share of the trust were there, but money is not what interests me—despite them splitting their estate down the middle between us, to treat us the same for once. It was when I read the tiny clause entitled *Joint Ownership* (the one regarding shared assets) that I knew what I needed: the family home to be sold. To put to rest the memories of a childhood rocked by neglect and disappointment, given their insanely demanding careers. After I reached out to Mr. Decker, to see whether he could draw up that paperwork, he said you rejected the idea—effectively blocked it, per the joint ownership clause. I can guess what your reasons are, but think about mine, please. Let me put to bed the reminder that I'll never get to repair the hurts I inflicted as a pissy teenager—none of us will. Can you do that for me? You'll say the home means too much, especially now that they've passed, but I'm ready for everything to go away. You owe me that much after what you did to them. What you did to all of us. You do not deserve to decide anything anymore. You don't deserve anything from them.

I just. I can't.

For better or worse, ever since I pretended to be you for the eighth-grade presentations that rocketed you to the best science classes, you have always been Mom and Dad's favorite. In turn, after that massive favor, you harped on my mood swings—said they made you feel unstable or threatened or *whatever* as kids—but think about what you're doing to us now. What you've done. You know this last thing is what they would have wanted. Us working together again, finally, to find a compromise here. Us being the powerful duo they always said we would be. Don't be so proud or so blind to your narcissism that you can't see you're still acting the favorite. Even when you don't deserve that title anymore.

Think of someone other than yourself, Shayna Astrid. Otherwise, I don't know how we can continue.

Chapter 15

Inside the Sorbonne's courtyard, large cobblestones stretch from the immense domed chapel to the Legal Sciences wing—all pillars and Greek influence—uninterrupted but for a large fountain in the middle. The sun dips on its downward trajectory now in late afternoon, and shadows climb the opposite stone walls like in a Charlton Heston film.

One good thing to come out of Valentin's visit: a checklist. Now I know exactly where Angela went in the days prior to her initial disappearance. *On Friday, the twenty-ninth, she was at the Sorbonne. On Thursday she only left her apartment to perform dissertation work and to go to dinner at Les Deux Moulins with Bronn. On Wednesday she visited Emmanuelle Wood, and Tuesday she was seen on the Champs-Élysées.* I can unofficially stalk my sister much in the way her abductor might have. Finally having an outline of a plan is a relief after the last several days of bumbling about wearing my sister's face, practically baiting someone to finish what they started; they call me the type-A twin for a reason.

I head straight for the humanities department, dodging clumps of students and a man handing out leaflets in the courtyard. Delphine Rousseau's assertive voice travels from her office on the second floor to the lobby, but I circle the scuffed tile below. Another *Divine Research*–style sign is unlikely to be here on campus, but it was damn near a unicorn to begin with. A pass at the baseboards and the ceiling molding confirms my disappointment—not even a trace of ambiguous graffiti to misinterpret. Polished benches and lacquered stairwell balustrades lining the walls could be featured in museums; their sheen glints in the sunlight cascading through the latticed glass panels forming the ceiling. Students casually lie on the benches, studying or taking afternoon naps.

This nonchalant intersection of modernity and history seems so Angela—the integration of cell phones Snapchatting images of the fountain sculpture, as easy and obvious as passing the Eiffel Tower on a daily commute. Certain statues were made in honor of real people who walked these grounds at one point, according to a few plaques; students send text messages beneath them in the narrow shade. Sadness slows my steps as I recognize how my sister traveled six thousand miles to find her proverbial tribe, before a comforting thought replaces it: my sister was happy here.

Across the plaza, author Victor Hugo guards the entrance to the library. My heart beats faster with each step closer to the site of Angela's disappearance. According to Valentin, she came here that Friday doing something. Checking out a book? No one knows what, exactly. Witnesses say she was walking the many aisles when the shooting occurred. I did an internet search on whether school shootings were as common in France as they are in the United States and discovered highly regulated French gun laws, consistent with Nour's commentary. Everything I found on French news websites and then translated via Google made a point of saying how surprising the shooting was, considering universities are respected throughout the country, if not necessarily revered. The shooter himself was high on a few substances and cited difficulties with his peers, as well as recent indoctrination by the Red Brothers. Armed guards on campus fired shots before he took his own life. The chaos of hundreds of students running to safety made the aftermath hard to track. Angela was last seen in the library.

Rows of tables with generic desk lamps greet the eye upon entry. A normal scene, excepting the destruction opposite: panes of glass are completely missing. Yellow tape, with the words **ZONE INTERDITE**—prohibited zone—repeated over and over protects the closest walkway area in a three-foot arc. Shards no longer line the floor after three weeks, but a clear plastic tarp covers the section of glass still needing to be replaced.

In spite of expecting it—of being surprised I didn't see anything earlier—the visual of the moment's violence is stunning. Was this the moment of the shooter's death or before? Did he spend time here, did he care about these aisles of books, or did he run here by accident?

My fists clench. I pass along the side aisle, imagining my sister studying with exchange students and French students, commingling with all, unaware that anyone could want to harm her. Maybe the shooter didn't target her, but he did other students and faculty. And his actions ultimately gave someone the opportunity to snatch her. The thought squeezes my chest when I reach the tall columns of the archaeology aisle. I withdraw several books from a shelf, waiting for a title or cover to leap out as the one Angela needed—the catalyst to this whole disaster.

Diving deep into pages about urban planning of the eighteenth century, I search the table of contents for words in French I recognize. I move to the next shelf and barrel into a young woman. We each cry out before sharing a laugh at our mutual reaction. I apologize, *Pardon*, but she dismisses it before I can breathe the second syllable. *Pas de problème*, she says. Confusion tenses my mouth. She's not annoyed I knocked her book to the ground and kicked it under a shelf? Dark hair falls from her ponytail as she bends down like it's the most normal thing in the world, bumping into a stranger in the library weeks after grief and violence struck here. She smiles again and shrugs small shoulders. Without another glance, she turns down the next aisle.

Another fifteen minutes offers nothing of use before I realize the catacombs will be closing soon. Regret tinges my second goodbye to Angela's university, along with the nagging thought that I'm missing something.

Crowds ebb and flow while I stand across the street from the green tool-shed, observing like the voyeur I am. At the front of the line, a Japanese couple uses animated gestures while speaking to the cashier. They pay, then pass through the revolving turnstile and into the informative foyer. People's expressions alternate between excitement and obvious dread. Individuals cast longing glances toward where I stand, far from the entrance, beside a terrace table belonging to an Irish-themed bar.

On Thursday Angela went straight from her apartment to the cata-combs around ten in the morning. She came home around six for din-ner with Seb. A whole day was spent underground doing work on her dissertation, like a less athletic version of Lara Croft. The archaeology director, Dr. Leroux, told Valentin he saw Angela come in; they had lunch together around one o'clock, right when his belly started to rum-ble. Otherwise, she left around five. In the interim she photographed piles of bones relevant to her research. She was a staple often seen below-ground at that point, going on nine months of interning. According to Valentin, the director implicitly trusted her with everything down there, both to ask if she needed help and to respect the significance, the history of the tunnels.

From outside, everything looks the same as it did two days ago. I didn't see anything significant aboveground or below when I did the self-guided tour with Seb, and I have no intention of descending again on the off chance I missed another sign. As Seb explained, the cata-combs are two hundred miles long. If there is some clue buried one hundred and fifty miles in, in the dark, behind a stack of skeletons (a stack identical to the dozens of others down there), it's as good as nonexistent for me.

Without a more specific idea of where to look, I was hoping some intuition would strike me outside the entrance.

A young boy pitches from the queue to hug a tree on the sidewalk. His parents raise their voices, motioning for him to get back in line, but he refuses, tightening his grasp around the trunk. The mom and dad take turns cajoling the boy as the line moves up. By the time they are three people from the front, they give up and join their kid on the sidewalk. A joyful whoop bursts from the boy, then he tears across the street. His parents follow at a grumbling distance while I high-five him on his way inside. I wish I had done more of that growing up—held my boundaries and waited them all out: my parents, Angela, our friends and teachers who categorized and made assumptions about me as soon as they saw my mirror double.

Other people take notice of the boy's quick escape. Several heads turn my way from beside the ticket booth, including a set of gelled curls that looks like a riptide of Corsican chocolate. Seb and I lock eyes. He makes his way across the street while my stomach knots remembering our last moments together. The memory of the heady scent of his cologne returns well before he stops a foot away from me.

"Hello, Shayna." He speaks to my feet, as awkward as I feel. The short-sleeved white button-up he wears strains at his chest.

"Hi." I shift my weight to my other foot. It's been two days and at least a half dozen apologetic texts and calls from him. I haven't replied to any of them; what is there to say?

"I was just—um." Seb gestures behind him, back to the catacombs kiosk. "I was wanting to . . . Were you thinking about—?" He points downward.

"Oh no. Definitely not. I was . . ." My voice trails off, imagining the words said out loud: *I was just following your exact suggestion to retrace Angela's steps today. This is my second stop.* He did have a good idea, but

I can't allow Seb to think we might partner up again or let him know where to find me—even if we're so in sync we end up at the same place at the same time. "I was just people watching."

Seb sinks deep into a nod, puckering full lips. "I see."

A moment passes in which we both look around, at the patio chairs, at the catacombs queue, at the clear sky, rather than at each other.

"Well. I have sent you a few messages, but let me say this in person," he begins. "I am sorry for what happened between us, Shayna."

"Don't worry about it. I'd rather . . . We're not . . . There's no need to talk about it," I babble.

Seb places his hands in his shorts' pockets. "In any case, I hope you'll forgive me. It was wrong, and I take full responsibility. For kissing you," he adds, squinting, as though I forgot. "I hope that we can continue to work together. For Angela's sake."

Hearing him speak our shame knocks immediate sobriety into me. Whatever small flame flickered upon seeing him, it's quenched. "Sure. Listen, I gotta get going, though. Good to see you, Sebastien."

He shrinks backward. "Seb."

"Good to see you."

With another nod, he turns around and crosses the street to the kiosk. I watch until he reaches the corner, then passes out of sight toward the city center. Relief, dismay, and something like loneliness all mix together in my throat. Our random encounter felt less serendipitous and more like a heavy reminder: I've elected to do this without him, and I better get it right.

The sun slopes in a decline, nearly touching the narrow gray Haussmann-style chimneys of the city skyline. I take a seat to plan out my next move and order a café au lait and pain au chocolat from an older woman. She is distinctly not Irish in her greeting: *Bonjour, mademoiselle!*

An online search turns up little using *Emmanuelle Wood + Paris*, but the white pages database produces options within Paris proper.

Buttery pain au chocolat flakes litter the steel folding patio table, and bittersweet dark chocolate coats my tongue as I scroll through results. Heaven. I cross-reference with social media to find only one choice under the age of fifty—a heavy pout fills the circle of the profile picture. Online presence: strong. My own Facebook account contains sporadic posts from over the years, since I never really got into it. Angela's timeline used to bubble with action, but as I saw a few weeks ago when I started researching her world, that tapered off. Manu's About section practically triangulates her address. Through a thorough study of the last year's posts (and check-ins from her apartment) it's easier than I hoped to find her.

I text her address to Jean-Luc with specific directions (Metro stop Rue d'Alésia, two blocks south, across from a MarchéU grocery store, tomorrow morning), though nothing about the purpose of the visit, then I wait for his response. The line across the street maintains a constant flow of anxious visitors even past dinnertime. The longer Jean-Luc doesn't reply, the more nervous I become he won't be able to join me tomorrow; maybe he's working or sick of following me around like a shadow. Just in case someone, Manu or otherwise, is there, I want my form of French insurance with me. The hopeful arch of Seb's eyebrows fills my thoughts, but I shake my head.

The waitress returns with the check as my phone pings:

Be there at 8:30. Almost thought you'd forgotten about me.

The corner of my mouth twists into a smile. Is Jean-Luc flirting with me? Part of me likes him toeing the line after our emotional last parting. It's encouraging that we can forget the whole thing and move forward these next four days.

Footsteps come fast and quick around the corner, children's voices blurring together at a high-pitched frequency. I look up as they hurtle past the restaurant and a small hand snatches my phone from my lap.

Before I can react, five pairs of feet take off running faster than I would, had I not been sitting buffaloed in my chair. Their laughter carries from the corner crosswalk as they sidestep a group of teens and disappear from view.

"I lost a camera to those little vagrants my last trip to Paris." The woman sitting alone at the table next to me shakes her head. Her accent is American, and she wears a baseball hat with the words *Las Vegas* stitched across it. She leans conspiratorially toward me. "Sip your coffee with both eyes open—my advice."

I nod, not fully absorbing her tip. Instead, I stare in the direction they barreled. My phone is gone. *Gone?*

Regroup. Losing my phone is a serious blow—to my afternoon, my search, and all the notes I was keeping on it—but I have no desire to rant about it with a stranger, and all my files are uploaded to a cloud storage platform anyway. Although my phone was old by technology standards—almost two years—it will fetch a good price on the black market. Judging from their faded clothing and dirty knees, those kids (or their parents) need the money more than I do.

Seriously? Now is when I get all humanitarian?

I have no phone. I'm in Paris. With no phone.

"You don't live here, right?" the woman asks. Large sunglasses dwarf sagging, rouged cheeks. "You're visiting?"

"Yeah, just for the week."

"Do you need to call someone? Maybe your hotel?" She offers up her phone, a BlackBerry with built-in keypad.

My only source of contact with home, and the tiny circle of people I know in Paris, is probably halfway to Normandy by now. No doubt clanging around with a few other phones, tablets, and pairs of earbuds in one of the backpacks I saw bouncing along. Valentin has no way of reaching me. Cold shock drips through my body, fully absorbing the significance.

There's a tiny phone retailer next to Angela's apartment and I'm sure a few on the Champs-Élysées. I'll have to buy one. Shit. Valentin mentioned some disturbing new details to be aware of; this is not the time to lose lines of communication. A serial killer may or may not think I'm my sister, and I can't look up any new information or destinations until I reach Montmartre and my laptop tonight. At least I managed to text Jean-Luc Manu's address beforehand. Staying too long in one spot when I might have an unknown pursuer is frivolous and/or lazy. He or she could be watching me right now.

"Hey, are you okay?" The woman stands beside me, metallic lenses reflecting my anxiety. She looks toward the restaurant's interior and asks someone for a glass of water. My breath snaps in and out of my lungs, a rubber band sound. In out in out in out. Faster and harder. *Inoutinoutinout.* A mother with a baby stroller walks by, stares straight ahead, pretending I'm not hyperventilating, not having a panic attack, not imploding into a snotty mess.

"Tiens." Someone hands me a glass, and I drink it back in three gulps.

"What's your name, honey?"

I look up. Farther on, behind the woman, a policeman with a cap pulled low and *CHiPS*-style sunglasses betraying nothing stares at me. He approaches from down the block, and I suddenly realize I'm making a great big scene in public. People across the street in line stop to point at me, remarking on the spectacle.

"Astrid." I reply with my middle name, loudly. I slap a few euros on the table, thank the woman, and hail a cab.

The driver looks wary of my red eyes and blotchy cheeks, but I clear my throat. I give him Manu's address instead of Angela's. The first thing that comes to mind.

We head to the southwest part of Paris, cutting through long side streets and busy boulevards to the Moulin de la Vierge quarter. The blocks here are seedier than those of the housing projects I encountered at Nour's. No empty lots, just abandoned buildings. An affront to the beauty Paris is known for, and confirmation there's a backside to those picturesque postcards. A stooped woman pushes a shopping cart while a child stands alone in a full diaper, surrounded by weeds, watching me pass; cardboard boxes form water-stained forts in front yards beside disabled men in berets who reflect my own leering back at me from folding chairs on the sidewalk.

Here are the forgotten Parisians, immigrants and fringe members of society. As the car circles the block back up toward the main boulevard and the flickering streetlamps fade into the darkness behind me, I can only hope my phone buys a few weeks of groceries for those kids' families. Even as I cannot believe my fucking luck.

Chapter 16

Day 5, Thursday

The empty lots and cracks in the sidewalks appear more numerous in the bright sunshine. Dark tenements and tent towns are like postindustrial grave markers tallying the unexpected death of a dream held by each resident. My driver slows down at a stop sign but doesn't stop.

Last night when I returned home to Angela's apartment, well past store hours of the phone retailer, I fell asleep, exhausted from the day's informative-slash-unproductive activities, and the morale suck of having my phone stolen by grade school kids. I muttered plenty of curse words against them each time I felt the knee-jerk reaction to check the time/texts/emails. But I can't bring myself to get angry—the tiny toes peeking through hole-riddled shoes won't let me. Those kids reinforced a valuable lesson: no moment here is safe.

The dilapidated building at Manu's address squeezes in between two brick residential structures, both clearly more recent, judging from the stark white trim hugging their windowsills, in contrast to the peeling dark-green paint of Manu's building. I should wait for Jean-Luc, but I'm early. Instead I pay the driver and go ahead on my own.

A gentle push cracks open the building's metal door. I don't have the apartment number, but a row of mailboxes sits in the lobby, each labeled by tenant last name. WOOD 12 marks one box of a dozen.

The week of her disappearance, that Wednesday, Angela was seen at the convenience store around the corner from her building (scene of my disturbing swastika encounter). Then, a few hours later, she was noted entering Manu's apartment by a neighbor. We only know this because when Manu went missing, the police interviewed everyone in her building; the neighbor recalled a female visitor that day fitting Angela's description. When she was shown a photo of my sister, it was confirmed.

Sounds more common to nightlife swell in the stairwell. Moaning, bass music, glass breaking, scuffling, crying, and a baby's coo. I turn back, deciding to wait for Jean-Luc after all, when a man descends the stairs. I press myself against the side as he squeezes past without making eye contact. His ducked head and rumpled pants could mean he's late for work, but curiosity drives me to the landing, up to the fourth floor, where the bass music emanates. A door is partly ajar; the apartment is dark inside, its shades still drawn. A woman in a negligee sits within counting cash on a table.

The floorboard beneath me creaks. She snaps her head up. She's young and beautiful, and at first glance the bustier she wears might suggest a wife titillating her husband. Then she shifts forward into the light of the single lamp, and dark roots blend into shabbily bleached hair, revealing an ache in her expression and accentuating circles under haunted eyes. She rises with purpose, walking to the door slow enough to make my heart pound in my chest—then slams it shut in my face.

Emmanuelle?

Panicked, I scan for the apartment number and realize she's a neighbor. *The* neighbor? The one who saw Angela enter Manu's apartment? Before I think better of it, I knock on the door. No answer. I knock again. "Bonjour?"

Movement is audible inside, but I can't tell if she's still sitting at the table counting money or has disappeared into a back bedroom to ignore me. I try again—"Hello?" There are at least a dozen residents in this building, and any one of them could have reported Angela's visit.

I move down the hall to Manu's apartment. Blood pounds in my ears. "Bonjour?" I tap my knuckles against the door. It falls open. "Emmanuelle?"

Inside, the tidy front room, devoid of electronics and clutter, could belong to a middle-aged woman instead of an early-twenties college student. Shoes are lined up neatly in a row beside the door, and an orange, knit blanket is folded artfully on a modest love seat, one section peeled over like unfinished origami. A pile of magazines on an end table is squared up along each edge. The dead bolt dangles from the door as though someone kicked it in from the outside.

A punch of sharp air hits my nose, churning my stomach. Something rancid was forgotten here. Dishes are piled in the sink, and I turn in the opposite direction if only to get away from the stench. The bedroom resembles a San Francisco apartment, no bigger than a shoebox. Photos blanket every flat surface from the dresser to a bulletin board. A young, heavyset woman with curly waves of hair, a stern nose, and a small chin smiles in most photos or pouts with girlfriends. Photo after photo shows a girl full of life, happiness, and deep thoughts. Pensive, artistic photos of her facing away in desert landscapes have the prized location on a shelf facing the made bed, crisp corners tucked in army-style. As though she would see these last before falling asleep at night.

I scan the space, searching for an indication that Manu is alive and safe—maybe a receipt from yesterday's lunch. Some hint to clear Angela's name so Valentin can focus on my sister as the victim again.

One lacquered wooden frame sits in the middle of the dresser top, plain and unique among the other sparkly frames, protecting a picture of Emmanuelle and an attractive man. Their cheeks press lovingly against one another, rich skin glowing in the sunlight behind the camera. Stubble lines his jaw, while his green-gray eyes carry a weight absent from Emmanuelle's. Dimples dot each cheek, and a curl of black hair hangs above one eye. I grab the photo and examine it up close. He's the same guy in Angela's photo. The one I found that first day with Seb, searching through boxes. Is this Emmanuelle's boyfriend? Did Angela steal her boyfriend?

A floorboard moans in the hall. My heartbeat pounds in my ears, and I hold my breath, straining to hear movement. Sliding the frame into my handbag, I peek into the living room.

"Shayna?" Jean-Luc nudges the door open. Techno music begins to blast from the apartment across the hall, with the lyrics screamed at the top of the singer's lungs.

"Hey, Sherlock. Come on in."

He closes the door, shutting out some of the noise. He pauses beside the broken lock. "Whose apartment is this?"

"Angela's friend. This morning I knocked on your door, but you weren't there."

Jean-Luc pinches his nose, coming too close to the kitchen. "Yeah, I had an early meeting at the office. Bitch work is required at all hours." He steps back, examining the faded couch and patchwork throw pillows. A pile of mail is stacked on the kitchen counter. "What are we doing here, Shayna?"

I shush him with a finger, and his eyes nearly bug out of his head. "I'll be quick," I whisper. "I'm looking for something. Take a seat if you want."

Although his cheeks begin to burn red, looping Jean-Luc or anyone else into details is not part of my plan. And if I'm honest, that hasn't been my mode of operation for years. That's probably why no one has contacted me, worried or concerned when I disappeared from San Diego and didn't tell anyone—not even my aunts. I know Jean-Luc could get in trouble, but I'm all selfishness this week. And I learned my lesson against getting too close to Frenchmen on Monday.

Jean-Luc spreads his hands. He hasn't moved from beside the doorway. "Shouldn't we say hi at another time when she's home? I don't like this. Seriously." His gaze darts around the room like he's afraid the love seat cushions will come to life. "What are you looking for, exactly?"

I adopt an innocent expression, all wide eyes and parted lips. "A photo of Angela and her friend. Or something that might look good at the memorial for Angela."

He nods too deeply and slowly to be buying my story, surveying the space. There aren't any windows here. Only a door beyond the kitchen, leading to a bathroom or pantry, probably. He toys with a stack of beer coasters, then marches into the bedroom. After a few seconds, a drawer is opened and shut. He stalks back out, furious.

"We're leaving."

"What? Why?" My hands are full of coupons from the sideboard.

"You lied to me, Shayna. I can't be here. I've seen this girl's photo on the news—Emmanuelle Wood. She's missing." He grinds his teeth, wavering between the exit and the back wall, where I stand. "I'm a *fucking* embassy employee, Shayna. I can't be here."

"Shit." I smack a hand to my forehead, making a show of it. His eyebrows plunge deeper. "Hey, I'm sorry, I didn't even think of that. Give me a few minutes, then we'll leave. Cool?"

"Shayna, no, I can't. Not cool. You know, for someone who's gotten the short end of the stick in life—you sure don't hesitate to poke people with it." I open my mouth to object, but he lifts a hand to stop me. "I have to leave now. Can't believe you brought me here." He uses the bottom part of his shirt to wipe the coasters he had just been touching, then wipes down the doorknob, muttering in French. He knocks it open with his foot.

"Hey, wait—where are you going?"

He turns back, slowly. His eyes narrow, taking me and the scene behind me in. "Somewhere else, Shayna. This is . . . not okay."

We've only known each other a few days, and he's been beyond helpful to my search even without understanding it fully. He's the first person I've felt some human connection to in a long time. The realization leaves me feeling cold, clammy. Seeing his angry expression now tightens my chest.

"I'm . . . I'm sorry, Jean-Luc." The words sound bulky in my mouth, unpracticed and unrehearsed, and he knows it. His face sours like he can see the struggle my tongue makes to wrap around unfamiliar letters. Once, they were familiar. Back when I had anyone to apologize to.

Jean-Luc steps through and shuts the door with his foot as much as it will let him. My chest buckles hearing him clamber down the rickety steps, fills with regret at the greedy impulse to bring him along, knowing full well he could get in trouble if caught. Flickers of panic lick my neck and clench my throat before I push the old emotions back. Jean-Luc won't forgive me for this. I could see it in the sneer of his mouth.

Fine. Add him to the list.

If Manu really is missing, she won't mind that I took her picture frame. I just need something to vindicate Angela—maybe a recent note from her to Manu with a #BFF in the postscript. Anything to prove my sister couldn't actually have a role in making another person disappear.

Jean-Luc is right. I shouldn't be trusted.

My belly growls. I have half a mind to dig around Manu's pantry but for the overwhelming stench of molding cheese. No. Something more substantial, heavier. A weightier stench that pricks my eyes the closer I get to the kitchen. My stomach seizes as I pass the front door. On the dishes in the sink, I can see rotting leftover dinner—cabbage, half-eaten beefsteak, and peas so shriveled they could replace BB gun ammunition cling to the plates. The closer I creep, the more crushing the odor becomes in the unventilated apartment, and I cover my mouth, bile threatening to climb my throat. Still, dirty dishes don't seem like enough to account for the smell. With forefinger and thumb, I move a few plates here and there, checking under each for the culprit, when a new stench reaches my nostrils. From beneath the counter.

I step away from the closed cabinet below the sink. My heart pounds, louder than the neighbor's bass. A new wave of nausea clenches my stomach. It could be a garbage can or expired food stuck in the disposal.

Used diapers, though I didn't see any sign of children.

A dead rat.

My hand shakes, reaching for the handle as I mentally try to place the odor. I bite the inside of my cheek, wishing Jean-Luc had stayed. When were the police here last? I tug on the handle, only the cabinet won't open. I tug again. It's stuck. I pull harder and brace a foot against the other door.

The cabinet falls open. Discolored flesh highlights black veins that spider along an arm, a leg, a naked body bunched and folded at the hips to fit into the cubed space. Glitter nail polish shines in perfect condition on hands folded across the chest. Black hair hangs forward, covering the face. My eyes shoot to the door, but it's still closed, trapping us in here together.

Hysteria claws my chest, building into a scream, but I clap both hands over my mouth. Valentin's accented English echoes in my ears. *Neighbors. Series murderer.* A keepsake bracelet dangles from the body's wrist, little symbols extending from the main chain. The Eiffel Tower. A heart. A dog. A boy and girl holding hands.

Counting to ten does little to calm my heart rate but allows me to watch the arm, alternately hoping it moves and that it doesn't. The fingers don't twitch. I don't touch anything, but I toe the cabinet door open a bit farther to see inside. Black rings circle each ankle. Ligature marks.

My belly contracts, and I heave, the croissant I ate for breakfast splattering across the floor, amplifying the smell. I lurch to my feet and slam against the counter. Everything I touched and marred with my fingerprints—the doorknob, the cabinet, the dresser—flashes across my vision and is enough to make me dry heave again. *Angela is implicated,* Valentin said.

Floorboards groan somewhere else in the building. I wipe my chin with the back of my hand and grab a dish towel from the counter to mop up my sick, then shove it in a plastic bag I find in the pantry. I wait a full minute before tiptoeing to the front door. The stairwell is empty. Body odor lingers in the air and melds with the underlying dust.

Who killed this woman? How long has she been here? Valentin's assertion that Manu is a missing person just became even more frightening since there's a body underneath her sink. Is that Manu? What kind of past does Manu hide—a history of violence? The body could have been placed there after the police did their sweep. Right? Even as I try to logic through this, nothing makes sense. I can't think straight with the arm so close, so stiff. What the fuck is going on? What was a hopeful visit to find some clue, some hint of evidence to vindicate Angela from Valentin's suspicion, just turned into another nightmare.

I should try to ID her; I know it.

My fevered breathing turns to ugly sobs, and I stumble downstairs, techno music amplifying my frenzy.

The neighbor. The john descending the stairs. Jean-Luc. All the people who saw me here, wearing Angela's face, surge to mind in a torrent of regret. All witnesses, capable of identifying me and confirming my suspicious actions. I spin along banisters, no longer touching anything, no longer careless and naive about the record of my being here.

I land on the first-floor foyer with the same thought repeating over and over in my head: two dead bodies in one week. The front door swings open as a gust of wind catches it, and I barely break stride, pounding the pavement in my flip-flops. Rhythmic human screams nip at my elbows, stay with me and ring in my ears the length of the block, until street noise finally drowns out the neighbor's stereo.

Chapter 17

Deep gulps of air burn my throat and batter my lungs. Pollution hangs low on the outskirts of Paris, and a bakery truck belches a cloud of gray past me. New tears sting my eyes, but I don't slow my pace. I run until I spy an empty cab with an illuminated UNOCCUPIED sign, then get in and lock the doors. My breath catches, and I struggle to tell the cab driver where to go.

"Eh, mademoiselle, ça va?" He turns to me from the front seat, neon reflective sunglasses revealing little.

"I'm fine. Just go, please." When he hesitates, I add "Allez!" We merge into traffic to join the stream of cars navigating the morning rush hour. People honk and gesture while staring at their phones, cutting off other drivers. The routine is calming, the normalcy what I need in a place and situation that feels like a constant out-of-body experience.

As I withdraw my hand from my bag, it cramps, bent in the shape of the picture frame, red where my grip wedged to it. The grooves of the wooden frame imprint a right angle on my skin, an L that remains like a pointed finger after we cross over the Seine. *Thief. Evidence. Implicated.*

The driver slams on his brakes, and the frame flies from my hand. It clangs to the floor and knocks against the middle console, breaking the frame's stand. "Hey!" I look up; we are two inches from a delivery truck's bumper. The driver shoots me an annoyed glance in the rearview mirror. I pick up the pieces of splintered wood and the frame. The glass is intact, at least. "Watch the road, please," I mumble.

His hands scroll for a new song on his phone, ignoring me.

"Hey, s'il vous plaît, the road!" I nod my chin at the empty space before us, the delivery truck already thirty feet ahead. The car behind us honks. "Allez?"

The driver has been muttering in French since he slammed on the brakes, and his stream of commentary ticks up in volume here. He yanks the parking brake, yells that if I don't like it I should drive in morning traffic. Then he points to the door. We're more than a few blocks away from my destination, but I pay him for the total thus far and get out.

"Nous sommes arrivés, mademoiselle!" the driver yells when I slam the door shut. As he peels away to merge back into traffic, I try to collect myself. *Nous sommes arrivés, mademoiselle.* We're here. The same words (in a much different tone) were spoken by the driver on my first day as I arrived in Montmartre. Stepping onto the sidewalk I feel exposed, raw. Like the universe is telling me a riddle in pig Latin after a round of Seb's Calvados. There's a trash bin nearby, and I toss my plastic bag of sick in.

Five blocks later, the crowd swells and carries me beyond the curb to the busy storefronts of the Champs-Élysées. Angela's Tuesday outing. Two women pass wearing matching wide-brimmed black hats, exclaiming over the lucky buy they found. I find a store window with mannequins in swimsuits modeling the hats, then duck inside. Planting myself beside a rack of clothing, I wait for my pulse to settle. After what I just ran from then ran into, I wonder if I should have left Angela's apartment at all today.

A body. There's a body in Manu's apartment. Another thought strikes me, and my hand flies to my mouth. What if that was *Angela*?

"Shayna?"

I yelp and knock into a rack of camisoles. The flimsy tops fall to the ground in a pile. Seb studies me from beside a table of women's jeans, dark eyebrows stitched together. Yellow squash pokes from a reusable shopping bag slung over his arm.

"This is why you did not return my calls or texts? Because you would rather shop than recount Angela's steps together? Did I catch you between stores at the catacombs yesterday?" The pain in his voice makes me glad he's standing against the storefront window, the sun behind him hiding his face. The satin top in my fist might as well be a smoking gun. Fury fills me at his accusatory tone.

"Actually, yes. I would *love* to be shopping rather than recount . . . *retracing* my sister's steps!" The noisy cluck of saleswomen at the back counter pauses. "Look, Seb." I run a hand down my jaw, try to act normal. Try to remember what that is at this point. What is he even doing here? Is this his normal jaunt home? Was he following me? "I needed some space after . . . after Monday."

He takes a hard step forward. "What happened does not matter, Shayna. What matters is learning Angela's fate before you leave." He grips my arms. "I cannot do this alone, Shayna. I have tried. I did not want to push you yesterday, but seeing you here, I need your help. Please." His voice cracks.

Blue eyes stare with such intensity, I can't tell if it's meant for me or Angela. "Are you listening?" His eyes are bloodshot, like he hasn't slept well. A loud buzzing flits past my ear, then a fly lands on Seb's shoulder. He slaps it, leaving a trace of wing, before wiping his hand on his cargo shorts. "My apartment is nearby across the river. Will you come with me and work together again? I worry about you."

Etiquette would suggest at least grabbing a coffee. But I've used up my quota of niceties for Seb. I eye him again, with Valentin's claim about his dishonorable discharge in mind; Seb still seems lonely, sad, and in mourning. No outward sign of imbalance. The yellow tank top he wears emphasizes thick shoulders and beefy arms. A tattoo of a rooster peeks from his neckline above his heart. He shifts his weight, waiting for my answer, and the tension leaches from his frame until he just appears neglected, needy.

"Shayna, we could—"

"No, Seb. We are not a team. You and Angela were a team, maybe, but not us."

He straightens. His jaw pulses as he meets my gaze. "You and Angela are the team. Always."

A few days ago, I would have stopped to puzzle over his words, to wonder whether he truly felt that way all along and whether it was me who misinterpreted, out of jealousy, their *twin-like* bond. On day five, I'm happy I haven't revealed anything I shouldn't. "Seb, I want to know what happened, too. I will figure this out."

His eyes dart back and forth between mine, then he crushes me with a bear hug. Conflicting emotions rise in me—relief and aversion—and make me grit my teeth against the impulse to shove him away. I pat his back instead. Words of stumbling reassurance muffle against his shoulder.

"Thank you," he whispers. "Please excuse me, I—I am not sure what came over me." His eyes turn red as he stares at a framed handbag on the wall. "Angela and I used to buy groceries together. She loved walking down this street toward Napoleon's arch."

"I promise I'll email you if I find anything useful. Okay? I need to get going now."

Once he waves goodbye from the storefront, I grab the wide-brimmed black hat I was eyeing and head to the cashier to pay the thirty-six euros. It's the least I can do since the staff didn't chuck us from the premises. Added bonus, I'll own a first line of defense against serial killers: camouflage.

Behind the counter, two teen girls discuss something hilarious, heads tilted back, mouths agape with silent laughter. They stop when I approach, and a mean little voice inside me says they witnessed my reunion.

Outside, a movie theater across the street presents advertisements of recent films—a macro reminder that the world still turns while mine is at a standstill. A group of women passes, and glittery nails fill my vision. Did Angela like glitter, or did she think it was a form of warfare from the way it stuck to everything? Why did I leave Manu's apartment without doing what I should have—identify the body?

I buy a ticket for the next movie so I can sit in darkness and digest this morning's events. Angela once received a birthday card whose front was covered in rainbow glitter; she threw it away after opening it. (Definitely, warfare.) Those nails weren't my sister's. Was that Emmanuelle's body, then? When did she go missing, exactly? How could Angela be implicated in Emmanuelle's disappearance if she herself is missing? An ugly thought surges forward, along with the immediate sting of regret: What if Angela is missing *because* of her involvement in Emmanuelle's disappearance?

In the movie, two friends are in love with two sisters, and they scheme to convince the women to accompany them to a destination wedding. When one of the sisters disappears and the heroine turns to her lover for help, the theater stops being a safe place. I get fidgety and leave.

Wandering back among the crowds, I clutch the shoulder strap of my bag and pull my hat down low. The picture frame adds a new weight to my tissues and passport, one that announces itself with each bang against my hip—*I will not be ignored*—clang clang—*I am here*—clang. Angela is not typically the Other Woman. It's not her style; she believes in love and white horses too much. It seems outlandish she would go after another woman's man, disrupting their lives so much she earns herself a stalker. She would never fight for a man to begin with, instead insisting he should recognize her value on his own. A street performer calls to me on his microphone, but I walk faster and move out of range.

Something is off about the romantic photo of Emmanuelle and the heartthrob. It was the only photo of him in the bedroom. Did they break up and she burned the rest of them? Is he photo shy and that's the only good one of him? The *GQ* picture I found in Angela's box says otherwise.

If the neighbor hasn't realized there's a dead body in Manu's apartment by now, she will soon. That acrid smell will grow worse—and lead police straight to my fingerprints on the doorknob. A shudder crawls across my shoulders despite the morning heat. Jean-Luc had the right idea in wiping down his prints.

Five days have come and gone, and I'm no closer to discovering what happened to my sister. *Five days.* Bits of clues and a list of people to avoid keeps growing, but Angela's whereabouts remain just outside my understanding. I've done everything people in the know have done or suggested: Seb's idea to retrace Angela's steps, Valentin's police work telling me those precise last steps, Nour's suggestion to visit Delphine, and even Jean-Luc's cautious guidance at the restaurant. Each form of advice was offered with other priorities in mind. Official constraints placed on each move. This whole time, I've been chasing someone else's idea of how to find my sister. Someone else's idea of Angela.

I set off toward the hill of Montmartre at a brisk pace.

Angela's apartment was turned upside down and inside out by the police, judging from the box of evidence in Valentin's office. She knows I would never gain access to something the police would consider important; every clue she thought I'd need I must have already seen, back at home base.

I have to stop chasing this Paris Angela and reexamine everything I've already looked at and ruled out because I haven't been honest with myself. My review of her apartment has been through a filter of distance—the Angela I assumed she was in Paris, the one who ran half marathons and charmed everyone. Other than that brief conversation with Jean-Luc—and let's admit it, even then—I've resisted probing the ugly memories from our past, the darkness of certain deeds that shaped us as much as the moments when we bonded over an invented language. Any clues Angela would have left would be meant only for me, and our ghosts.

"Mademoiselle, excusez-moi," a man calls from behind. An officer in a dark uniform with POLICE stitched across his baseball-style cap waves me forward. Large yellow teeth contrast prim pink lips. I glance around me, but the crowd continues without pause. They are already certain he's speaking to me.

"Oui?"

He replies in French, too formal and complex for me to grasp. He beckons me again. "You must be coming," he adds in a thick accent.

"I'm sorry?"

"You must coming," he repeats, his voice dropping. He looks beyond me, lifting his head so that I can see his nose appears once broken, off balance in an unnatural way. A stiff patch reads POLICE NATIONALE and cups his right shoulder. "Now. I am police—we go now."

Fear spikes my heart rate. Did something happen? Was there a break in Angela's case? Why would the police dispatch someone to pick me up at the Champs-Élysées (has he been driving around looking for me?) if there wasn't something important? The man's poker face should be on an ESPN live feed.

"What happened? Did Valentin send you?" I cross the three feet that separates us just as the breeze picks up, carrying with it the rank smell of body odor. It is deep, stifling, like the man hasn't bathed in days. Instinct clenches my belly and freezes my steps. The smell from the stairwell. I lift my eyes to his face, still partially covered by the wide brim of his policeman's cap. This man was in the stairwell of Manu's building.

His lips twitch. "Yes. Valentin have message for you. Come." A black car with tinted windows stops at the curb. Tourists crowding the sidewalk scatter before it, their selfies ruined. He clutches my elbow, directing me toward the open door. My mind races. I haven't seen

Valentin with this man, and I don't recognize him from the station. Valentin has no way of contacting me without my phone, and I left too early this morning to buy one. Sending another officer is not such a stretch. But why would that officer take me away in an unmarked car with tinted windows?

Numbness radiates from where the man grips my skin. We approach the door, and a pair of sneakers and a T-shirt are visible in the first foot-well. The back seat flows into the front, no metal grid barring the way. The driver wears a baseball-style cap with the word POLICE, too, pulled down low, obscuring his face as he scans the crowd. It's a regular sedan. But for the duct tape and zip ties that litter the cushions.

I scream and shove the man away, then turn and tear through the crowd of tourists. Women cry out; my hands push through their photo op as I strain to hear footsteps behind me. I leap past a small hedge around a restaurant and run another twenty feet down the next street before I pause at a covered bus stop to suck air into my burning lungs. My hat is gone. From here everyone passing at the corner is visible— three taxis zip by; a stooped man with a rolling shopping basket waits at the crosswalk. Shaking spreads through my limbs, and my elbow throbs with the memory of the man touching me.

Green light. The man with the shopping basket hobbles across the street as a black sedan glides into the adjacent intersection—hesitating, slowing, searching. Someone honks from behind, and the sedan speeds up and out of sight. I collapse onto the bus stop bench, into a bed of fabric scraps and newspapers. My breathing comes jagged and the rags sit upright, eyes wild until they land on me.

"You okay?" the man asks in French, but I can't speak. He repeats something, undeterred and alarmed. *Comptez jusqu'à dix. Comptez jusqu'à dix.* Count to ten.

Comptez. One, two.

That man came to abduct me. *Three, four, five.*

Possibly to kill me. *Six, seven, eight.*

147

He was in Manu's building. *Nine, ten.*

Which means he's been following me.

I fill my lungs with air, and a sob-hiccup escapes. A grimy hand touches me as calm settles over me like a blanket, shock spooling through my core.

"You okay?"

I nod. A yellow cab turns the corner, and I let fly my dad's shrill whistle, the one that he taught me when we were thirteen and which I lorded over Angela because she never could do it. The taxi rolls to a stop beside us. I thank the bus stop man, and he repeats, "Comptez jusqu'à dix."

I climb into the back seat of the cab, the plastic partition and prominently displayed ID already a comforting sign that this driver is legit. We veer left toward the hill. With every black vehicle we pass, I slide farther down in the seat until only the wide, leafy trees lining the road and approaching clouds fill my vision.

These last few days were driven by the assumption that Angela was hiding from someone. And that I should be, too. Knowing now for certain how true that is, the arresting fear in my chest diminishes with each kilometer we drive. While my hands coil into fists.

Chapter 18

Ready for your burial, Moon?

My toes still poked through mounds of sand. The coolness of the lapping waves rushing my ankles was refreshing, although it made Angela's job harder; each time she succeeded in covering my toes, water would rise and wash away her progress.

We were ten years old, sprawled across the bumpy sand along the water of our inlet. The sun bore down harder than usual, but a breeze kept things bearable, dancing across the skin exposed by my one-piece swimsuit. Angela started pouring sand on me with her toes—*finger toes*, she called them. *The better to grab you with.* It turned into a game: I'd lie still while Angela covered me with as much sand as her finger-toes could grab in one footful. The sand kept spilling off, creating triangles along my body. Angela suggested she could use one hand and one foot to make it go faster, to build on the triangles, and I conceded.

Clear blue reigned above us, with only one airplane toting a banner passing by in the ten minutes that followed. The sound of wind chimes carried from somewhere close. Sunshine bathed my face, a delicious contrast to the cool sand cascading down my legs. It was a relaxing summer day—until suddenly it wasn't. Tiny stinging rocks woke me. They were attacking my cheeks, my eyes, my mouth. I tried to open my eyes, but the constant stream of sand made it impossible. I moved to shield my face from the sand, but my arms were pinned. Panicked, I screamed and kicked, fueled by sudden terror, and succeeded in rolling onto my stomach. I threw off a mountain of silt and a driftwood log. Angela stood over me with a soda can and plastic pail filled with sand. Horror drew her face long. "I'm so sorry, Moon. I don't know what happened. I'm sorry," she repeated, over and over again, gulping sobs stifling her words until she lay down beside me. I stayed on my hands and knees and threw up a mouthful of sand. Apart from the thousands of grains of beach stuck in my hair and my irritated eyes, I was okay. Okay but confused. Scared, when I remembered Angela had been angry with me that morning for playing with her doll, the designer one I loved. Her retribution, delivered. We ended our visit to the beach earlier than usual that day, but not before she swore up and down she would never do anything to hurt me. That I was her best friend and the most important person in the world to her. Even as our mother separated me from Angela for days afterward, until it was safe to play together again.

Early morning turns into late afternoon with the ease of a sick day at home—agonizingly slow then quick, to where I look up and three hours have passed. The memory of body odor returns cyclically, every so often. Panic siphons the air from my lungs, and I replay the event from start to finish in my head: attempted kidnapping in broad daylight in the middle of the crowded Champs-Élysées; I escaped. Deep breath. Through the nose. Breathe.

I sat in bed for a good hour when I got back, debating going to Valentin right then and there, imagining the hypothetical conversation. *Miss Darby, are you sure? Miss Darby, what did he look like? Where were you coming from? What were you doing at Wood's?* Wrapping my head around all the different turns this conversation could take left me feeling as unglued as when I got in the cab. If the fake cop somehow actually does work for the police, I'll have to bob and weave in the moment. But cowering in fear is not how the next three days go. They can't.

Someone has been following me. Someone is growing both impatient and bold.

Shadows stretch across the hardwood floor and the paper I've organized into piles. I nod off twice before deciding on a cup of instant coffee I find in the kitchen. My bones ache from little to no sleep last night. Was that only last night?

Think, Shayna. I've reviewed all the boxes of papers and knick-knacks first opened with Seb. Where would Angela hide a clue? I climb onto her desk chair and peer down from above: nothing. I get down on my hands and knees to look beneath her bed (again), then her armoire and find a farm of dust bunnies. And . . . and remember something.

Seb looked beneath here and added two pieces of paper he found to one of Angela's folders—nothing interesting, grocery receipts, I think, but Seb didn't want to throw anything away. I launch over to the desk, to a manila folder titled SORBONNE RECORDS in my sister's slanted hand. My fingers shake as I riffle through the pile, passing over receipts for pasta and tomato sauce, then pausing on two receipts I skimmed my first day here. One is for a nightclub and the other a historical tour of something called *bordels.* The web browser on my laptop translates it as brothels. There's no website for the company listed on the receipt, but user reviews in French say it's great for native Parisians, and other stuff that doesn't make sense with subpar translation engines.

Holding up the receipt against the afternoon sunlight, an image ghosts through the paper. Excitement drains the moisture from my mouth as I realize I know these shapes. I flip it over. A sun and moon are drawn in pencil with a plus sign in between.

Angela's light cadence whispers in my head: *Good day, Moon.*

No one else thought the nickname was anything but sweet, except for me. To me, it was a callout, salt in the wound, a reminder that everyone outside our family preferred her charismatic, sunny disposition.

Disappointment, anger, and hurt all collide in a ball that lumps in my throat, then mingles with hope as I stare at the drawing. I found something no one else did. Angela must have left this for me. After staring at—savoring—the receipt a minute longer, I zip it away in the inner pocket of my bag.

The sun dips in the corner of the window behind apartment buildings, casting somber shade on the crowds of people heading to dinner or out to the bar. My stomach knots thinking about my morning. The body. The sedan.

I grab the Taser and my bag, then clamber out the door. Cedar incense burns somewhere in one of the apartments and snakes into the hall. I reach the stairwell and cast a glance above. Jean-Luc hasn't come down after his angry goodbye this morning. Probably for the best, considering he can't like what I exposed his budding career to. If he is home and hears me, he doesn't stir.

As my sandals slap the hard tile of the foyer, the door marked CONCIERGE moans inward. A mop of gray-streaked black hair emerges. Madame Chang.

She beckons me with a hand. "Venez." I look behind me and feel even dumber when I turn back to her and she's rolling big brown eyes magnified by thick glasses. "Allez," she adds. *C'mon.*

She opens the door wider as alarms ring in my head not to trust strangers, even tiny ones that reach my shoulder and recall my Chinese grandmother. But she waves me in in a way that is charmingly familiar. The front room of her apartment is both living room and kitchen, and she mutters, "Aiyaa," then something in Cantonese I don't understand. Warmth spreads in my chest at this sound of home—my mother's preferred exclamation. She motions to a plate of individually wrapped almond cookies and a pot of tea all prepped and ready on the modest coffee table. A coup of courtesy. After sitting in a sofa chair with a blanket buffering the plastic covering beneath, she points to the love seat. "Là." Now I don't know if she speaks Chinese or French again, but I sit, anyway.

"I'm sorry your sister is missing. She always lights up a dismal day." Perfect English. She tucks a strand of black hair back, artfully cut asymmetrically to complement a round face. I wonder how many languages she must speak, and whether being multilingual is just a thing here. Like inexpensive madeleines.

"Thank you," I reply, automatically at this point. "I'm Shayna, by the way."

She extends a small hand and shakes mine in a dying-fish wiggle. "Louise Chang. If there is anything I can do for you while you're here— I assume to handle some paperwork—let me know."

The ring she wears on her left hand looks like one of my costume jewelry pieces, but I doubt hers cost only twenty dollars. "Thank you. Were you and Angela very friendly?"

"Amicable, yes. We talked shop occasionally. I was very intrigued by her research on the catacombs."

"How so?"

"They're such a storied part of Paris's history. Now they've been reduced to a tourist attraction—or a hub for traffickers in Europe, depending on who you ask."

My first day here, passing Chang's doorstep, I'd read the headline emblazoned across the newspaper lying on her doormat. The word *trafic* stood out among the rest. I didn't realize it meant traffickers—not congested car traffic. Once again, the reality of how little I understand about this city slaps me across the cheek.

I smile at Chang. "Do you own this building, Madame?"

She pours me a cup of tea. "Chang. Now I do. After my husband passed away—that's him there." She points to a wall of photos above an entertainment stand, where a television might normally be, and to a frame holding a photo of her wearing a beautiful red dress—a cheongsam. In it, her head reaches the shoulders of a dashing young man with a thick mustache. It could have been taken ten years ago for all she's aged, but the faded yellowing of the image would suggest the eighties. "Maxime de la Chapelle was a good businessman—have a cookie, *eat, eat*—I miss him every day. That's him in his Serge Gainsbourg phase— all broody eyes and cigarettes."

"Wasn't there a biopic a few years ago?"

Chang leans forward and clutches her knees. "Oh yes. Serge was an icon here—still is. Most of the world wasn't ready for him—did you see that duet with his daughter?—but France was. His outrageous songs mainstreamed women's sexual empowerment for a hot second." She sighs, the action curving in her small shoulders. "Maxime loved him."

I nod, my mouth full of almonds and sugar. After half a sandwich for lunch, I didn't realize how hungry I was. "That must be hard . . . losing a spouse."

"Yes. Unbearably hard, for a while. As hard as . . . well. It's a difficult loss." She adjusts her glasses, then tightens the lavender knit shawl around her with a sympathetic nod. "At times it's challenging to manage all the real estate he left me. Worse—everyone thinks we weren't married because I kept my last name. Makes for more red tape and headaches."

Part of me wonders why she's telling me all this, remembers I need to get going, and another part just wants to sit here all day. A lunar calendar drenched in celebratory red hangs beside a series of French cookbooks lining the narrow counter of her kitchen nook. The army-style backpack she was digging in my first day sits beneath on the hardwood floor. A grappling hook hangs over the canvas flap, and a set of knitting needles beside it.

"Why did you? Keep your last name—if you don't mind my asking. If it made things easier for you, why not take your husband's? Plenty of women don't nowadays, but earlier I'm sure it was assumed you would." I sip from the teacup she laid out for me, painted with gold accents and delicate flowers. Hot liquid courses down my throat.

Chrysanthemum tea, my favorite growing up at family events, and at dim sum on Sundays. Warmth pools in my belly, in this other world away from the chaos sharpening its knives outside; I could purr.

Chang smiles. "You're right. If I had, it would be easier. I didn't want my identity to change simply because I moved from Singapore to France and married a Frenchman. I was still myself. I've tried very hard not to let the world change that."

I swallow another bite of cookie. "Makes sense. Seems like you've lived quite a life."

Chang waves a hand to the wall of photos. "Oh, I've done a few things. But I haven't had a real adventure in ages." Her voice is wistful. Mahjong tiles line the granite kitchen counter.

I thank her for the tea and cookies, then tell her I have to go. As we stand, I cast a sweeping glance at the framed photos lining the space around her wedding picture. Images range from lush green jungles to Chang and Maxime in ripped jeans holding up peace signs, the pair of them on a boat against an ocean backdrop. One photo in particular catches my eye: Chang, on a stage with a hundred people below her, cheering. Beneath, on the entertainment center itself, a crowbar is propped up against broken-in boxing gloves.

Another dozen questions beg to be asked, but my internal clock pushes me toward the exit. She tucks two almond cookies in my hand, then shuts the door behind me with a small bow of her head.

I stride toward the main entry of the building with new energy. The receipts add a certain heft to my bag, while the tea allowed me to recenter and regroup. Hearing how Chang rebelled against social expectations and pushed the envelope of accepted behaviors is reassuring; at least one person in Paris won't judge me for my evening ahead.

Chapter 19

Locals hurry past on foot outside, baguettes in hand and pointed heels clicking the sidewalk. The homeless man sits slumped against the wall in his usual spot, but he wears a change of clothes, at least. Tired eyes blink as I walk past him to the phone retailer, where a line of customers winds outside along the wall. A fold-up sign on the sidewalk advertises the latest smartphone release. Shit.

I get in line behind a tall man with a messy bun of hair and wait. Whatever the length of the queue, it would be better to have a phone on me than not.

A man in the store's blue polo uniform steps outside and begins speaking to the crowd. He waves his hands, then retrieves the fold-up sign. A collective groan sounds from the people waiting as everyone disperses. *No, no, no.* I approach the storefront. The man shakes his head from behind the glass doorway. He turns the lock, then points to a sign listing store hours showing they're closed for the night.

I hail a cab. My driver sets off for the police station, down the hill and across the river, while I try not to let disappointment dampen my verve. The closer we get, the harder I gnaw on my thumbnail, remembering those pencil-thin lips and zip ties. That man who tried to abduct me might pop up again tonight, and I won't have a phone or any means of calling for help when he does. I unwrap another cookie, searching for the sense of calm I felt back in Chang's apartment. Despite the moment of reprieve, my nerves are on full alert again, out in the cacophonous city with its dark corners and concentrated crowds.

It's fine. Everything's fine. As long as I speak to Valentin, I'm still making progress.

He's been investigating Angela's case and others that may relate without knowing everything I'm doing. Without understanding the nuanced clues Angela is leaving or having all the puzzle pieces that have plagued me since I arrived. But he has access to more information than I do, and a network of people to help him pursue leads on both Manu and Angela. Hopefully, he's willing to share some of that insight if I begin by confessing some of my morning.

The taxi rolls to a stop beside the grim stone building. I scan the groups of homeless people loitering in twos and threes out front. Whiskey fogs and imaginary friends occupy the men and women present, and I breathe a sigh of relief that my anti-American attacker is somewhere else. I ask the driver to idle in a no-parking zone, then take the steps two at a time. The lobby is empty. A young man in uniform staffs the reception desk. He rests his chin on his palm until I tap the counter.

"Inspector Valentin, please?" I ask in French.

The young man shakes his head. "Sorry, miss. He's in the field."

My heart sinks to my toes. There's no way of finding Valentin without a cell phone. When I ask for Valentin's location (and for the young man to breach protocol), he only smirks.

"Alors?" The cab driver leans a tattooed arm against the plastic partition when I return. His skin is deeply cracked, tan like he spent decades at the helm of a fishing boat before moving inland. Light-brown eyes cast a glance at me through the rearview mirror while I slump into the back seat. Speaking to Valentin was my best plan for the next hour.

A police siren cuts through the noise of evening rush hour, halting my garbled reply. "To follow! The police, now!" I say in French and point a finger toward the sound. My driver gives a dry chuckle before explaining he's not that stupid. Then I throw a hundred-euro note through the square opening into the front seat.

He steps on the gas. We take a hard right on a one-way street toward the Seine River. Parked cars flank each side of the narrow road, and I hold my breath, expecting a stroller or dog to appear out of nowhere. The siren grows louder, closer, as though we're speeding alongside it but obscured by the string of buildings to our left, until the driver slams on his brakes, catching sight of a stop sign at the last second. He swears, loud and long, like the sailor I suspect him to be, as his head whips back and forth, searching for oncoming traffic. The car rolls forward, but he slams on his brakes again as not one but two police cars come soaring past, the rocking wail only catching up to their speed when they're well out of sight.

I don't even have to butcher the verb for *follow* again. The driver takes off automatically. We join the throng of cars on the motorway and dip into the tunnel until we are flush with the river. The hum of vehicles and the rush of water beside us echo the length of the tunnel, the longest I've ever been in. Sounds from the mini television embedded in the passenger seat are overwhelmed, but the crawl at the bottom of the screen reports breaking news: a body has been found. Another one. Exhaust swells around us, invading the car cabin through the cracked window, making me light-headed the deeper we travel. A dozen vehicles separate us from the two police cars, but we weave in and out of lanes like a gnat, barely idling in one space before flying forward again. I buckle my seat belt. When I look up, we're three cars behind, and I debate my next move.

This is crazy.

Who's to say the sirens aren't leading to a break-in, unrelated to the murders?

What am I doing?

Thoughts of logic and good sense pinball in my head, but I ignore all of them. We exit the motorway past an open park with ruins. A sign we pass says BASTILLE, and I rack my memory for the plot of *Les Misérables*. Only a tiny Peugeot separates us from the police cars. They make a sharp left, then abruptly stop beside a residential building with two-foot-wide wrought iron balconies along each apartment window. They cut the siren. My driver parks three blocks down. Taller buildings here cast long shadows as though imitating my sneaking mind-set.

"Should I wait for you?" He turns to face me from the front seat, causing the Polynesian bird tattooed on his neck to flap its wings. No hint of flirtation, greed, or even excitement colors his face; concern presses in lines around his mouth. I thank him, tell him no, and tip more than I should. I shut the car door, then walk toward the flashing red and blue lights. Loneliness cuts into my giddy adrenaline, my newfound independence and renewed sense of purpose. Being more alone than ever in a foreign city is the consequence of finally embodying Angela's instructions.

The scene pulses with uniforms. Compact cars parked along each side of the street offer little in the way of protection, but I stoop and hide as best I can. Voices ring out as another pair of cars arrives, the buddy system all the rage among police. I scan the group for anything resembling the build of my fake cop and even close my eyes and inhale. The only offensive odor I can identify is dog feces on the spit of grass beside me. A lanky woman with skin so dark it could be blue strides from the driver's side of the first car we followed, all legs and little torso. The pink-faced man from the passenger side of the vehicle jogs to join her on the sidewalk. His crown of curly brown hair and balding center catches the light as he passes into the building vestibule. Valentin.

Conversation swells the closer I dare to slink. Passing between cars unseen is difficult in my white shorts and blue tank top, one of the dumber camouflage choices of my life. I succeed in wedging between a Renault and a Peugeot about fifteen feet from the entrance.

"Well? Is he dead?" A woman's husky voice in French jumps above the noise of the crowd. Her counterpart mumbles something in response, and she sighs loudly. "What? Speak up."

"He's been dead for around a week, but he was moved from somewhere else. Shot to the head. Still all dressed up for a night at the opera."

"Same ligature marks as the others? Tattoo?"

"You got it."

"Might be the serial, then."

"Captain thinks so. Hey, don't!"

"What?" the woman growls. "It's only a fly. There. See? It's gone."

"Well, it's a living being. Better to shoo it away than kill it."

The woman snorts. "Okay, Buddha."

Their conversation fades into the controlled chaos. Dead for a week and moved from another location. Whoever is in there died two weeks after Angela went missing.

"Can I help you?" The lanky woman towers over my crouched mass, wearing a stern expression. I'd even venture she does not want to help me. When I don't respond, she yanks me by the arm and plants me on the sidewalk. Voices around the front door of the building pause, and I'm sure my panicked heartbeat is audible to everyone. I don't know anything about French police except they don't mess around. Images of Valentin's own disgusted expression when I sassed him in Angela's apartment return, and suddenly I can't remember how to say anything in French. I can only stare at her while the police officer repeats her words more slowly.

"Are you lost? Are you a tourist or are you French?"

"No, I . . ." Sweet crap, how do I conjugate? Sweat breaks across my temples, and I cast a glance at the front door, searching for Valentin. Only tall men walk in and out.

"Are you Mexican? Chinese? Your embassy is around the corner." She points with a blunted nail down the street, then waves her hands, dismissing me in that direction.

"American. I'm here to see Inspector Valentin." My English rings out, and the bustle pauses. If she's going to dump me off at an embassy, at least shove me toward the right one. A pair of plainclothes cops moves into the building just as someone exits.

The officer places both hands on wide hips. "Why you are sitting . . . derrière . . . a car?"

I search for a plausible excuse when heavy footsteps pound in our direction. Inspector Valentin glares at me, sidestepping a man in a black slicker with yellow letters on the back. His mouth forms an angry curl.

"Thank you, Tremaine," he says in French. She frowns, then cedes my guard to him.

"What are you doing here? This is a crime scene, Miss Darby." Rather than rage at me, at my insolence, my audacity, Valentin's face gathers into a pinch. He raises a hand, as though to rub my shoulder, before it drops to his side.

One of the many subjects Angela and I always disagreed on was people—their intentions, their motivations, their treatment of others. While I've never been trusting of people—call it a remnant of being picked last for kickball—Angela has always sensed them and given them exactly what they wanted. *Why not?* she used to say. People see what they want to see, so why not give them what they want if it works to your benefit? Always the socially aware sister. The emotive twin. Staring at Valentin's exasperated mien, I know she's not wrong. A swift punch of longing hits my chin, and tears pool behind my eyes, missing my sister—needing her expertise to balance my default behaviors beyond this week, and throughout this life.

It's been so long.

Valentin regards me on the sidewalk, alone and apart from his colleagues. His expression softens.

I clear my throat and push the sudden emotion aside. "Well, I had my phone stolen so I couldn't call you, and I had to tell you something. I went to Emmanuelle Wood's apartment."

Valentin sucks in a breath. "And?"

Nothing comes to mind that will lessen the impact or better couch this news, so I just go for the truth: "There's a dead body beneath the sink."

Call me the tactless twin.

He takes a step back. His eyelids shut several times, maybe focusing blurry vision. "That's impossible. I was there last week."

"Could be it was moved there recently. Makes sense to deposit it after the police finished looking around."

He nods slowly, as though disturbed by my candor. "Anything else?"

I consider taking his hand but think better of it before I do. No need for theatrics. "Do you think it's Manu?" I need her to be alive, to prove Angela wasn't implicated in anything, that they were actually good friends despite obvious conflict.

Valentin exhales, staring at his feet. "I hope not. You had better get inside and remain there. I hope you're not talking to strangers anymore, Miss Darby."

"No. Not anymore. Did you learn anything else?" I can't help pressing him for more information, more detail. Especially when I recall my visit to identify Angela's supposed corpse. Valentin must know more than he's saying. "I meant to ask: the morgue director said Angela's gunshot wound and tattoo were administered postmortem. Why would anyone do that?"

He sighs, annoyed. "He should not have shared that with you. Once we confirm how those details align with the cause of death, I will update you. You can be assured."

"What about this dead body?" I motion to the apartment building. "He has the tattoo and the gunshot to the head, too, right? Is this the work of the same serial killer that went after Angela?"

Valentin rubs the bridge of his nose. "I wish I had more to divulge. Really, I do. We are working at all hours, given these developments. I, myself, am performing on three hours of sleep." He glances over his shoulder. "Have you ever heard of Michel Fourniret?"

Jean-Luc's Ogre des Ardennes. "The serial killer, right?"

Valentin nods. "Fourniret killed nine people. The inspector working that case blamed himself for not being able to apprehend Fourniret sooner. Over time, this failure became the inspector's legacy. I have no intention of these murders here becoming mine." He locks eyes with me. "Do not move. I'll get someone to take you home."

I watch him dodge a procurement team taking bags to a white industrial van before he disappears inside the foyer.

No one comes for me after thirty seconds, and I sneak closer to the entrance. The officer who found me must be inside; I don't recognize anyone else from the station. A crowd of locals gathers beside another van with direct line of sight into the building. Three men flank a well-dressed woman in a suit speaking into a camera, the same woman I saw on my taxi's seat screen—they're a news crew. *Monsieur Leroux,* she says, gesturing behind her, along with other words she speaks too quickly for me to grasp. The ticker flashes to mind, the text regarding a body.

Delphine mentioned that name in her office—Dr. Leroux—and Valentin confirmed it.

Could this body be Angela's archaeology director?

At the end of the ground floor hallway, a door is cracked open. Feet protrude from a black tarp beside a yellow shopping bag with black cursive writing. The letters look familiar. I make out the word *L'Opéra* before more policemen enter the hall and the view is blocked.

Valentin emerges alone from another door some fifteen feet removed from the main entry. Something glints in his hand before he pockets it. He looks up, directly at me.

I push through the crowd, ignoring the angry huffs from people, knowing he won't leave to follow me. If I'm lucky, I'll find another taxi waiting, go to my bordels tour, then squeeze in a visit to the Paris Opera before they close. Yellow bags with the same black cursive lettering were sitting in Nour's living room; she's a costume designer at the opera. And she might know more than anyone thinks.

My sandals smack the pavement, noisy in the quiet residential streets, until small convenience stores and restaurants bloom toward the city center. A thrill courses through me with each pump of my arms. Faster and faster, like adrenaline spurts in my limbs. The sun sets, and a breeze sweeps through the roundabout square. A yellow cab idles by the curb, and I'm panting like a dog when I come to a stop beside it. The driver rolls down his window to fully look at me. He hesitates to say hello, peering behind me for a pursuer, as I slip into the back seat. My heart swells, feeling the satisfaction of making tangible headway, on my own terms—on our terms—and like I finally have a grasp on next steps. Disregarding the declarations of outsiders who believed *Angela would do this* or *Angela did that* leaves me feeling empowered, and in control in ways I haven't experienced in years.

Even as Valentin's expression of surprise, locking eyes with me as he exited the building, lingers in my mind. And it registers the object he was taking care to conceal was a pair of shiny steel scissors.

Chapter 20

Once a year, we went to the San Diego Zoo as a family. Always in the summer and with a battery of antics. Angela and I would stand next to the monkey enclosure and groom each other while miming finding tasty bugs in each other's hair until a small crowd formed around us. Then I would get shy, and Angela would bow.

Things changed between us after that day on the beach. We lost the implicit trust that we shared as children; I never fully let my guard down with her again. By the time we went to college, long gone were our hammy bits and the comedic routines we both got such a kick out of. I began to feel that we were strangers; I didn't recognize the fluctuations in Angela's emotions, which dipped and peaked wildly. Reactions to mistakes in school or to hard words from our parents were twice the level I felt was appropriate. Everything was heightened for her. My therapist, Dr. Poucer, symbolized the undoing of our bond, according to Angela, even though our parents had always appreciated therapy and had sent us to a psychotherapist when we were fourteen to ensure we each had our own identities and were having our individual needs met. In Angela's mind, she, as my twin, was supposed to be my source of comfort and understanding—not the therapist.

Her feelings weren't unfounded. I did need an outlet I could confess everything to. An impartial ear to my twin worries, the pressures of *twin for the win* being our sister slogan, urging togetherness for success.

My fears of Angela's outbursts—for what they were doing to our family, and to her own relationships after she broke up with her boyfriend, then keyed his car—were making me jittery. It got to the point where I would receive a call from her and a cramp would form in my stomach, anticipating conflict I couldn't reason with, that refused to be fair. I didn't want to feel that way about my sister when I was there for her. I would always be there for her. Our parents loved her, too, just not always in the way she wanted.

Somehow, after they died, Angela's tirades, originally aimed at our family, her friends, and her boyfriends, landed squarely on me. A fact that royally pissed me off, in the midst of grieving, graduating college, and being tasked with managing my parents' testaments. Although we received equal halves of their estate, and that might be enough for other siblings, she never forgave my not selling the family home. As the executor, I didn't want to, so I didn't. About a month after the funeral (and several nasty exchanges by email and phone), we stopped talking. Just quit altogether. I was never entirely sure of Angela's reasons, but I couldn't take it anymore, the guilt she insisted I should feel regarding our parents' favoritism—knowing the crushing guilt I felt was far worse.

Posters of American metal bands and images of women in animal-print lingerie posed in various attack stances line the walls of the bar—far cries from the beasts Angela and I first encountered at the zoo. A furry claw curls under my bartender's jawline, an arm tattooed down to the collar of his white tank top. The fur color matches his surprised eyes—red, like he just smoked a bowl or contracted pink eye. He looks me up and down, then points past a pair of men at the counter—drunken regulars, from their looks of quiet stupor.

I double-check the address on the receipt I found in the folder as I head to the shadow-filled courtyard behind the building; we're near the

Pantheon, a secular mausoleum—shudder—on the Left Bank, and it's still eerily quiet before the night gets underway in the Latin Quarter. It's not that I expected a historical brothel tour to be rainbows and daisies. But an official sign would have been nice, or a pamphlet describing the tour itself; instead, broken glass lines the doorway of this bar like a crunchy *get lost* mat.

The tour guide grimaces when I emerge into the brick enclosure, then takes a beat to stare at my chest.

"Bon soir." I try to make eye contact with the other civilians, three young men, if you can call them that—maybe late teens—but they're all absorbed in the cracked cobblestone at our feet. Cigarette butts layer the ground.

Mathieu, the tour guide, introduces himself with shifty eyes. Dyed jet-black hair hangs to his chin in strips, but from the parentheses around his mouth, I bet he's at least forty. He turns and leads us through a side exit; I follow the throng of black jackets into an alleyway. Crowds begin to form before the adjacent bars and clubs and amplify the silence among us. We walk for ten minutes, alternating our route with sidewalks on busy streets and narrow alleys. The air is cool, allowing the constant sheen of sweat on my chest to finally dry at ten o'clock at night.

Our guide pauses beside a brown door. The muted space is couched in neon spray paint lining each side, and the only other business on this stretch is a convenience store. Bells chime as two men exit the store carrying paper bags. They see us, then burst into laughter.

Mathieu clears his throat. "Here is the location of one of Paris's most infamous brothels." He gestures mechanically, using practiced movements. He explains this was a favorite haunt of top Nazi brass during the Occupation, but it has since been turned into a storage unit. I'm the only one who seems to have any questions, searching for reasons why I'm here. *Does the Sorbonne study these sites? Do classes study sex workers?* Mathieu dutifully explains prostitution has long been decriminalized in France. Only the johns are fined now.

We move to the next location. Mathieu uses a flashlight when the streets become crooked and unlit, while thoughts of every horror movie ever swirl in my head. *Girl goes to Paris. Girl bonds with locals. Locals attack!* Why did I come here? Why did Angela? She clearly wanted me to find this receipt—she drew a sun and moon on it. The tour isn't on TripAdvisor, and I only found the one review on a French website that stated it was a good time for Parisians.

Mathieu halts in front of an abandoned three-story building, the structure leaning like a tenement. "Here we see the business of Madame Trudeau, famous proprietor of Trudeau's Home for Girls." Mathieu seems to zone out again while he recites this site's history. I have a hard time staying focused. I'm only able to catch his meaning when he uses swear words I recognize. Lots and lots of fucking occurred here.

We move on, heading back toward the sound of glasses clinking and bass pumping. Mathieu assures us our final stop is coming, and the boys all perk up, fidgeting and adjusting their jeans. Groups of people clad in their Thursday night finest crowd the sidewalk, forcing us to pass through single file, with me bringing up the rear. Cigarette smoke mixes with the smell of sugary cocktails, engulfing us.

Mathieu nods to a hulking bouncer outside a club bursting with young and beautiful patrons dying to get in; we're admitted without a second thought. We trail Mathieu through the entry until he leads us to the crowded bar. A red claw twitches from the same bartender's neck. I squint past an army of gyrating bodies and spy the heavy metal posters and photographs of animal-print women adorning the walls. We're back.

"Excuse me," I shout in French. "But we had three stops on this tour."

Mathieu shakes his head and points to his ears. He hands us each a shot of something green, tosses one back himself. The boys follow suit, but I eye my tiny glass, feeling my heart beat against the bass's rhythm.

Mathieu smirks. "It is to relax," he shouts in English. He mimes gulping it back, then he rubs the belly of his torn Iron Maiden T-shirt like it's a warm ladle of soup. "Relax. One more stop. You must drink— part of tour."

I open my mouth to argue with Mathieu, to say I didn't sign up for alcohol or being obligated to drink, but he crosses his arms. "Part of tour," he repeats. "No enter without this drink."

"That's not fair. That's not legal."

He shakes his head to show he doesn't understand.

"Goddammit." Not seeing another way, I take a sip. "There. Happy?" Its sweetness contrasts the bitter taste I was expecting. What is the point of this visit? Why did Angela come to this shitty excuse for a historical tour of Paris, paying fifty euros for an hour-long walk of nothing and a shot of something warm and green and altogether delicious that makes me suddenly parched and tickles my insides? *The green fairy.* Like a scene from one of Angela's favorite films, *Moulin Rouge*, this is a shot of absinthe. Instead of a musical number, images of the dead bodies I've seen this week jostle behind my eyelids. A girl bumps into me, sloshing the tiny cup.

I hand it back, empty, to Mathieu. He presents another, already prepared, but I shake my head. "No."

With a wink, and the first show of genuine interaction since I started following his cracked leather jacket, he leans into my ear. "You have need . . . extra relax." His French tongue grapples with the English, near swallowing the words. The boys, who only got one shot as part of their ticket fee, exchange a glance; I pass this second one to the red-headed boy when Mathieu isn't looking.

Colors seem brighter as we leave the bar and weave our way through the crowd, while the air feels thicker, covering my exposed skin, my tank top and shorts, like a sleeve. The sip of absinthe ignites my senses by the time we leave the brick courtyard and pass into the alleyway once more, its fierce mint flavor continuing to tingle my mouth.

It's been so long since I've had the slightest bit of alcohol; enjoyment registers before a wave of shame courses through me.

Words in French from smokers and drinkers outside pass over and around us, encircling me, and I accept them without thinking, or overthinking, and swear I become fluent in the course of five steps. Frustration knots my fists. I still have no idea why I'm here, and with my crap tolerance, I have a buzz.

Mathieu pauses down the length of the courtyard along the same wall, before an unmarked door I hadn't noticed. He opens it and ushers us all inside a scant lobby, looks backward, then pulls it shut. A cozy fit for the five of us. Dirt covers the ground beneath, except for a large, circular metal plate I stand on—a manhole. Bass from the adjacent club vibrates my chest, and I'm not sure if it's the absinthe or bad wiring, but the one light bulb illuminating the space flickers.

The panel in the metal door before us shifts two inches to the left. A beady eye lands on Mathieu, lingers on each of us—longer on me than I'd prefer—then slides shut. A bolt is undone, and the door with no handle swings inward with a groan. Mathieu and the boys step forward. The absinthe only allows for a quick jolt of nerves, a sudden fear for my safety and whether someone who's been trailing the tour since it began might follow me inside—then the impulse is stifled. Excitement at what lies beyond bubbles in my chest. Maybe this is Angela's favorite French speakeasy, like the one we visited in San Diego's Gaslamp District once.

A grizzled woman greets us in the somber foyer darkly decorated like something from a red-light district in the forties. Two antique parlor chairs and a table with a chessboard carved into its face occupy the round enclosure. She offers to check any belongings we might have. Heavy bags beneath darkly made-up eyes make her welcome ominous, as though we might not get our belongings back. The lamp behind her augments the scowl she reserves for me when I shake my head. She withdraws five tickets from a pocket and warns us not to lose them. When she gets to Mathieu, she speaks to him, dropping her voice and throwing me a side-eye. Serious shade for a glorified hostess. They argue, with her pointing at me, and I hear Mathieu say *Américaine*, but she shakes her head, wiry hair quivering in a bun. The words for *trafficking*, *police*, and *United Nations* tumble from her mouth in quick succession before she plants herself in front of me.

"Are you police?" Sharp eyes narrow, daring me to flinch.

I shake my head.

She says something snide, judging from her lift of one eyebrow. Then she nods over to Mathieu. Without further pomp, she turns on her heel and motions for us to follow.

We move down a skinny hall with red cloth lining the walls. A large man waits for us at the end, bald and pink cheeked in the warmth of the low ceilings and stunted environs. One at a time, he pats us down for objects, and the small voice that fought through my intoxicated haze pipes up again. *Part of the tour?* The man pats me down as thoroughly as he did the boys, and I focus on the crisscrossed pattern of the walls as he slides his hand around my waistband. Mathieu watches intently. When I'm released, we step through a restaurant-style door that swings behind us with an aggressive flapping sound. The dim lighting continues. A red haze grows the farther we walk in. Classical music thrums from speakers louder than I've ever heard violins, along with a deeper noise I can't place. I stumble along, behind Boy One and Boy Two through another empty vestibule. Boy Three takes off to the right like he already knows the drill. Mathieu leans into me and says, "Excited?"

A figure approaches from a counter tucked off to the side. Alcohol bottles line glass shelves, with no bartender in sight. Maybe this is a real speakeasy, with no liquor license. That's what I was getting the side-eye from the hostess about.

The man wears a hat with a large brim, and for a second I panic, thinking it's the fake cop. Then he leans in, and his accent purrs in my ear, trilling his *r*'s. Not a French accent. "What are you looking for?"

he asks. "Old boyfriend break your heart? Best friend cheat with him? I can help."

I jerk out of reach, though the movement is much slower. Mathieu says something to make the man turn back to the DIY bar and takes my hand. I watch him pull me to the right, following the group. My chest burns, warming me beyond the temperature of the small space. I wasn't supposed to drink anything. I shouldn't have drunk anything. He pushes a velvet curtain to the side, allowing me to enter first, and I almost trip on a couple making out on a footstool. "Sorry," I mutter. But neither one bats an eye at my slurred English. Mathieu pushes me forward with a hand on the small of my back, past an aisle of four doors, then left down a series of curtains. The deeper we travel inside this speakeasy, the more heightened my senses become.

This is not a tight space, not the family chest Angela locked me in when we were kids. But not knowing what lies ahead arouses my anxiety. I go to crack my pinkie knuckle, and it won't give.

Mathieu peers at the red drapes. Painted numbers are next to each golden rod suspending the velvet material, and he gestures to me—whichever one I'd like. Confusion adds to my buzz. The security I understand; the hostess's third degree makes sense for an illicit bar. These curtains, the empty foyer and vestibule, the lone couple making out, his hand under her shirt, are all strange. Where are we? Where are the patrons, eager to be seen and posted on social media, like in the Gaslamp speakeasy?

I choose curtain number two, and we pass into a tight space with a view that stops me in my tracks. A glass partition presents a room with a bed. Folded chairs are propped against the walls of our viewing space, and Mathieu unfolds two for us. The glass is streak-free; the smell of window cleaner lingers, and something else. Antibacterial. Beyond the bed, a velvet drape of fabric hangs at the back, probably leading to one of those doors along the adjacent hallway. I turn to ask Mathieu what we're doing here, but he is already seated, leaning forward, waiting. The curtain sways.

A woman enters, clad in nothing more than a slip. Nothing fancy, with barely any lace to the hem. But the silk clings to her slender frame, moves with her hips, becoming provocative and more than just a precursor to bedtime. She approaches the glass, and I'm not sure if it's a two-way pane or one-way from the manner she blows a kiss to the corner neither Mathieu nor I occupy. She's young. Far younger than I would expect someone to be at a peep show, with heavy makeup and rouge, like she's prepared for a theatrical performance. Is this burlesque?

My heart races, titillated by the sheer taboo of being here. Never in a million years would I have bet Angela set foot in a place like this. She believed ardently in love stories and shunned anything that suggested the contrary in romance and sexuality. Anything that suggested sex was a base act instead of a form of ethereal lovemaking.

The young woman massages her breasts for her audience. Pale skin glows in the red light, her blonde hair showing platinum from root to tip. The slip she wears appears nude so that she could already be naked were it not for the fabric gathering under her palms. The curtain sways again, and Boy Three enters the scene. I gasp, but Mathieu doesn't move beside me. Boy Three, naked from the waist up, only wearing the jeans I just saw him in, approaches her from behind, and if she hears him, she doesn't let on. He grabs her by the waist, then climbs his hands to her chest, but she doesn't flinch, instead allowing her glossed lips to fall open as though she enjoys his touch. As though this is a performance she's acted multiple times. Boy Three slides his hands to between her thighs, lifting the slip to show us her red cotton panties as his fingers search for skin. Here, she purses her lips, then turns to him, lifting her slip over her head and allowing it to fall to the hardwood floor. He leads her to the bed, undoes his pants, then climbs on top of her. She lets her face fall toward us, then licks her lips in a wide arc.

My skin turns cold. The warmth of the absinthe dissipates, replaced by nausea and a creeping understanding. Sickness builds from my abdomen and climbs into my rib cage. The third stop. This is no longer a tour. And not just a peep show. I am in a real-life brothel.

Mathieu's breathing intensifies beside me, and I'm unable to look at him. He clears his throat. "I am so glad you returned. I thought you might not, after your last visit."

"What?"

He tears his gaze from the couple and withdraws a small tube from his pocket. He offers me a tiny round pill. When I shake my head, he takes it himself. "I am sorry about last time, Angèle. I do not remember all, but the scratch you gave . . . endured one week."

My chest tightens. "Angela?"

Mathieu groans, watching something the couple is doing. He rubs his neck, licks his lips, then turns to me again. "That hurt, Angèle. I do not remember when you left, but it is rude to leave without saying au revoir. Come closer. Stay this time."

He grabs hold of my wrist and yanks, and I fall against him. "Angèle," he breathes. A lecherous gleam clouds black eyes. His sweaty palm climbs my thigh. "I was so angry when you left."

"Let go!" I push his hand off and struggle to stand, but he wraps both arms around me.

"Angèle," he says again, louder. His grip tightens. "Arrêtes, Angèle! You did not go to the police, did you? Did you?"

I wrench out of his grasp and bolt from the room. People extend their half-full glasses of liquor like barriers to the exit, and I dodge left then right. The deep noise I couldn't place when we entered registers as intense moaning, thrumming beneath the ache of bass strings. The hostess yelps when I barrel into her in the foyer.

Pushing past her and her questions, I don't stop until I'm back at the main street, glitter and sequins reminding me the night is just getting started. A cab stops a few feet down from me, and I cut in front of a pair of girls, then slam the door shut. It takes another minute before I can muster speaking a second language.

I thought I was out searching for my sister and only I could decipher the clues to her whereabouts. That I owed this search to her. What I've learned so far is that she's not the person I grew up with.

Academic Angela. Reclusive Angela. Sexually deviant Angela.

The lights of Paris blur together at the speed of my cab as I try to recall any mention of Mathieu in Angela's files. Bruises begin to form on my upper arms. Mathieu, slightly intoxicated, not exerting his full strength, was stronger than he appeared.

Now, certain that my sister was here before, I'm not at all sure she left in one piece.

Chapter 21

Snaking through the city side roads forces me to steep in the images I just saw. The questions they raised. The words spoken. What did that man say beside the do-it-yourself bar? *Old boyfriend. Your best friend. I can help.*

Angela went to that place, maybe alone. What was she looking for? Could she have been approached by the same thug for hire? A thought burrows into me: What if Angela hired that man or some other man I saw slouched along the walls—uninterested in the curtained rooms—to intimidate someone? To go after Manu? My hand grips the armrest on the taxi door as the idea takes root. What if Angela did have something to do with Manu's disappearance—or her death?

Spotlights illuminate the green arc of the Paris Opera's dome against faint stars dotting the sky, a megawatt OPEN sign to music lovers. Groups of people attending tonight's performance linger at the box office in sequins and coattails. Wide, flat steps lead to several windows for ticketing while pigeons hang on virtually every inch of the plaza at midnight.

I pay the cab driver and get out, expecting my knees to buckle, but they hold fast. The air is cool with the sun long gone, sloughing off the grimy feeling that's encased me since I ran away, providing the energy to finish out tonight's itinerary. With each step forward, my body falls into a rhythm on autopilot. Pigeons peer up at me, then flutter aside at the last second, the parting of the gray sea. A white-and-black one stops sprinting away to peer at me.

I want to go home. Back to San Diego, where I was devastated but things made sense.

Inside the square box office window, a young woman with an emerald nose ring picks at a fingernail. A hijab patterned with skulls drapes her head down to her chest.

"Nour?"

Vanity bulbs that frame the window highlight her beaming smile. The tension in my shoulders releases seeing her familiar face. Maybe that's residual shock.

"Shayna? What are you doing here, love?"

"Hey. Any chance opera tours are still going?"

Nour tilts her head, her pink lipstick pressing to the side. "Done for hours. But I can give you the VIP tour." She slips me a stub that says *Gratuit*. Free. "Meet me inside."

The lobby remains crowded, patrons discussing in groups or taking photos. People mingle along a large reception hall leading into the main theater. A thick, polished railing winds along an ornate staircase covered in rich carpeting and golden rods that restrain the fabric from bunching, while crystals forming a chandelier overhead chime with the gust of air I bring in. Nour skips down the steps from the main level to kiss me hello on both cheeks. Her hijab comes loose, but she pins it back with a practiced motion.

"What do you want to see? I have a small break right now before we close up and can show you around." She smiles and reminds me how easy it felt in her apartment. "There's also a set of costumes from the Metropolitan Opera here on loan, if you like that sort of thing."

"Actually, I was hoping you could tell me about someone who came to the opera recently. Is that possible?"

Nour squints until her eyes are all mascara. "What do you mean?"

"There's someone who may be related to Angela's disappearance. He was found dead, and I overheard the police say they think he came to the opera the night before he died. Do you have access to video surveillance or anything from Friday, July 13?"

A woman passes by carrying an identical copy of the yellow OPÉRA DE PARIS shopping bag I saw at the crime scene.

Nour laughs, a husky sound that contrasts with her petite frame. Her hands shove deep into the pantsuit jumper she wears, but she doesn't teeter in her four-inch heels. "I don't. I'm just the costume designer, filling in for someone on holiday. Wish I could help."

I try to remember why I thought this was a good idea. What I came to do, exactly. "Well, I think they said his last name was Leroux. Could we at least see in ticket records if he came here with someone? Is there someone I could ask?"

Nour's amused expression turns tense. Her gaze shifts past me then back toward the main hall of patrons. "I'm sorry, Shayna. The police were already here this evening, so I doubt anyone will show you anything without a . . . what is the word? Certificate? Warrant? I could tell you anything you'd like about the last month's designs."

"Do you have any idea what the police asked for?"

She sighs. I'm grasping at straws and possibly pushing Nour too far, but I don't really see another choice. The coincidence of the yellow bag obligates me to ask, to beg.

She fingers the edge of the headscarf's fabric, rolling it between thumb and acrylic-tipped forefinger. "Sorry, love. I wasn't even allowed in the room. They went through the ticket office, and I was asked to step outside. All opera traffic was shut down for a good fifteen minutes."

The tiny flame of hope snuffs out in my chest. Too much of my search has been contingent upon what-ifs. What if Nour saw something, saw someone? It was a fool's hope, anyway, to ask Nour to risk her job integrity and dig into opera records. After Jean-Luc's reaction to me leading him into something similar, I'm lucky Nour hasn't slowly backed away. I shouldn't be wasting time on random hypotheticals with three days left before I go home, but desperation is creeping up like the flu. A shudder traces my neck, and Nour sees. The cream skulls of her hijab twist against light-green fabric.

"Are you finding your way around the city okay? How has it been? I hope you've at least been able to enjoy—" She pauses, catching herself. "To see a few things."

I rub my arms, recalling the warmth of the brothel. "Yeah, discovering a lot. My phone got stolen, though. A pack of roaming kids grabbed it."

"Seriously? That's terrible," she huffs. "They're everywhere lately. Probably because school is out."

I nod, taking a second to admire her English.

Nour sniffs. "You should be careful walking around. Those children sneak through crowds and pick the pockets of tourists or French people who look lost."

"Yeah, I'll be wary of them from now on. Thanks."

Nour takes me into the lobby and points out a few highlights—the chandelier installed in 1769 as part of the opera's centennial celebration, the woven drapes commissioned by one of the King Louises, and the room down the hall to the left that used to be a dressing room and is supposedly still haunted. I listen as best I can, but my thoughts skitter back to her previous words. Nour's warning against a band of (thieving) kids recalls the American woman with the Las Vegas hat and her suspicion of those children. Although both women are right to be on guard, I can't help wondering if Valentin brings some kind of bias, too. My Google search turned up one result related to *missing + Emmanuelle Wood* from a local news outlet, the one I'm guessing Jean-Luc saw on television. What if the police are doing a shoddy job of investigating Manu's disappearance, simply because she's Roma? If they're not giving this investigation their full efforts, Valentin's suggestion that Angela may be implicated in Manu's disappearance takes on a darker weight. Would the police allow Angela to be named as complicit, simply because she isn't a native French person? How deep does this social disdain for the *other* go?

"And that's basically it. Our tour is finished. Everywhere else is forbidden to the public," Nour adds. "You don't want to get lost in the maze of a basement we have." She cocks an expertly threaded eyebrow.

I smile. "Probably not."

"Any other questions for me?" Nour places both hands on her hips. She's spent her entire break with me already, but I can't leave yet. Not without something of value.

I inhale a sharp breath. "What do you know about brothels?"

Nour laughs, then stops short, seeing my face. Her cheeks blush a dark red. "Prostitution is the oldest profession known to man?"

"What's its history in Paris?" *Why would Angela send me to a brothel?*

Nour eyes me hard, examining my face, probably absorbing just how unlike my sister I am. "There hasn't been much activity since the Second World War," she begins, cautiously. "The Nazis were big clients during the Occupation, but the administration afterward considered the prostitutes traitors. No one thought to interview the women and get their knowledge of their clients."

I nod, remembering the platinum sheen of that young woman's hair before Boy Three entered the room. "I'll bet they have stories to tell today, too."

Nour shakes her head. "Brothels were outlawed decades ago. Now prostitution is decriminalized and the customers are fined, but there are no houses left. Why do you ask?"

I stare at her, debating my reply. She matches my gaze with increasing worry the longer I don't. "I think I saw something about them in Angela's research. Just . . . trying to connect some dots."

"Well, that's easy," she says, brightening. "The catacombs were Angela's doctoral subject, right? They used to link every major door of vice in the city at one point. The black market was conducted underground for a long time, and brothels were a part of that—some scheme to allow husbands to sneak away from their wives." Nour rolls her eyes toward the gilded ceiling.

My breath comes shallow as images of the last few days, the last few hours, return. The round metal manhole of the brothel entrance.

"Remember Hugo?" Nour continues. "He's a total history fiend. If you have any other questions about Paris, you should ask him. Plus, his schedule is less crazy than mine. Launching this production of *La Bohème* is such a time suck." She offers a crooked smile.

The hurricane of thoughts in my head pauses at her suggestion. Another guide? The memory of my last two and their issues stops me from automatically accepting. Following someone else around with so little time left in Paris sounds as terrible as showing up on Nour's doorstep unannounced. No, that's another chance I can't take. Jean-Luc's quiet guidance came with restrictions. So will Hugo's.

"Thanks, but I don't think I'll have time. I'm leaving Sunday night."

She shrugs, her hands back in her pockets. "Well, if you change your mind, he's usually at the same spot on Fridays. He deejays from eight to eleven, before the main act at— Oh! I almost forgot." She disappears inside the box office. A few seconds later she returns, rummaging in her purse. She withdraws a paper flyer, then scrawls something across the back. "Et voilà. Hugo's number and your note."

I pause, accepting the square. "My note?"

Nour cocks her head to the side. "It's yours, isn't it? On the back. Your do-tos? To-dos. You know what I mean."

I flip the sheet over to examine a list of handwritten items:

Land in Paris

Go see Nour

Go clubbing

Go home to San Diego

"Thanks, but this isn't mine."

Her skin creases between her eyes. "It was outside my door after you left my apartment. I went to get groceries, and it was partially under my doormat. If not yours, whose?"

I struggle to think back to Tuesday. So much has happened in the last three days, a mad-dash recap of scenes would be helpful, like when sitcoms offer their viewers a visual summary after a long hiatus. As is, I remember leaving her apartment, then sprinting to the police station. "I don't know, I—" And then I see it. In the lower-left-hand corner of the flyer, in our secret twin language, the word *help* is penciled in at a slant, uneven, like Angela wrote while resting the page on her pants leg or the wall of a building.

Nour taps my arm. Her rounded eyes narrow. "Shayna, you okay? You look really pale." I know her hand is on my skin, but it's like she's touching someone else. I can't breathe. I did not write and lose a note to self. I went to the police station, then to the Sorbonne, then to Montmartre and searched Angela's apartment, without ever grabbing a flyer or leaflet from one of the many bus stations rife with them. The whole morning is a blur because that day I had decided to stay longer in Paris, but it's not possible I wrote an itemized list in an unconscious burst of thought.

"When did you find this?" I gasp. "I mean, what time do you think you left the apartment? Was it daylight?"

"Maybe a few hours after you left? Around noon."

"Was there anything unusual about the hallway? Any other papers? Anyone out front?" I want to press her for more, for specifics, for the exact temperature outdoors and the color of the sky, whether there was the sound of footsteps as she opened her door or whether a woman of my build and face was lurking out front. God, I want to ask her a thousand and one questions because . . . Angela must have left that note under Nour's mat. There's no other way. My sister is alive. She followed me to Nour's and saw me go inside.

A dam of tears, joy, and confusion threatens to overwhelm my voice, so I cough. Hard. Harder, trying to loosen the lump. I don't dare look Nour in the face until I feel able to ignore the figurative fireworks exploding in my mind, the sparklers flaring in my heart. *Angela.*

"It's going to be okay, Shayna. I didn't see anything else in the hall, but it wouldn't surprise me if you're forgetting stuff lately. You're going to be fine, love." Nour rubs my shoulders, then leads me back outside to the square teeming with streetlamps and people, dozens of doors, and hundreds of hiding spots. A labyrinth of possibilities, each of which could house my sister.

She's alive.

When Nour kisses each of my cheeks goodbye, I respond on autopilot, barely feeling her touch. My skin is numb, pure electricity, vibrating hope.

The front entry of Angela's building slams shut with a bang, contrasting the muted click I created when I tiptoed in thirty seconds earlier. I withdraw Angela's key from my pocket, suddenly eager to get inside her apartment, safely behind her fireproof metal door. Footsteps clamber up the stairs in time with my attempts at unlocking the door in the dark.

"Shayna?" Jean-Luc pauses at the landing, breathless. Shadows from the skylight above cast an angry glow, draping his high cheekbones at menacing angles. "Hey. Listen, I'm sorry I walked out earlier. I freaked." He drags a hand through his hair. It falls in thick curtains beside his ears.

So much has happened since this morning, when he ran out from Manu's apartment building and then I followed. More than twelve hours ago. Before I started embodying Angela's warning to me completely.

"No worries. I looked around a little more without you. Thanks for coming there." I jam the key in the dark lock of the door again, but the metal grooves don't align.

"So what's the plan for tomorrow? I came by three times today, but you weren't here. Did you get a new cell?"

I've literally spun the key in all possible directions with no dice. Swear words torpedo from my mouth.

"Shayna? Hello?" Jean-Luc hits the wall with his palm, and a hall-way lamp flickers to life. I insert the key again. The door clicks open.

"Thanks."

"Listen, I said I was sorry about this morning. Can I go back to translating fascinating items like lunch menus for you?" The levity in his voice matches the easy smile he wears. He takes a step toward me. "How does that sound?"

I would love having a local with me, a partner on this sojourn into the bizarre and unbelievable. I thought that was Jean-Luc, but he's gotten too close. Learned too much about me and is frankly too much of a distraction. I see it now, after spending the day apart. He would only ask questions and balk at the direction I'm taking, because how can't he? He doesn't know the real reason for all my traipsing around. He can't. He has to go.

"Shayna, don't push me away because of this morning, please." He stops before me, within the grasp of a strong hug. The distance of the lean of a kiss. He smells like fruity shampoo, the faint scent of strawberry.

I steel myself for the millionth time this evening, it feels like. Harden myself against the creeping softness that funneled through my limbs at the sound of his voice. "I'm not pushing you away, Jean-Luc. I don't have some desire to isolate myself, contrary to what you may think. You may feel some insurmountable guilt from your past, but not me. I just don't need your help anymore."

Jean-Luc lurches backward like I swiped at his chin. "What's that supposed to mean?"

"Nothing. Just that I'm not drowning in guilt and acting out some textbook reaction. I know I'm not responsible for any of the tragedies that have touched my life, and I'm just trying to get by here. Whereas you breathe every day as a self-appointed surrogate for the life your friend Benoît forfeited. I don't need your help anymore, and it's not rooted in anything else. That's all." My voice tapers to a wavering fraction of what I began with, reduced a little more with each horrible word that tumbles from my lips.

Jean-Luc shakes his head slowly, disbelieving. "Wow. Is that what you really think?"

I step inside the apartment and partly close the door. I'm unwilling to cede the inches of progress I made today, not for anyone. A small voice inside me notes the familiarity in pushing people away. The voice questions what might happen if I didn't. Jean-Luc stares at me from the hall. The wide-eyed shock he wears fades to resignation. His shoulders slump in green-and-black plaid.

"Good night, Jean-Luc. Thanks again." Before I can second-guess myself, I close the door on his defeated expression. From the other side, I rest my forehead against the cool metal until his shuffling footsteps dissolve into the carpeted landing above.

Chapter 22

Sunshine warms my cheeks, rousing me from a sticky sleep. I tossed and turned until three in the morning, when I finally passed out, but not before I replayed every moment of last night in my head. Did I imagine everything? Was the sip of absinthe that potent? To tell myself it made the images I saw at the speakeasy exaggerated wasn't logical. After all, the ticket receipt I have is real, and so are all my memories before returning to the bar and afterward at the opera.

Angela is alive.

A sob of relief bursts from my throat, and I flip over and scream into a pillow until my throat closes. The sound turns to crying, and my lungs ache from breathing into cloth. My flight takes off Sunday night, in two days, at 10:00 p.m. I can't leave without finding her. Bodies entwined and writhing was absolutely a part of my night, along with the disturbing offer of a stranger. *I can help.* And I doubt he meant sexually, despite our location at the time.

If I'm being objective, the question of whether I simply forgot writing some note that I dropped at Nour's is legitimate. Grief is a bizarre beast that can make us see and do things that don't make sense. Memory adjusts and omits with the slightest nudge, let alone under circumstances like mine. But did I write myself a to-do list, then drop it outside her door? The answer has to be no. Otherwise, I'm forced to question everything I've done here.

If Angela was following me on Tuesday, she may have been following me this whole week. Something must make her hesitate to approach me outright. Even though I'm in her personal space, her apartment, her neighborhood. Something, or someone, won't let her.

Ducking beneath the tiny faucet in her bathroom, I mentally review my progress. Late last night, a poke under the armoire for other possible clues came up empty. A Google search verified some of Nour's and Seb's tidbits about the catacombs. Most disturbingly, the Nazis did use the network of tunnels during their occupation of Paris. One named Josef Molinare tortured concentration camp prisoners—he was obsessed with twins. Molinare gave them gifts of blankets and extra food during the day, but they always disappeared at night.

I shiver as I exit the shower, memories of the encyclopedia webpage feeling too personal. Once I'm dressed, I continue sifting through the piles, reexamining everything. At least a dozen notecards were thrown in her trash—

The trash.

I dive to my knees and clutch the round waste bin to my chest. I pull out the notecards and tissues I've added, eyeing each one. Seb didn't think we should throw anything away, not yet; I was the one to dismiss and disregard these items, so intent on doing a surface scan, not probing further.

A brochure lies squished at the bottom. A giant cross and a stone facade grace the cover, along with a fearsome-looking gargoyle. *Les cryptes de l'église Notre Dame.* No ticket or receipt is squished with it to let me know how recent this excursion is, but it's a church—a clear link to the clue *Divine.* And better than divining tissues.

Turning the brochure over, searching for another drawing, I almost miss it—a pattern. Of dots, much in the way Angela and I used to send messages in Coke cans from the beach.

On napkins, we wrote out what we imagined were mysterious images to the untrained eye—dot drawings, unknowingly imitating pointillism—attempting to re-create Magic Eye images that could only be seen for what they are by holding them far away from your face and crossing your eyes. The dots on the back of this brochure string together a rectangular shape, with an oval top and a tab: a soda can.

Happiness clamps down on my chest.

Opening my laptop beside Angela's, I search through my inbox for the list of the embassy's emergency-only phone numbers. If ever there was a time to reach for help, it's now. I use the Skype account I last called Angela with years ago, and a man answers after two cheery rings. "American Embassy Emergencies Abroad, how can I help you?" he says in perfect English.

A sigh chokes in my mouth, hearing the warm accent of home. "Yes, I'm wondering if the embassy can help reschedule nonrefundable flights."

When I rebooked my flight to San Diego on Tuesday, American Airlines made it clear they would happily assist with booking new flights at the low rate of three times what I initially paid, and they would not credit me with anything. If I rebook my flight again, from this Sunday to—a week from now? A month?—I could lose that entire sum. I explain the sad context of my visit to the embassy employee, but he offers no alternatives.

"Unfortunately, the embassy can help book a flight, but we can't negotiate terms with privately owned companies. If you do reschedule, you'll probably lose the amount you paid for the nonrefundable flight. Sorry. Have you already been contacted by embassy personnel while in Paris?"

"Yeah. I've had a guide, kind of, since I arrived. Jean-Luc something or other."

"Hmm."

"Is there a problem?"

"I don't see anyone named Jean-Luc in the citizen assistance department."

"I think he's in the repatriation group."

"Our French interns are usually in another sector. I'm trying to load his information to see if he's working today. He might be able to help you navigate French airline websites, if you want to explore your options."

"No, that's fine. Thanks, anyway." I hang up, feeling the weight of my ticking clock heavier than before. There are no outs here. I didn't expect them to pull diplomatic privileges for me, but I had to ask. Throwing on one of Angela's sundresses, I tuck some extra tissues into my messenger bag.

On the street, people migrate toward the metro, window-shop the boutiques, or set up artwork on easels. As I step from the tall entryway, an eerie feeling of déjà vu comes over me. Montmartre looks much like it did six days ago when I arrived. A cab slows to a stop beside me as my corner's homeless man asks for spare change. I offer him what euro coins I have in my pocket. He accepts without speaking, eyes planted on the ground.

The light, sugary scent of fresh crêpes wafts from a street vendor's stall. Two children drag their parents into line, leaning at earnest forty-five-degree angles. All around me people go about their normal Friday, unaware of my compacted timeline. There's no line in front of the mobile phone store this morning, and I head toward the fold-up sign on the sidewalk.

My sister is *here*. Somewhere. I know it as well as I know she's always enjoyed messing with me, staying hidden ten minutes too long just for the fun of it. There is no way she's playing some game now.

"Miss Darby?"

I whirl to find Valentin ten feet off, standing beside a bench covered in magazines. His nose is red, as though he's been out in the sun since yesterday. Abundant eyebrows are askew like he ran a hand down his face or fell asleep on the metro.

"Inspector." Valentin's track record has not been to bring good news.

"May we go somewhere quiet? Perhaps your . . . Angela's building? You left the crime scene after I said to wait. I desire to speak with you."

Now it's my turn to hesitate, knowing how the apartment looks. How I am trying to find my supposedly dead sister alive. How I have packed next to none of her belongings with two days left. "You know, actually, I'm air-drying all my underwear right now. Not really a good time."

He frowns, creasing the bridge of skin above his nose. A pair of rowdy high school–aged boys passes by, and he takes a step closer toward me. "Please, Miss Darby. Here will do."

I sigh, taking a seat on the bench.

Valentin pushes aside a magazine featuring a hand-drawn cartoon before he sits. "Miss Darby, I imagine your trip has not been an easy one."

The urge to snap at him—*You think?*—balloons in me, but then the classical music of the brothel echoes in my eardrums. For a second, the idea of telling Valentin everything about my would-be kidnapping, of blurting out each of the supposed clues and messages from Angela, makes so much sense that the scowl wipes clean from my face. My lips quiver, fighting the words.

Valentin sees my struggle and leans in. "Shayna, I am here to help you. And help Angela in any way I might."

An-jel-ah. Hearing her name in his accent yanks me back to reality. Telling him anything would only add surveillance to my path, or worse, well-meaning house arrest. "Thank you, Inspector. I know you are."

He straightens. "I come with an update. We found the cadaver in Emmanuelle Wood's apartment. As you said, it was beneath the kitchen sink and placed there recently; the police are examining it now. We are trying to get in touch with her twin for Emmanuelle's whereabouts. Did Angela engage with the Woods to your knowledge? Did the three of them interact—perhaps bond together as twins?"

My mouth moves slowly, forming the words: *Manu is a twin?* Does that mean she was more, or less, enthralled with my sister? My stomach tenses at this revelation, confusion and concern braiding my insides.

Valentin watches me, no doubt cataloging my expression. "You did not know?"

"No," I mumble. "I told you I hadn't spoken to Angela in ages when I arrived here. Are the Woods suspects now?"

He blinks, giving away nothing. "If this situation is linked to your sister's case, I will keep you informed."

"You do think it's odd a body was found in Manu's apartment, right? Is it Manu? Did the serial killer put it there? Does this guy even exist? I haven't heard anything about it on the news." As soon as I finish speaking, the number three pops into my head—the body count I've personally seen since arriving. More than most people do in a lifetime. Even before Valentin presses his lips together, I have my answer.

"Miss Darby, do you recall what I shared about your sister's investigation your first day here?"

I scan the pudgy cumulus clouds overhead. "Nothing?"

"There are multiple murders I suspect may be linked to Angela's death. Three bodies were discovered before your arrival, bearing similar marks to those present on Angela's body. Clément Gress was the first body found, in the garbage dumpster behind a frozen foods store."

"I do remember that. What kind of marks?"

"Restraints or some kind of binding material. Tattoos. And a head wound inflicted by a firearm."

Exactly as the officers confirmed at the crime scene I followed the police cars to. *Ligature marks. Tattoos. Shot to the head.* "Why are you telling me this? Why now?"

"Officially, we're not confirming anything. Unofficially, the city has not seen this level of repeat murders in many years. The person or persons responsible would be calculating and patient individuals. Binding their victims for such a period of time, and then dispatching them by a gunshot to the skull, suggests these murders are impersonal. Clean. Driven by a higher need. The perpetrators appear, at the moment, to be abducting men and women arbitrarily; aside from the mode of execution, we have not yet determined any commonalities that apply to all the victims. Angela's gunshot wound was the only one to be administered postmortem. Victims are of varying ages, men and women, of various occupations—two homeless—but, on a rudimentary scale, we can confirm each victim bears little known ties to family, and at least one tattoo. With these facts in mind, I would advise staying in tonight. For your safety."

I sit dumbfounded. Finally, with only two nights left to me here, he offers all the details. "So the body below the sink is one of the serial killer's victims? She has the same markings?"

"No. The body bears the restraint marks, as I'm sure you saw. But that is where the similarities end. The cause of death was a gunshot to the chest."

"But aren't the restraint marks significant? Where did you find the rest of the bodies? Were they also in the Seine? Maybe the killer is trying to throw you off by choosing overtly different victims. They must be linked in some substantial way. Right?" Thinking on Angela's body double—"Were you able to determine Angela's cause of death?"

Valentin stares out at the passing traffic. "Our forensic sciences team should turn in a final report on Monday. I would caution against too much optimism, however. Sometimes the elements remove all final clues. Bonne journée, Miss Darby."

"Wait, I need more information here. You can't expect me to—" I'm still reeling from this deluge of information when something about his words stops me: *the elements*—nature—as the most powerful of all, a belief Angela always championed.

"Miss Darby?" He leans his head in a way that is eerily familiar, like I've seen it before. Suddenly, his tone, the apologetic *wish I could help you* shrug goodbye, all ring insincere. Deliberate. Empty. The image of Ted Bundy giving interviews outside a Utah courthouse lunges forward in my thoughts. Jean-Luc's voice follows: *Psychopaths—those are the ones who sneak up on you.* Is Valentin hiding something?

"Inspector, why did you take scissors from the crime scene earlier this week?"

"Pardon?"

"The crime scene I saw you at. The opera lover who died from a gunshot to the head. I saw you pocket a pair of scissors as you were walking out. Shears."

A smirk, full blown, stretches his face. Newly grown gray whiskers twitch the corners of his mouth. "What is your meaning, please?"

"Were they the murder weapon? Why would you take them?"

He regards me a long while before speaking. "Miss Darby, I understand your . . . query. Some might say paranoia. I want to find your sister's killer as much as you do, truly. And I am not the person who should worry you."

Valentin nods goodbye, then stands and crosses the street. I keep him in sight until he disappears behind another red-and-white-striped awning toward the river.

Conflicting emotions push and pull within me. His smirk dropped as quickly as it appeared, replaced with unease. Whether I believe him—that a serial killer is randomly targeting people, that the body double's cause of death is unknown—he won't be sharing additional details.

Manu is a twin. The photograph of the smiling young woman in the desert suddenly seems material, and I regret not grabbing them all from the dresser. Was there a photo of Manu and her sister? Manu may be dead—may not be related to the serial murders—but Valentin didn't say Angela had been cleared of involvement. The framed photo of Manu and that man, the same one Angela has a photo of, further punts any premature relief. The photos form an undeniable link between the two women. And I have both hidden in my duffel under sweaty tank tops.

I lift my hand to another cab, then stop midwave. The pamphlet. A quick rummage through the sections of my handbag, the zipped outer pocket against my hip, and the inner adult pocket that hides bandages and aspirin, confirms my burst of clarity: it's still upstairs. Using a few choice words in English, I trudge back the whole block from the building I managed to travel.

The pamphlet lies on the desk, right where I left it, next to Angela's illuminated laptop screen, still bright from my earlier use and displaying her inbox. I've been very careful to check my email on my own laptop, to avoid signing Angela out of hers. For a reason I can't place, instead of grabbing the rectangle of paper and leaving, I slide into Angela's desk chair. My back presses flat against the cool wood. Gliding her mouse along the left-hand margin of her inbox folders, I hover over an arrow I'd ignored before; I click on it, and a hidden list expands, revealing a folder entitled UPDATES. I click again.

Emails are shown in order by drafts then sent date—there are seven of them. Most were sent during her first few months here, and I remember replying to them. Drafts that she never sent—*Update #1* and *Update #2*—seem to be written a few months after our parents passed away; I've never seen these.

The final draft email seems to have been written a week before she disappeared. I hesitate over the subject line, *Update #18*, then click on it.

Chapter 23

from: Angela Darby <ange.d.paris@smail.com>
to: "Darby, Shayna" <shayna.darby93@smail.com>
subject: Update #18

Salut, dearest sister! The party was *hyper chou-ette* last weekend. Carine got so wasted I thought she might puke into Serge's hat like last time, but the giant baguette we ate for dinner balanced her stomach. That and the late-night kebab at three in the morning. Me, I got so drunk I started calling her *Karen*. God bless French drunk food! I miss burritos bad, but I'll take a French fry kebab until Mexican culture makes its way here. I got my best grade yet this semester on my final research paper for my third year of graduate school and really feel like I'm getting the hang of my French slang. *Salut, ma poule!*

Summer is here! FINALLY. Although I've been so busy with research recently I don't know if I would have noticed except for the summer solstice tomorrow. The internship is trucking along as usual. When I began, back in Update #11, I had no idea I'd come to spend all my free time with dead people. Imagine! Obtaining the internship with the Archaeology Society was a lottery (I guess everyone wants to be underground), and back in November when I started, I could not have known it would develop into a lifestyle of mine. Going from every Thursday to most days seems like a leap, but not when you consider all I've learned down there. The smell of decay, the thrill of discovery, and exploring paths that have not seen warm bodies in centuries is intoxicating.

On another note: I think I have a stalker. I wasn't worried at first—his style of clothing is colorblind hipster, so I always see him coming when he follows me round at the Sorbonne—but he moved into my building last month. Now I sleep with the Taser I got on the black market here (since they're illegal), but I can't shake the feeling that he's watching me whenever I exit my door. Sometimes, although he lives on the fourth floor, I think I hear someone in the hall. I wish to God the French employed lookholes in their door designs. If anything happens to me, you'll know where to check.

Eventually, dear sister, I hope to send all these updates to you and catch you up on my life, instead of saving them as drafts in my inbox. Until then, I'll wait for our reunion of minds via our twin connection.

Twin for the win,
Gelly

Chapter 24

My eyes fix tight on the doorknob from the farthest corner of Angela's studio apartment. Her bed frame, armoire, nightstand, and writing desk block the entry in my frenzied attempt to Tetris myself a barricade. Each time the building creaks, my heart seizes, like I'm watching a movie of my life, the one where I usually bellow at the woman to sprint for the exit. Rereading Angela's email for the twentieth time only heightens my impulse to scream.

If I'd opened this UPDATES folder yesterday, nothing would have changed. I still wouldn't have seen him. I still would have refused to call him for help. But I would have known. Days were spent with Jean-Luc. Before I learned he stalked and abducted my sister.

All the emails from the folder, I printed, then arranged on her floor. I recognized most of them from earlier—before radio silence ensued—from when Angela first moved to Paris after New Year's. Emails from when she was getting settled and when we fought over our parents' house. I set those sad memories aside to focus on the new additions, the latest written only a week before her disappearance, it seems, and never sent. So many things don't add up. While so many other things about this coil my guts.

Updates numbers three through seventeen are missing. I stared at update number eighteen, trying to comprehend for an hour. *Summer Solstice. Colorblind.* The confusion in the embassy employee's voice this morning returned in sharp detail: *no Jean-Luc in the citizen assistance department.* Then I snapped to action, moving furniture against the door—the bed frame, the chest of drawers—moving quickly and quietly. I set the mattress in the corner, then took up my vigil.

Jean-Luc is above me. Jean-Luc held me. Jean-Luc abducted my sister.

Floorboards moan overhead. *Shit, shit, shit.* I draw my knees into my chest and resume rocking. How did I miss this? Footsteps descend from his apartment, the wood groaning with his weight. What badge did he show me the first day? I hold my breath, waiting for the sound to soften, for his feet to find the thick carpet of the hallway before my door. What kind of idiot believes the coincidence of him living just above?

The tempo continues with the curve of the railing. *Step. Step. Step step. Step. Step. Step step.* Silent tears rack my shoulders. This is all my fault. I had one job, one clear message from her. *Trust no one.* My eyes pull wide remembering the moments passed with him, the man my sister basically named as her attacker. How did no one else find this folder? Wasn't her apartment searched a dozen times over? But Seb didn't mention this folder. And she didn't implicate Jean-Luc by name. Valentin took photocopies of everything. What is Jean-Luc's last name? Filler? Fuller? The police seemed to have everything they want in that box marked Preuves.

I dial Valentin's number from his card via Skype. No answer. I try again with the same result. The chipper, bouncing ring is a frustrating contrast to my anxiety. Chewing the remainder of my thumbnail offers something to focus on. A terrible habit, and painful when you get down to the base where flesh meets the nail plate, as I have. A sharp sting jolts through me as teeth catch deeper than before. Blood pools beneath the translucent shell.

⚜

Before long, fatigue steals up behind me and strikes. My throat is scratchy when I wake, my body achy all over. A dreamless, heavy nap leaves me feeling more exhausted than when I lay down. It shouldn't come as a surprise, but the review of what meager meals I've eaten, and the stress, the grief, leaves me feeling bitter—angry—that this is my constant.

I open my laptop and log in to my email inbox. The emails Angela originally sent me are all there—confirming she never hit "Send" on updates one through eighteen. Several advertisements for cheap plane tickets and discounted surfing classes appear as new mail, along with a chain letter from my auntie Meredith. Her note above the chain message wonders how I'm doing; what plans did I have for my upcoming birthday? I haven't heard from her since February, when she asked for a loan she insisted my father would have given her, and our birthday is in late September; I shake my head. The communication is a reminder no one from home knows I'm here.

The whiteboard's message—ALIVE. TRUST NO ONE—remains stark in black marker. The black dots and even planes that so confused Seb add an air of alien hieroglyphics, even to my practiced eyes. I haven't touched it once, for fear of ruining evidence and somehow losing the one link I feel confident relates to my search.

My heart drops into my stomach, tightening my belly until I could mistake the pain for menstrual cramps. Anguish leaves a chalky taste in my mouth. An empty wine bottle—Seb's? Angela's?—rests in the corner of the kitchenette. It is old, long exposed to the air and elements at this point, but I cross to the kitchen and lick the top lip of the bottle. The alcohol hits my tongue, spreading like a fire across it. I search every cabinet of Angela's for liquor but come up empty. Disgust and desire alternate, flooding my core.

I sit down on the mattress again. Angela's list on the back of the Danse La Nuit flyer juts from the flap of my bag. How much longer can I stay here? How much longer should I?

Knock knock.

My eyes fly to the door. A noise comes from the other side, followed by swearing. Someone is trying to get in.

I grapple for the Taser that I shoved under the pillow and watch as the lock rotates back. The door cracks open. I scan the room for a hiding place, anywhere to duck into, but the floorboards will creak and give away my position if I try. I sit frozen as the door inches backward, the bed frame, chest of drawers, and writing desk moving at a glacial pace. A hand slides in, then flicks the light switch in the afternoon shadows. Dark hair violates the space.

"What do you want?" I ask, my voice trembling. The person moves fully into the room, and I blink hard, not sure what is happening.

"Exactly as I thought. We're leaving this apartment, Shayna." Chang stares at me. A reprimand is on her lips, but she peers at me with concern.

"You . . . Did you just break into Angela's apartment?"

Chang's thin eyebrows lift. "From where I stand, I just interrupted a very depressed afternoon. Come with me."

I struggle to my feet. The pamphlet to the crypts remains on Angela's desk, now pushed to the wall. I grab the folded paper, then meet Chang at the door.

Chapter 25

from: Angela Darby <ange.d.paris@smail.com>
to: "Darby, Shayna" <shayna.darby93@smail.com>
subject: Update #1

Hello, sister.

Although you may not know it, today is All Saints' Day in France—Toussaints. It's the day after Halloween, which I celebrated with a trio of American girls from Wisconsin, and the beginning of the holidays—aka the Period of Unrelenting Solitude for Those of Us Alone. It's been three months since our last email, our last fight over Skype. My guess is: You did not sell our childhood home? (My spidey sense is tingling.) And while I meant what I said, that I needed space, indefinitely, I can't deny the gnawing need to communicate with you, dear twin. To tell you all the things I've been withholding, as I've begun to climb out from the muck, from the bottomless pit of mourning, and the Camembert. O, the Camembert.

School has been rough this semester for obvious reasons. It continues to be hard to focus, mostly late at night. When I come home after a long day, the emptiness creeps in to fill my chest, like a slime I can't siphon out. I know I don't need to describe it to you.

The less obvious reason is I'm not French and am learning the French are quite aware of this fact. Well, yes and no. The less-less obvious reason is I don't *look* French. I don't look American, from what our movies have told the locals here, either. For all their laïcité, their desire to remove religion from government affairs, any obstacle that might impede societal cohesion, the French are hyper-fascinated with my *pays d'origine*. What is your country of origin, they ask. "Well, I'm American," I reply. But they shake their head. No, no, where are you *from*? They won't relent until I say my mother is from China and my father's family is Scottish and Dutch.

Whereas, when Piper from Wisconsin is beside me, all she has to say with her dirty blonde hair and blue eyes is "American." There seems to be an underlying racial theme: if you're not Anglo-looking, you must not be French or American. As though I'm expected to return one day to a country I've never visited.

At a time when I already feel isolated and alone, being called out not only as the Other, the foreigner unfamiliar to France, but also being categorized as semiforeign to the United States—the Other Other—stings. This in-betweenness has been a theme for us before we became aware of it, vacillating between enjoying shrimp and pork dumplings with the family and attempting to administer Kelly Clarkson's chunky highlights on each other. I've grown to let it go at home. To feel the itch of offense and release the emotion back into the wild from whence it came. But here. At this moment in life. After losing you. Mom. Dad. It's a reminder I'm neither wholly your twin anymore, nor someone's daughter, nor American enough, nor White or Asian enough. I'm somewhere else. Somewhere in between.

Are these the ravings of a woman experiencing dairy product withdrawal? Maybe. Certainly that, coupled with starting a doctorate program, could lend itself to the argument. Or maybe I'm tired of smiling and releasing the emotions, and just want to be accepted.

Although I won't send this (ever?) for a while, it feels good to write to you. Maybe I'll continue.

Update #1: complete.

With madeleines and un café allongé,
Angela

Chapter 26

The roads to Notre Dame are packed at four in the afternoon. Chang was enthusiastic when we got to the ground floor and I mentioned I wanted to go—but now, with the windows halfway down and exhaust hitting our lungs, I wonder whether I should have suggested Les Deux Moulins for the easier route.

Traffic jams slow our pace, crossing into the Île de la Cité, the tiny island that houses the church and—shudder—the morgue. Both Chang and I are quiet as we pass. Tourists and locals alike enjoy the warm summer day, a few families and couples eating pastries along the River Seine. When we roll to a stop beside the church and the concrete plaza before it, the overall meaning of Angela's second clue hits me. *Divine Research.* Maybe Angela wanted me to go to Notre Dame all along, a place steeped not only in divinity but who knows how much research over the centuries.

Tickets for the crypt tour are sold inside the church vestibule. I buy one for myself, then I lean beside a slab of stone a foot thick that reaches my shoulders. After I assure Chang I don't need an escort, she waves goodbye and joins the throng of people exploring the crowded nave of the church. According to a plaque on the wall above, the stone was knocked loose from the rectory during World War II bombings. A dusty smell lingers here, like these massive columns first began supporting the marble rafters a thousand years ago and have witnessed countless major events in the time since. Angela would have glowed here in all this history, while all I can feel is impatience for the tour to start.

Blonde hair flashes in my peripheral vision, and I snap my gaze to a woman with a chin-length bob. Not Jean-Luc. A scan of the vestibule confirms tourists surround me, their bulky cameras poised to capture activity. I raise two fingers to my neck and count to thirty before my pulse slows back to a normal rhythm.

A man in a black robe cuts toward a thick wooden doorway, gated and locked, leading to the crypts. Beyond the iron bars there's a spindly railing descending below. Groups of people bunch together while the man wields a ring of keys, trying this one and that until we hear a click. The gate swings open. A few of the prayerful in the closest pews raise their heads our way. When I look again for Chang, she's out of sight behind the choir.

The spiral staircase winds down into darkness. We make four full turns, then all eleven of us find ourselves on a dirt floor. I'm the only one who hangs back near the stairs, taking slow, measured inhales until my eyes adjust. A green-lit sign, SORTIE—exit—sits on the wall opposite behind another gate; cracked steps climb up and out of sight. Construction lamps, the handheld kind, are suspended on hooks and positioned at intervals along the ceiling, offering comforting orbs. The crypts are larger than I expected, with several chambers branching off the main artery we stand in. Deep stone compartments are stacked three high along the walls. Our tour guide, Loïc, recounts the history of Notre Dame and the famous cadavers that once graced these shelves. I wander into the first adjoining room, taking care to duck a protruding section of rock. One of the family's little girls twirls by herself in the back, her red backpack providing extra momentum to swing round. She sees me, then stops, running to join her mother in the main area. Loïc asks our group what we know about embalming.

I run a finger along one of the empty shelves and trace a thick line in the dust, like a scene from an old wood-cleaner commercial. A sewer entrance lies near hidden by a grate, but the space is otherwise empty. Loïc elaborates on the mortuary practices of the crypt. I keep hoping he'll drop in something relevant to my search; instead, he switches to tidbits about *The Da Vinci Code*. Apparently, a sister tour is offered at the Church of Saint-Sulpice. Fabulous.

Divine Research. God's studies. Angelic academia.

The crowd ambles forward like bored cattle exiting the atrium. Chang and I meet at the front. "Did you find what you were looking for?" Chang asks.

"What do you mean?" I lead us down a side street back toward the river. More taxis tend to idle that way.

"Well, I always go to church—any church—mosque, temple, public park, wherever God plants before me when She knows I need help. Especially when I'm feeling lost or confused. Seemed a little odd to me that you went down to the crypts instead of a pew, but to each her own."

Thinking back on the dusty shelves I touched, and the anecdotes Loïc tossed out, I'm not sure I gained anything. "Probably should have chosen a back row."

Chang shoots me a shy smile. "Hey, we have another two days until you go, right? We could always come back. Have to fill that time with something."

We return to the apartment building, and Chang follows me all the way upstairs. I unlock the door and step inside. Chang surveys the space from the doorway. Without a word, she sets about righting furniture and organizing half-full crates. Replacing the bed frame and mattress against the wall takes some doing, but together we make it happen. Chang scans the items at her feet—clothing, untaped boxes, stacks of papers—then rubs her arms. Like she's trying to get warm. Slowly, she turns reddened eyes to me. I sit perched on the twin bed, legs tucked underneath like I'm ten years old again. The solid white comforter is soft, worn in a few places, and a cigarette ring has singed a square of fabric. Chang asks me something, but all I can think right now is how Angela would never smoke. But maybe Paris Angela would. "Sorry, what?"

"I said you're doing really good, Shayna. This isn't easy, and I see you doing the best that you can here." Chang steps across a box to the bed and gives my shoulder a squeeze. "Angela gave me permission to enter her apartment if I ever felt it was necessary. So now I'm going to give you the same: Come downstairs whenever you need anything, all right?"

I nod, because my throat is clenched tight.

Chang smiles. "Good girl." Then she shuts the door behind her.

⚜

Music pulses from a string of venues while patrons navigate the sidewalks to the beat. Revelers pack the Marais quarter. Men and women hug in the shadows, men with men gyrate against cars, and mini outfits peacock in the streets. My black dress with matching heels might as well be a parka. A wizened man in all white carries a bucket of roses from couple to couple. Groups laugh, dance, and mingle outside while the bars and clubs are only beginning to fill.

A hulking woman stands outside a fluorescent entryway. Impressive forearms cross beneath a muscled bosom. She nods as I approach, not so much as glancing at my purse for ID. I pass beneath the flashing, neon sign for the club—DANSE LA NUIT—each word illuminating individually in sequence—the club whose flyer Angela wrote my to-dos on. When I called the number on the back this morning, the line went straight to voice mail. Did Angela mean for me to end up here tonight with Hugo, one of the resident deejays, or was I supposed to be here Tuesday night when she slipped the leaflet under Nour's mat, making me days late for an appointment I didn't know existed? Anxiety sears my blood as I step inside, and I look over my shoulder to see whether Jean-Luc or anyone is behind me.

Techno music bumps on the speaker system while rainbow-colored strobe lights form a disco pattern on the black-painted floor. People huddle in twos and threes. Two bars flank the dance floor on opposite sides, and I head to the closest one next to the entrance. The bartender smirks at my request—Diet Coke with lime. Ignoring him, I raise the plastic to my lips, craving something sugary.

A deejay spins from a booth in the center of the floor behind the protection of a plexiglass case; grinding dancers press against the panels. Song lyrics strike with the pounding rhythm, and my chest aches unwillingly along to each verse. The deep questions the singer asks—*Will we be admirable or will we be detestable?*—seem to hang in the air made smoky by dry ice and cigarettes. A woman throws back her head, cackling with laughter along the far wall—everyone with her joins in, including Hugo.

He looks much like he did in Nour's apartment—all smiles, wearing a fashionably unbuttoned dress shirt with a smart blazer—but somehow more aloof, aware that people are looking at him here in his element, as a deejay. His gaze lifts and peers into the semidarkness directly at me. I duck behind a pair of broad shoulders. Sipping my diet soda, I move to a wall, putting a dozen bodies between us, and farther into the shadows. I didn't come here for another chaperone.

All pairings—ages, races, and genders—slink in the crowd together to a mysterious melody. Black walls are empty save for the purple beams projecting upward from fluorescent lamps on the floor. Where would Angela be? Would she hide here? What does she want me to find?

"Shayna?" Hugo stands before me, a plastic cup with clear liquid in hand. Vodka, probably. Or rum, on the rocks. Good choice.

He says something else, then breaks into a grin; I can't hear him so close to the speakers, and he gestures away from the dance floor. We move into a hallway beside the restrooms. My eardrums throb with the volume change while I take the opportunity to scan these walls for more of our secret language. Two unisex bathroom doors line up adjacent to an unmarked door. I take another step down the hall when the door opens. A young man emerges, donning an apron. A barback.

"Shayna?" Hugo waves a hand in front of my face. "Good to see you again, chérie." Full lips pout at the end of each word, mirroring his mild accent. He kisses me hello on both cheeks.

"You, too. I didn't mean to take you from your friends."

Hugo smiles. "No worries. Nour said you had questions about Parisian history. I love that stuff."

I peer behind him, back into the growing mass of bodies, then eye his cup. The dry scent of vodka tingles my nostrils. "Actually, I had some questions about the layout."

He leans against a framed photo of a couple dancing. "I know Paris better than anyone. Above and belowground."

A shiver skips along my back despite the venue's raging body heat. "You mean the catacombs? I've already been there."

"If you want the boring, sterile tour, then you have it available Monday through Friday. There are entrances that offer more interesting scenery, though not as pretty as the main one. Sorry—am I going on a tantric?"

Two excited girls flounce past and give Hugo a flirtatious giggle. He wrinkles his nose at me, and we share our own laugh. "No, I'm interested," I reply, understanding he meant *tangent*. "How do these entrances differ from Denfert Rochereau?"

Hugo casts his eyes to the side. "In the unofficial doors, you don't have the fancy stairwell with railing that takes you one hundred steps underground. You have to earn the catacombs, ma belle. There is one good entrance left on this side of the city that hasn't been shut down by police."

The reminder of so many steps beneath fresh air and daylight constricts my chest. My pulse races, but I muster a smile. "I almost puked on that staircase. Don't know if I could do anything else less luxurious."

"Suit yourself, chérie. But Impasse de Valmy is full of history, if that is your goal." He smiles, then turns back to the dance floor. "Shall we?"

We talk about (shout about) Nour above rap music mashed up with a house beat. I learn he's known her since they were seven, during their parents' tenure as part of the Muslim Association of Paris. Bodies crowd into the area, bumping against me when someone calls to Hugo. A girl shrieks with laughter to my right. A stranger's sweat slimes across my cheek in a YMCA move to the love ballad playing, and the scene tilts away from me. I steady myself on a random elbow and focus on the ceiling's lattice of flashing lights to calm my breathing in the suddenly cramped space. *In out. In out.* The neon filters provide enough visual clarity to find Hugo and say goodbye. He cozies up to a cute boy with glitter across each cheekbone, probably the bare minimum age to enter the club (eighteen). We do the kisses on each cheek, then the boy reclaims him. Purple nails claw Hugo's pants pockets.

As I pick my way to the front entrance from this side of the club, I have a view into the deejay's booth. Her fingers dance across the dials of an electronic board, turning settings up and down, before she preps the next track on the tablet she holds in her small arms. Neon makeup, like war paint, accentuates big eyes, high cheekbones, and makes bright-green lips pop. Asymmetrical black hair sways beneath giant headphones. She pops her head up from her board and waves to someone in the crowd. She must be five feet tall.

"Hugo? Hugo!" I turn back and grab his shoulder. "Who is that woman?"

"The deejay? That's DJ Chyn-noisette. A legend! She's been spinning since the eighties, on *actual* turntables. Owns a ton of property in Paris, worth a billion dollars. I met her in the tunnels once!"

Hugo spins back to his dance partner, leaving me to gape open-mouthed at Madame Chang. She leads the crowd in punching the air to a slowed-down remixed version of the *Will we be admirable will we be detestable* song I heard earlier, masterfully bringing the energy down low only to turn up the bass and speed and make everyone jump and dance with more excitement than before. Without Coke-bottle glasses, she looks thirty.

"Chyn-noisette est trop vielle!" Hugo's friend lurches forward to slur French in my ear, only the music fades at that moment and his shout knocks me backward. The yellow bandanna he wears glows in the black-light strobe flickering across his pale cheeks. I can't tell if he means she's old as in aged, or old as in boring, irrelevant news. Either way, I glance at Chang to see if she heard; she adopts a stiff smile, scrolling down the screen of her tablet. Hugo playfully pushes the younger guy and says something I don't understand; he shakes his head, then repeats, "Legend. Le-*gend,*" drawing out the word in English. A rocket ship noise kicks off the next song, and the debate is forgotten. I cast another eye at the booth, and Chang is already shaking her fist, revving up the crowd.

I exit the club, feeling more bewildered than when I entered. Fresh air fills my lungs, expelling the smoke and tension from inside.

The sidewalks are sparse around two in the morning, everyone finally inside a bar or club. Cool night air is a relief from the daytime's fumes. I raise my gaze to the starry sky, searching for constellations familiar to me at home, when an airplane passes overhead.

For a moment, my internal reprimand—that I didn't learn anything useful from Hugo, from the flyer Angela left me, and all I'll have to show for my efforts in the morning is a slight hangover from the sugar—falls quiet. I watch the airplane pass over Paris with nothing more, no thoughts, disappointments, expectations—just observing a massive steel machine that could drop out of the air at any moment and rain disaster on every last unsuspecting fool, unaware of how good they have it on this block. Then the plane travels behind a cloud and out of sight.

I wait a good minute in front of the club on the sidewalk, but the plane doesn't reappear.

I step into the road in the direction of Angela's apartment. Darkness extends beyond the corner ahead, and I scan the block for pockets to avoid. With no cabs in sight, and the discovery of Chang's deejaying and Hugo's insight behind me, I focus simply on placing one foot in front of the other. Before the next red, blinking light falls out of the sky.

Chapter 27

The nightlife disappears and the street opens into a wide, flat square. A sign affixed along the side of a building reads RUE MOUFFETARD. People I recognize from the row of clubs lie passed out on the few available benches. The sight of them is reassuring; if they feel safe enough to pass out in this communal plaza, I shouldn't feel like someone has been following me the past ten minutes. And yet, I do.

Cobblestone magnifies the echo of high heels and clinking glass. I resist the urge to look over my shoulder again. The sound of footsteps overlapping my own began around the curve in the street, where the bars were no longer visible and the next set of businesses was closed. No taxis seemed to be running, despite this being a sort of rush hour, near closing time and along a frequented bar block. I kept walking, picking up my pace and telling myself I was being paranoid, when Valentin's words of caution resurfaced: *Murders are impersonal. Perpetrators abducting men and women arbitrarily. Stay inside.*

One bench is being half used by a slumbering man, and I sit down to bide my time—there's got to be a taxi at some point. Another couple stumbles from down the road, heading toward me, along with a single man behind them.

"Shayna?" Someone grips my shoulder, and I whirl to face a shaggy fringe of hair.

"Jean-Luc."

He steps back with his palms up, like he did that first day in the stairwell. Big green eyes look brown in the yellow wash of the streetlamps, larger than I remember. His hair is disheveled, looking much like an assailant's should. Fear spikes through me as I twist round searching for a friend, an exit, a weapon, without alerting him: *I know what you did.*

"Good to see you." Jean-Luc leans forward, but I stumble away, using the flat stone bench to maintain my distance. Confusion draws his face in the shadows. "Shayna, I've been trying to get ahold of you, but you haven't gotten your phone back. Did something else happen?"

His easy cadence of English stings, both tempting in that it sounds like home and safety, and painful because I know it's a violent lie. The spoiled cherry to this week's horrors, a reminder that he was calm, polite, helpful when I was taciturn, in order to finish the job. Jean-Luc has been targeting me since I arrived, the way he targeted Angela. Since he was unable to keep her, he must want me to replace her. Sweat breaks across my chest in the high-neck dress.

"No, nothing else. I've just been soul-searching, alone. Excuse me." I step away, toward the main road, wishing I had worn flats or sneakers instead of Angela's stilettos, but he jumps into my path.

His features tense like he's caught me cheating. "Shayna, I don't believe you." He steps toward me, glancing at the man sleeping on the bench. "I was at a bar down the street and saw you leave. I saw someone else start following you."

Despite the warm temperature, a chill ripples across my skin. Were those the footsteps I kept hearing, or were they Jean-Luc's? Or is he lying to get me to trust him again? Were they the fake cop's? Are they working together?

A sphere of headlights grows in the crooked road. Panic riles me, closing my throat, and I take another step away from him. "I'm fine. Thank you for your help this week, Jean-Luc."

People still drinking and stumbling around us snicker, mocking my English with thick French accents. *"Zahnk yeu, Jean-Luc!"*

As the headlights near, I thrust out my hand, and a taxi rolls to a stop beside us. I climb into the back seat.

"Shayna. If you need anything, you know where I live," Jean-Luc says through the open window. He raises a single palm. "And I know where you live."

My thumb pushes down the door lock. "Montmartre, s'il vous plaît," I say to the driver. The front seat is dark, so I can't tell if he heard or understands my accent until the car pulls forward. We veer left toward the river. I count to five before I let myself look behind. Jean-Luc is in the same spot. It could be simple coincidence that he saw me leaving, or he could have been following me since I ducked out of Danse La Nuit. Since the baggage carousel at Charles de Gaulle airport.

The driver asks me something in French I don't grasp. I'm shaking my head when a high-pitched wail reaches us. Loud, fast, rocking toward us from the main causeway of the river. A police car speeds past, narrowly missing our cab. Valentin. Could that be him?

"Follow that car, s'il vous plaît."

The driver looks at me in the rearview mirror. "De . . . quoi?"

"My sister . . ." I lift a hand to my head. The throbbing I felt inside the club returns. My cheeks flush as an uncomfortable warmth spreads down my chest.

"Everything okay?" he asks in French. Streetlamps blur along the riverside boulevard. Turning my gaze to him aggravates the growing vertigo. Darkness flits across his concerned expression, and I mumble that I'm fine, *mal de tête*. Headache.

"Please follow that car. My sister is missing; she needs my help. Please. Help me look for her." My vision turns hazy. Exhaustion and sleep deprivation burrow into my temples. My dress seems too thick, too hot, even though the driver wears a jacket.

"Your address," the driver attempts. "Miss, where you live?" Something about his voice in English is familiar, but I can't place it.

I mumble what I think is the street in Montmartre. Offer the closest metro stop to better orient the driver. The car pitches right. The leather seat is cool on my cheek. Brightness glares through my eyelids. Someone touches my shoulder. "Angèle. Nous sommes arrivés."

"What?" My eyes fly open, and I find Mathieu, the bordel tour guide, holding open the door. I scramble out of the car, but he grabs me by the shoulders.

"Angèle, you are okay?"

"Get away from me!" I struggle to tear free, to get inside.

He says something in French, raising his voice.

"Let me go!"

"Angèle, you know I drive on Fridays. Why do you not call me?" His grip tightens, towering over me. "You cannot keep running, Angèle. We must talk of what happened!"

I dig in my bag and yank out the stun gun. Mathieu sees it and releases me, throws me forward, so that I catch my balance against a garbage bin.

His upper lip curls in a sneer. "First, you would . . . scratch me? Now you would hurt me again?" The streetlamp above casts him in darkness.

I don't respond, not trusting my voice. His outline blurs in and out in my vision, and I know a full fever is on its way.

He growls. "How you were there one second at the bordel . . . and gone the next?"

"Listen to me. I don't care what happened between us earlier. Leave me alone." I step back toward Angela's building without breaking eye contact.

"Angèle, wait . . ."

I throw a twenty-euro note to him and turn and jam the jailer's key in the door.

"Angèle!"

The entry slams shut, and I pause behind the safety of six inches of metal. The curved handle jiggles underneath my palm. "Angèle!" Mathieu cries, his voice muffled, though his angry expression is clear through the glass. "Angèle, return, please!"

I make my way to the stairs, shaking, and ignoring his words in English, then French. Based on my experience with him at the brothel, the way in which he described Angela's escape the last time they met, and his behavior now—Angela might have been warning me about him, too, on the whiteboard, in addition to Jean-Luc. Although she wouldn't be this afraid of one person—so afraid she hasn't gone to the police, or come to me directly—would she? Are Jean-Luc and Mathieu working together, then? Mathieu probably has connections from the brothel, a network of black market muscle, like the man who offered me help in getting even with any heartbreaking ex-boyfriends. Does Jean-Luc have those same connections?

The three flights of stairs are my Mount Everest, and it takes all I have to stay upright. My balance teeters at every curve in the stairwell, and I stop twice to rest on a step. Mathieu is silent by then, hopefully driven far away, never to return.

When I get inside the apartment, I lurch straight for the medicine cabinet in the bathroom. I paw Angela's stash of over-the-counter medications until I find something that treats headaches, fever.

Lifting my eyelids requires herculean effort, so instead I fumble for the pills and swallow. Each feels like a brick against my dry esophagus. If a serial killer or anyone else wanted to kill me now, I'd probably thank them first. I stumble to the bed and fall deep into a dream.

Figures on my lids take shape. Menacing, limping bodies come closer, reaching out while I scramble away, my balance suddenly restored. They crawl toward me when they stumble, their limbs catching on rocks and crevices as the earth cracks and fissures, tearing feet and elbows from their sockets. They crawl forward anyway, using their chests, their foreheads, sloughing parts and tracts of skin. When heavy lead fills my core, a body catches up and reaches for me. I pull my ankles forward an inch with my hands, kicking and screaming internally, but no external struggle shows; it's not enough; it's never enough. One body extends its remaining fingertips, its hollow skull grinning with a shift of light, as its cold bones grasp my own.

I come to, standing beside Angela's desk. Pitch-black surrounds me. I pat around for the reading lamp and flinch when its click slices the middle-of-the-night quiet. The whiteboard is toppled to the ground, Angela's message to me in our twin language smeared and indiscernible even to my fluent eyes. The room is empty. No monsters. The door is locked, too. Bedsheets are rumpled in a pile on the floor, and when I reach for them, a rush of blood makes me dizzy all over again. Our hieroglyphics—Greek letters, even planes, careful dots—ruined. I want to curl into a ball and claw the whiteboard, break it in two, howl into a pillow again. Angela's one incontrovertible clue to me, gone—or at the very least affected and tainted by my sleep terror jumping up and away from monsters that weren't there.

Numbness seeps straight through my organs, staring at this visual of my carelessness. Poisoning me the way I deserve.

Something moves outside below—a pair of policemen. They're removing the homeless man who sleeps beside the front entry with his cane. He argues with them, then stands, rises with no wavering, and walks away like it's the most natural act in the world. The cane is under his arm. I rub my eyes. When I look up, he's gone. The two police officers confer alone. I touch the back of my palm to my forehead. Still warm. Did that just happen? I try to recall if I've ever seen the man walk before. Whether I've seen him carry his cane instead of using it to stand.

With both hands on the windowsill, I take slow breaths until my equilibrium stabilizes. This crusty, sick feeling is better than expecting my head to implode at any moment, but not by much. I make my way to the bathroom to splash water onto my face. Red veins spiderweb from each of my irises in the oval mirror. Freckles across my nose are amplified against pale skin. Behind me in the reflection, an image on Angela's corkboard stands stark against the notes to self and knickknacks she's collected.

I pick my way back across the room. The photograph is glossy, though faded from the years. I unpin it from the board. The four of us stand beside the World's Ugliest Moose. On the back of the photo, in my mom's perfect scrawl, it reads *San Diego Zoo, August 2002*. I cup the edges, careful to avoid prints. Sadness binds my chest, observing the way our eyes nearly disappear into our heads; we were smiling so hard.

Think, Shayna. I only slept a few hours, and the sun will be up soon. I should go back to bed to rest, but I can't. Not now. Not before I admit I did write myself a to-do list. That I've been grieving and that I blacked out for an hour or so. That my sister isn't alive. Maybe the real shame here is how I've been leading myself on a wild goose chase all week, instead of accepting the truth.

I set to biting my nails again, a habit I kicked when we turned thirteen and Angela told everyone I ate hangnails. My teeth worry my index finger, twisting and chewing. I sit down at Angela's desk and check my email. The essays Jean-Luc found in the Sorbonne archives sit in a pile against the wall. I pick one up and reread the first page.

Angela wrote about the plight of the Paris homeless during periods of extreme weather: triple-digit heat in the summer and fifteen below zero in the winter. There should be some significance here, some insight I can glean from the way my flighty sister settled down and married this research topic her first year in the doctoral program. She concluded that, if we only had better urban planning, we could provide protection for the homeless from the elements, especially the elderly homeless—public verandas to shelter people in known homeless enclaves, natural havens to exploit cooler temperatures, such as the Luxembourg Gardens and other geographic bowls within the city.

Divine. Research. Trying to figure out possible veiled meanings of each piece of her life leads me to switch hands after nibbling another nail down to the plate. Angela wanted more than anything for us to be one mind on the ethereal twin plane she mentioned in the early emails. She wanted to tap into it when needed, like a superpower she imagined when we were children that she never let go of.

Social welfare. Community. Brothels. Shelters. Heat waves. Death. My legs feel weak again, and I sit cross-legged on the floor amid other papers I think might matter. The brothel tour receipt is grouped with my Notre Dame crypt pamphlet; the drawings on each are poor comforts now. They could be useless, absentminded doodles rather than burning X MARKS THE SPOT signs pointing the way.

Key phrases pop out from my sister's notes, her emails, an image of the Gate to Hell.

Narcissism. Intricate underground tunnels. Twin for the win.

Sprawling flat on my back on the papers covering the wooden floor, I close my eyes. The tightness in my chest bursts into a sob that I swear carries down to the main entrance. Reaching out for Angela, trying to open my mind the way she always insisted we could, leaves me more frustrated as salty streams dry on my cheeks. This entire time I've felt like I was chasing the ghost of my sister, wondering if I even knew her anymore. Guilt crashes into me as I stare at this library of her hints. Everything she needed from me is stacked in haphazard piles, and I haven't been able to deliver on any of it.

Another headline surges forward from my jumbled thoughts: the dangers of trafficking as described on the front page of the lobby's newspaper my first day. I sit up, stricken.

If I stop to think, there have been hints everywhere I turned. The miniature TVs found in each cab I take, the ticker announcing the latest trafficking concern. Not vehicular traffic, but human trafficking. Chang mentioned the catacombs are one part tourist attraction, one part trafficking hub. Hugo even mentioned the police shutting down off-the-record entrances.

Psychopaths—those are the ones who sneak up on you. Jean-Luc stalked my sister, and like any good predator, he has been following me all week, relishing my discovery of the details of Angela's kidnapping, too arrogant to believe he would be found out, hiding in plain sight. Is he part of the trafficking ring? Is that how Angela came to be on his radar—through her research, spending time in the catacombs after hours, maybe stumbling across one of the tunnels they used? As Valentin suspects, the recent murders are impersonal. Clean. Driven by a higher need, with men and women being abducted arbitrarily. Human traffickers don't need anyone in particular; they need bodies.

I get dressed as quietly as possible, throwing on jeans and a long-sleeved shirt. My passport is already in the inner pocket of my messenger bag, and I add the Taser to the mix. My thoughts turn to Hugo, but he's not the person I need now. Not Hugo, Seb, Valentin, or even Nour. Creeping downstairs as quietly as possible at four thirty in the morning, I hope against hope I'm doing the right thing.

Chang still wears the white leotard and red plastic skirt she owned in the deejay booth, but the neon makeup has been removed. When she opens her door, she lets out a gasp.

"Shayna. Is everything okay?"

I pause. The memory of the matching twins in the photo on Angela's corkboard, hand in hand, a representation of singular happiness, quiets my nerves. "I need to go to the catacombs. Can you take me?"

A smile turns her full lips upward. "You're joking, right? It's the middle of the night. I've actually had a pretty long one this evening." She tilts her head to the side, and a pop issues from her neck.

"I know, and I'm sorry to visit you so late. But I was at Danse La Nuit and saw you deejaying. I just thought I would ask, since you used to be so adventurous—"

"Used to be?" Chang raises thin brows. "Were you with that rude boy who called me old? I think I saw you."

I suck in a breath, feeling the conversation teeter. "I know the guy he was dancing with. I'm sorry about him—he was rude, you're right."

Chang's tiny, slippered foot taps the ground. "Well, he's not entirely wrong. I've lived three of his unrhythmic lifetimes. But it's been a while since I've had a real rush." Opening the door wide, she motions for me to enter. "I'm in. Let me grab my hiking boots and some supplies."

"Really? You're sure?"

Chang grins. "Mahjong isn't my only hobby, Shayna. I think it's time for another adventure."

Chapter 28

from: Angela Darby <ange.d.paris@smail.com>
to: "Darby, Shayna" <shayna.darby93@smail.com>
subject: Update #2

Shayna, sister of my bones, breaker of my heart:

I've been thinking a lot about us. You probably recall the Period of Solitude is well underway, so maybe you were expecting me to draft this letter that I'll never send. I know you're going to Aunt Judy's in Boise for Christmas this year. I know a lot of things about you that you might not be aware of. Judy invited me, too, said she'd give me a tour of the German lager part of the brewery, but I said no. Not this year.

The truth is I've been thinking about that one day on the beach. The one you never like discussing and forbade me from talking about. In hindsight, the terror on your face is pretty laughable. Is that wrong? It's laughable because it's almost as if you didn't know the game we were playing, and you seemed to think I was some monster. Laughable, and yet it galls me in the middle of the night, when my apartment building creaks and moans like a weatherworn pirate ship, straining against its mooring—against the injustice punted at it from a past life. That day on the beach is simply another reminder you never understood me, never desired to. Rather than view my actions as well intentioned, you only see the end result. The product of pain and confusion instead of my meaning, my efforts.

The beauty of not sending you these emails is they allow me to shout from the rooftops all the things I normally would dilute and couch in compliments and empathy. Here, that's unnecessary. Here, I can say exactly what I should have, and should have kept saying, knowing you deluded yourself into believing otherwise.

If you ever begin to read this letter, you'll have stopped somewhere around "forbade," but in case your eyes scan down, I'll write this big:

YOU ARE NOT SOME VICTIM, SHAYNA.

You are no one's victim. And least of all mine.

Chapter 29

Sunrise is still a solid hour away. I can barely see straight in the semi-darkness, despite roaming to and from this corner all week. Sleeping bodies line the doorways of the block. Mathieu's cab is nowhere in sight. The glossy corners of the photograph are stiff in my hand, and I press the flesh of my thumb pad to each until a dull prick registers. This is not a dream.

My family and I stood beside the World's Ugliest Moose at the San Diego Zoo when Angela and I were eight. Out of frame and to the side was a wooden cutout of the animal (with warts, bald spots, malformed vertebrae, and all) for zoo goers to stick their faces into round holes with antlers. A banner above read **A FACE ONLY A MOTHER COULD LOVE!** When we finished laughing through a dozen pictures, my mother took Angela and me aside; she said, "Don't let anyone tell you you're unlovable." Holding the four of us in my palm recalls everything that was lost. And leaves me guessing when exactly I forgot those words.

In my other hand, a folded square of paper weighs like a brick—a scrawled note from Valentin I found wedged underneath the apartment door. He must have come by sometime while I was passed out. Yellow lights approach in the distance. I clamp my arms to my sides for warmth.

Bonjour, Miss Darby.

Apologies to reveal this info in a note, however, I did not want to wake you. A sixth body was found. Confirmed presence of series murderer in Paris, first in almost thirty years. City lockdown from now to sunrise for safety—no one wants additional death as their legacy. Check the news at 7:00 a.m., and get home to USA in one piece on Sunday, Shayna.

Best of luck.
Valentin

PS The body you found in Emmanuelle Wood's apartment, sadly, is her. Thank you for alerting the police.

Bright beams pierce my blurry sight. A taxi rolls to a stop beside me as Chang steps from the building's main door. She changed into cargo pants and a long-sleeved shirt and shoulders a canvas backpack. "Is this our trusty steed?" she asks.

A serial killer. Something Valentin has been alluding to for days now, and which my experience this week all but screamed through a megaphone. The information makes me feel exposed, raw. My eyes dart to the dumpsters of the next side street, the homeless man missing from my stoop. Cold fear slinks down my torso, curling into a knot in my stomach. Manu is dead. Officially.

If Jean-Luc stalked and kidnapped Angela to sell her as part of a human-trafficking ring—or if she was caught snooping and he wanted to get her out of the way before she told the police—is Jean-Luc the serial killer? Angela's body double pulled from the Seine could have been another one of his trafficking victims.

An easy gunshot to the head would be in line with Valentin's analysis. *Impersonal. Clean. Driven by a higher need.* Valentin didn't say where the most recent corpse was found, but extra police will be deployed in force all over Paris starting now. I wonder briefly whether Valentin knows it's Jean-Luc—has known this whole time, and that's what his warnings were about. *I hope you are not talking with strangers.*

A shiver runs along my neck, then I nod to Chang. "Our motorized carriage."

"It's a looker. What do you have there?" She points to the photo.

"Just a good-luck charm." I tuck it into my back pocket, and we slide across the seat of the taxi.

The driver catches my eye in the rearview mirror, wrinkled skin illuminated by the interior light. Most of his face is shrouded by a baseball cap. "Bonjour," he chirps. Chang gives him directions where to go while I settle into the worn cushions, my bag across my lap.

Hugo's words in the club—*I met her in the tunnels*—switched on a dozen light bulbs. Not only was Chang Angela's building concierge, a billionaire widow, and a deejay since Reagan, but the free time she gained during the day allowed her to pursue the less conventional interests I saw framed on her wall—cave diving, running with the bulls, and exploring the catacombs. She confirmed as much when I knocked on her door and caught her unwinding with a pot of tea.

My head has stopped throbbing, but I still feel disoriented, like a bubble encases my every move. Although I wanted to kick and scream going underground on Monday, I had to see for myself what beguiled my sister. I had to verify the question that felt so ridiculous to voice: Could Angela be hiding underground? Seeing it for myself—the cold darkness, the miles upon miles of chutes, passages, and cracks in the walls—cemented my suspicion that *No, no one could,* as Seb affirmed. No one could live underground indefinitely, but they could be held there in transit before being shipped off to a buyer in another country. Returning to the catacombs now is the right next step, now that I know what I'm looking for. I'll find the proof that Angela was taken there, that she's been hiding from her abductors—Jean-Luc and whoever he's working with—then go to Valentin with everything.

Alive. A deep breath rattles in my chest. The sight of Angela's whiteboard hasn't left my mind since I got here, along with the terror and exhilaration of reading her words. My stomach knots as I repeat my new mantra and know this time in my marrow it's true.

"I love sharing this world, Shayna, but you've been before—I haven't been in ages," Chang says. She rummages in her bag, withdrawing a roll of duct tape, then a cellophane-wrapped almond cookie that she offers to me. "Are you tired? We could always go later today—you leave Sunday?"

The variety of items from that bag never disappoints; I shake my head at the cookie. "Probably best to go now. While the crowds are low."

Chang doesn't reply to what I think is an obvious joke. She removes her glasses, then cleans them on her shirt. Seeing her with contacts at the club was weird.

"You're probably right. The scene—the network—used to be lively at all hours, but things have changed. Regular people go underground less with all the smuggling nowadays."

"What was it like before?"

"It used to autoregulate—a few kingpins managed it—but once the catacombs became a tourist destination—have you been to Disneyland? The main tour route reminds me of that—big names got arrested and black market activities picked up again. The powers that be sealed all the well-known entrances, but they missed a few."

My mind pulses with scenarios, but I can't focus with the French news being reported on the car radio. Words I don't grasp spew from the speakers. An apology for interrupting the usual music. Other words carry forward. *Tonight. Sunrise. Local forces.* The driver's dark eyes narrow in the rearview. He slows at a stop sign, then peers around him before accelerating, speeding across the Pont Neuf.

"Chang, what did that report say?" Relaxing music resumes, but no one listens. The energy is tight, nervous between the three of us. "Chang?"

She types search words into the web browser on her phone. "We have a problem."

The driver brakes to a stop beside a closed bakery. "Allez-y. Au revoir, mesdames." He pulls on the e-brake, then makes a shooing motion with his hands; he's not going anywhere. Chang tries to negotiate with him, mentioning more money in French, and I offer to pay more, too, double, if he'll just take us the rest of the way. The driver shakes his head and says something else. *Pas la peine.* Not worth it.

I pay for our ride here, to the middle of nowhere I recognize. When we exit, the sign on the cab's roof goes dark, no longer accepting fares. Chang turns to me with a sigh. "Who knew we had the one law-abiding cab driver in Paris?"

"What law is he following?" I ask. The car peels away from the curb, then makes a hard left out of sight.

"The report on the radio. There's a citywide lockdown from now to sunrise—I can't remember that ever happening. Must be something serious. They just announced it—anyone out will be stopped by police and questioned." Chang nods to where our driver disappeared. "Guess he didn't want to be stopped."

Shit. "Are you okay with being out still?"

Chang hesitates. The fluorescent lamp of a store selling insurance casts a red glow on her skin. Trash litters the doorway beside us. "I usually see the sun come up. We should stay out of sight if you still want to go underground—avoid the police. If we're caught, be prepared to see my best *old and confused woman* bit. You'll have to be my delinquent granddaughter." She smiles, revealing a dimple in her chin.

The street's silence is eerie. Dark shadows seem to multiply the longer we stand here. Along with my chance of being arrested, or worse— sent home to California.

We keep to the alleys wherever possible, cutting over to adjacent roads when we don't hear any cars. Twice, voices rise around a corner, and we duck into a recessed doorway. When we pass a sign directing people toward the Musée d'Orsay, I pause. "Isn't the main entrance to the catacombs behind us?"

Chang turns to me with surprise. "We're not going there. It's after hours, and there's no way we could enter that fortress." Forever ago, I stood in front of what I termed *a green toolshed* with Seb. Its metal doors would be impenetrable by my measly human hands. "Besides, there are police in that square by now—wonder why they're shutting down the city, very peculiar."

"Where are we going, if not to the main entrance?"

Chang resumes walking in the same direction. "An off-the-record entrance."

Slimy fear courses through me, touching everything, down to the tips of each limb. Hugo mentioned it in the club. No shiny banisters allowed. "Impasse de Valmy."

"Yes, have you been? Oh—!" Chang pivots into a deep doorway and waves me in quick. I leap in and make myself as flat as possible against a glass wall covered in flyers. The smell of urine is thick. A walkie-talkie radio sputters a message around the corner. Footsteps approach, several pairs of feet, one less steady than the other.

"Allez-y." A car door opens nearby. Not breathing, I lean forward and catch a uniformed man ushering a woman in dirty layers of clothing into the back seat of his car. POLICE NATIONALE is visible on the side. They're already rounding up people, anyone who is outside, including the homeless. Which explains why the streets have been so empty. The engine starts, then fades into the distance. Chang nods to me. We continue on, unspeaking, moving quickly across the parts of sidewalk pooled in light.

The mile we walk seems longer than it should, but I welcome the physical distraction. My feet ache in my worn sneakers, but each step forward is invigorating. It's a relief when Chang points across a large intersection. "Just around that corner."

We dash to the other side when a spotlight floods the square. "Arrêtez!" a man's voice bellows. "Arrêtez! Police!" Chang sprints behind a stone monument with me on her heels, along with the quick steps of a cop. She pulls left, charging onto a narrow road opposite the museum. A cramp splits up the side of my ribs, but I dig deep and round the corner. Arms reach out and yank me into another doorway. Adrenaline floods my brain and I shove, but the arms don't give. The policeman's footsteps breach the corner, and a uniform goes flying past, farther down the street. The arms release, and I look down to see Chang's grimace.

"You do strength training, too?" I hiss. She shakes her head with a finger to her lips. Voices carry from the left.

"See the large tree opposite the bank?" Chang motions for me to look, carefully. We're in the hood of a jewelry store doorway and awning. Frosted glass doesn't allow us to see inside or anyone to see us through the glass walls from around the corner. I peek into the street. An oak tree with a thick trunk surveys the commercial neighborhood.

"I see it. Two men are standing next to it."

Chang curses in French. "Then we're done for."

Regret pinches my stomach, watching her search for a way through this. Chang has only been generous and understanding since we met, and I deliberately put her in this position, one which could end in our arrest. If we step out now, we'll be rounded up. If we try and sneak back to Montmartre on foot, we'll be rounded up. God only knows what the French penal code entails. Some form of Miranda rights, probably, but I doubt they come with an interpreter. "Chang, how close are we to the Pantheon?"

She gives me a sideways glance. "Maybe five blocks. Why?"

"There's another entrance." I peer out onto the street again, but Chang's strong grasp pulls me back.

"I doubt it. Most of the entrances were sealed or grates have been put over them. This one is the last entrance that's still usable within three miles."

Pride tightens my chest. Excitement rises with the certainty that Angela left me all the clues necessary in her apartment. "Not all of them."

We pick our way along well-lit portions of street and sprint across each intersection after a careful pause. A siren screams past us once, but no cars stop. The sun is almost up and, once it is, our cover will be gone. When we arrive at the neoclassical mausoleum, I cut right and focus on hazy memories of Thursday night. The bookstore here doesn't look familiar, so I reverse direction down the street until I spy the convenience store, the one that Mathieu stood in front of on my tour of historical brothels.

"Shayna?" Chang's voice is strained. I push on, jogging to the next street, where I turn right. "Shayna," she says again. "Do you know what you're looking for?"

A brick wall extends the half block of the alley. Beyond it is a busier street, Rue du Renard, across from the Pantheon, and the one where I cut in line to grab a cab after escaping Mathieu's bruising grip.

"Shayna, you don't have to torture yourself by going everywhere your sister did."

I stop in the middle of the road, panting. "What?"

Chang walks toward me with her palms up. "I don't mean to overstep, but I spoke to Angela about her research on the catacombs. I know that's why you want to go underground. If what you need is to go home and take care of yourself, that's okay, too. You look like you might need sleep."

Though she speaks quietly and throws a glance behind her, her words fill my ears like the booming bass back in the club. I stare at the ground littered with broken glass and cigarette butts, weighing the truth of those options. It's possible I'll never find my sister. And, even if I do, things may not ever go back to the way they were, to being half of that happy family in the photograph.

"Someone is coming." Chang scans the alley in each direction. Tension serrates my belly as walkie-talkie audio fuzz approaches fast from down the adjacent road. I know the door leading to the brothel is unlocked before I touch the handle, and it swings open to the cubed foyer I crammed into with four men. As the last remaining brothel in the city, it serves a steady clientele twenty-four hours a day. Much like the crypts of Notre Dame, it's connected to a network more vast than I can fathom.

Chang's hand is sweaty when I pull her inside and shut the metal door. She looks down at the manhole cover and immediately withdraws a crowbar and workman's gloves from her backpack. Donning the gloves, she angles the crowbar, wedging it against the rim, and works it at various points around the circumference like a lever. She pries practiced fingers beneath the heavy plate, and I do the same until together we manage to push it up and to the side. Blackness peers back at us, and cold, stale air that reeks of sewage rushes my nostrils.

Aggressive voices call from outside the door. The police. Chang dangles her small legs into the hole and withdraws from her backpack a flashlight that could double as a battering ram. She points the light down. Rocky ground and a large trough of broken concrete lie a few feet beneath the hole. Chang surveys the space with an approving nod. "Ready?"

Beyond the circle made by the flashlight, darkness stares back at us, unyielding. Hysteria rises in my chest and threatens to piss all over the clean rug of my fake confidence. I lift my eyes to Chang's.

"After you."

Chapter 30

A moldy chill penetrates my shirt and jeans. The sweat on my back feels damp well after it would have dried aboveground. The coat of moisture in the air insulates and chokes like a wet sock shoved down my throat.

"You all right?" Chang shines her flashlight at my feet, where I've crouched down in a ball. We've been walking for five minutes, but I've been fighting the urge to run back to the manhole since we closed it. The halo of light exaggerates Chang's contoured cheekbones, making her appear ghostly. Concern indents her face and creates shadowy wrinkles you'd think would be evident in the daylight. Panic rips at my chest, clawing to climb out of my mouth in a scream. Counting to ten quells the itch by a small margin.

All of the dangerous things that didn't occur to me before fill my thoughts now. Like Mathieu saying, *How you were there one second at the bordel . . . and gone the next?* Angela scratched him—what if he knows about this entrance? What if it's where he and Angela scuffled?

I strain to hear any movement behind us, back at the manhole cover, and am met with silence. Using the pocket flashlight on Angela's key chain, I confirm no one is following me. But either Mathieu or

Jean-Luc could be around any of these corners, could appear from either end and sandwich us in an attack.

"Let's keep moving," I finally breathe. The dirt walls, though high and well packed, inch closer the longer we stay put. Chang nods, turning forward, giving me privacy to fall the fuck apart.

"No one knows how they'll react once they're down here," she says, generously. "Some people love it. And others . . . less so. What are those coordinates again?"

"Forty-eight degrees, fifty-three minutes, five-point-seven-five seconds north latitude, two degrees, twenty minutes, one second east longitude." I recite the coordinates of Angela's *Divine Research* blog post by heart, drawing strength from their sound, not even needing the note I wrote earlier.

Chang trails her hands along the walls, her wingspan just wide enough to touch. "Forty-eight degrees, huh? That will take us under the river—my favorite part. What's special about them? Your coordinates?"

It's just the two of us, and she already knows it on some level, so I mete out a bit of the truth. "I read it in Angela's research. And fully expect to find buried treasure there."

Chang laughs. The high-pitched sound is disturbing in the dark. "Don't believe everything you read on the internet."

She leads us straight, at a descending angle, for what seems like forever but is probably another five minutes. Crags of rock stick out from the otherwise smooth ceiling, and I have the wherewithal to admire the tunnels' architecture. Chang shares how she first got started down here with her husband back when it was a niche interest deriving from cave exploration in the south of France. I suspect she's filling the audio space for my benefit when I start to hyperventilate for the third time. My balance falters as the fever creeps back up, spiking intermittently in a way I've only experienced a few times in my life—once when I had mono, and another time when I ate a bad oyster. I stop to lean against the wall. When I'm able to breathe normally again, she resumes listing the people she's taken belowground over the years and who, I assume, came out alive after.

We step over a pile of trash, fast food wrappers, and an old pillow long since abandoned. An earthy hostel for the homeless. Angela surmised as much in her research paper, and now I can confirm. Yay. Walking along the creased sewer trough becomes a lesson in endurance and balance as the minutes drag on. Thank God the tunnel is empty, and it doesn't seem to have been used in ages. I wrap my arms around my chest for warmth, for comfort. Chang passes through a left turn but stops short in the doorway. "What is it?" I ask, joining her.

Skulls form a thick cross in a domed alcove. Dozens of them. A downward chute lies beneath the cross, a mouth of black the circumference of a human body. My hand flies to my chest, clutching at my heart, as the mental endurance I'd gathered threatens to crumble. "Are we going down there?" I point with the pocket flashlight, throwing shadow monsters around the hub.

Chang clears her throat. "Not here. The old sewer will lead us lower first to get under the river."

Lower. Of course. I nod, then follow her to the right of the two paths. The skull arrangements become more frequent as the concrete gives way to dirt and puddles. Chang barrels ahead, undeterred. I focus on tranquil thoughts, mantras, meditations. This is not the hope chest Angela locked me in. This is a tunnel matrix with dozens of exits.

This is the burial ground of six million Parisian unknowns.

Pools of water become more common as the ground dips more steeply. I try not to think about where I am and what I'm doing, because when I do my throat closes. Deep breath, through the nose. A drop of water hits my forehead. "Are we close to the river yet?"

"We're under it now." Chang's voice booms from farther ahead. The temperature is even cooler here, and my long sleeves feel nonexistent. Plink plink plink. A rock skitters behind me. I whirl, but the flashlight reveals the same pile of dirt I just passed. My mother's gentle reprimand comes to mind: *Pick up your feet, Shayna.* I jog to fall in line behind Chang. A metallic taste expands on my tongue as my teeth catch a dry section of skin—a reminder that I'm alive. Sane. *Alive.*

"What do you do back home, Shayna?" Chang picks her way along a jagged section. Large hunks of earth and stone block the path, and she offers a hand to help me across—a sight I would find comedic (tiny Chang, adult-size Shayna) if I wasn't so grateful she offered.

"Well, I start medical school Monday," I grunt.

"Wow. That's great. I know we've just met, but that seems like a good fit—or you could be a judge? Have you ever thought about deejaying?"

"Not really, no. Would you—?"

Chang spots me as I slide across a flat stone. The ground beneath is a good foot lower, and I steady myself with her help.

"Are you excited to start medical school?"

We continue forward in the semidarkness. For whatever reason, I felt a connection to Chang right off the bat, and that's only grown after hurdling over shrubbery together. I pause, examining the answer to her question. "I guess. I don't know, honestly. It's been this goal that I've worked toward so long with my parents, and now I'm not sure it's what I really want. So much has changed the last few years. Now it's almost a way to honor their memory."

Chang makes a clucking noise with her tongue. "Ah, I didn't realize they passed on. I'm sorry. What would you do if you weren't starting school on Monday?"

Cry? Stay here? Get hired as a waitress in the La Jolla restaurant where we had the med school mixer? Looking back on the last three years, I enjoyed volunteering at the veterans' hospital, dabbling in all aspects of its business. I couldn't do much medicine-related work, being unlicensed, but the hospital's administration interested me more than I expected. Going over patient profiles, sometimes assisting in managing legal files. It fed my overanalytical brain when I wasn't allowed to use it to treat real people. "Maybe something with law."

"I could see that."

"How did you learn so much about the tunnels? Trial and error?"

Chang laughs again. "A lot of error. At first it was a group of us that became interested, back in the eighties. We would get out of a gig—late nights led to many adventures—back then, taxis weren't so pervasive. The police weren't fans of the substances we were all smoking—it was the eighties, mind you—so we would take the tunnels under the city to get home and avoid the cops. Lots of people used to travel these tunnels, and I've met nearly all of them."

A set of stairs leads to another domed hub, bearing three different routes. Chang shines a light on the walls to reveal words, graffiti art, numbers, and dates, all written in various colors; a discarded spray can lies at the foot of the wall. A visual diary of everyone who has passed through here into this secret society. For a second, the sight is beautiful, and my muscles relax. Then I see it. Sharp angles and even planes across inverse Greek letters. Symbols foreign to most eyes in these parts, but I can read them with barely a light to see:

I am here.

"This was before most of the tunnel entrances were closed. There aren't any on the Right Bank now. Only a handful of us use them—some urban explorers, researchers, and those pesky smugglers I mentioned. The other remaining portals are on the south side of Paris, leading in from Spain—they're used pretty exclusively by the traffickers, and you don't want to run into them." Chang chatters on, passing through the route to the left, but I don't move. Researchers, like Angela. She knew of this entrance into the main network. She left me a signpost. I'm on the right path. *I am here.*

We approach a slight incline, and my fists clench tighter with each step forward. A narrow path stretches ahead, decorated in bone until it ends in a hub of skulls. Hollow cheekbones and empty sockets line up in neat formation, at least thirty in a circular space. Multiple paths converge there, but most are boarded shut, leaving only one open tunnel to the left. The stone tablet erected above the stooped entrance bears a message:

ARRÊTÉ
C'EST ICI L'EMPIRE DE LA MORT

Stop. For here is the empire of death.

"Chang?" I hardly recognize the shrill sound of my voice. We've paused in front of the door against my better judgment, inviting Death to come out and take what's his. I shift my weight, my bicep locked against my chest. My bones poke through the cloth more than I remember.

"Pretty morbid, I know." Chang stands by the doorway, just grazing the top. "The miners who first built the quarries—these tunnels—were fans of romantic language and poetry. You'll see more on the walls."

I follow her beneath the arch, muttering to myself.

With each step away from the hub, the angst in my body lessens. But we haven't climbed any more out of this pit, and the tunnel ceilings are still uncomfortably low. The light is nonexistent outside our flashlight halos and the temperature is cold, yet my muscles relax bit by bit until I let my arm fall to my side. Am I actually getting used to this?

A glow burns from around the corner. Someone is down here with us, after hours, and illegally. Traffickers? I cry out to warn Chang, but she turns past the bend. Peering around another corner, the words lodge behind my teeth. White bulbs illuminate the confined space, electrical cords spooling along the edges. Paths extend to the left and right. A plaque directs visitors toward a recommended route; the official tour is located ten feet ahead. This must be part of the longer path Seb wanted to take on Monday.

Chang stands past the corner, totally unfazed by my moment of absence. She checks a compass app on her phone. "This is about where I know forty-eight degrees latitude would be. You did great, Shayna. Not many people—"

"This isn't it." I motion for her to hand me her phone, and I consult her compass. "This isn't forty-eight degrees, fifty-three minutes, five-point-seven-five seconds north latitude, two degrees, twenty minutes, one second east longitude."

"What do you mean?"

"We're not here." Angela would not have chosen a well-lit hub of the authorized catacombs tour. A wall of skulls glares at me while I contradict my patient friend.

Chang looks at me with surprise. "It's as good as we're going to get. I don't know of any ways farther east from here."

The compass spins all the way around, then settles to point southwest. I show it to Chang. "Is this correct? Are we facing this direction right now?"

She shakes her head. "No, we're too far down; the mineral rock around us throws off the compass's magnet. What were you expecting to be here? The buried treasure?" she adds, showing her chin dimple.

A dank smell beckons from deeper in the tunnel to our left—decay and something else. Sweat breaks out on my forehead despite the goose bumps covering my skin as I wrestle with the impulse to believe her. If she says we can't go any farther, it must be true. She pioneered this place.

This is ridiculous.

This is all I've got.

Polished tour arrows direct me along a new, declining dirt path, and Chang follows behind. She doesn't even protest; instead she wordlessly allows me to take point. Skulls, skulls, bones, skull shelves, bone shelf, skull wall, skull wall. I become numb to the sight, no longer retching from fear at each new mosaic.

A tapering entrance, shoulder width at its widest, interrupts the macabre decor—one of several pitch-black passages veering to the right or left into avenues not recommended by the plaques. I slow down to focus on my sister—the way she charmed everyone in the room, her aura, her energy—and indulge her lifelong desire that we be mentally connected.

"Shayna?" Chang touches my arm. "There's nothing down there." She nods to the gap in the solid rock beside me. I ignore her and lean closer. Angela's presence always seemed warm to me, until it was cold. I try to recall what that felt like. I concentrate on any sense of my sister calling back to me, a gut feeling that returns my plea with *Here I am. I am waiting.* Adrenaline kicks ever-present claustrophobia from my back, while herculean strength drives me forward, deeper into my pit of hell. I slide into the black, tapered crack.

"Angela?" I whisper. My stomach tenses in sharp cramps, but I creep forward, hands out. The ground slopes downward as the three feet of light from the main walkway slivers to black. Seb said the catacombs were more than two hundred miles long. Chill, undisturbed air engulfs me, and I stumble to my knees, hands balled by instinct. I scramble upright, anticipating a sneak attack from a monster while my eyes adjust. One click of my pocket flashlight reveals the cavernous space and its secrets. Someone has been here before. Many people.

A projection screen stands before dozens of empty chairs. A full bar is set up against the far end of the makeshift movie theater, fashioned out of a tall table and three bar stools. The dome I'm standing in reaches at least fifty feet across and another thirty high. A carton contains old-fashioned film reels in the corner, next to a sleek, portable projector, something you might see on your favorite electronics website, and a vintage cinema projector, the kind with two rotating wheels balancing a wide base. Nothing about the space looks official. How many secrets do the catacombs hold? How much activity has gone unseen by the authorities?

A shiver traces my spine as I tiptoe back to Chang. She remains in the hall, her arms folded. "I think we should go," she says.

"Look, Chang. I really appreciate you getting me here, but you can leave now that we're on the official tour path. I should be able to find my way out." I adopt a confident expression and ignore the patterns in the bones behind her.

"No, you won't. The catacombs won't open for hours today. It's Saturday. You need another exit from here; the main one is back under the river and locked until ten."

Angela, Angela, Angela. My mantra plays on loop while I search for some sign of my sister and try to employ the twin powers, the psychic GPS or whatever, she swore by. Chang steps backward, watching me. "Are you feeling okay?"

A motif of femurs in a bowl shape, sunk into the tunnel's dirt floor, lies at the bend in the path. Something about it seems familiar; I've seen it before, in her research photos. *Angela.* I visualize a thousand tiny cables extending from my frame, reaching with a million follicles, alert and ready to transmit silent messages, less of words than of yearning. I orient the directions of the compass in my mind. East-facing pathways are nonexistent—until I spy an opening in one wall at knee level, just large enough for an adult body to squeeze through.

A dull snare drum kick-starts in my chest as I trip over my feet to jog-walk. Chang trails behind me, satisfied to observe and make sure I don't bash my head against a wall, until I slide to the ground and shimmy through the rock cleft. Her protests stop dead as I rise to stand inside a long tunnel shaft, pitch-black. Chang doesn't follow; she barks into another opening in the wall above, keeping me in sight and pleading for me to come back. I'm fumbling for my flashlight as the sound of movement stops me cold.

My fingers grapple for wall, rock—something to give me a sense of my inky surroundings—when a strong, bony hand clamps down on mine. I suck in a breath to scream, but another hand grips my face and yanks me farther into the shaft. It covers my mouth, seizing my jaw with such force tears pierce my eyes. I fumble with the flashlight button, then shine it in the eyes of my attacker, who doesn't flinch.

Dirt covers porcelain skin. Dust mars the apples of cheeks that haven't seen the sun in days. Disheveled dark hair forms a skewed halo around a head otherwise my height. Brown eyes contract like angry, light-averse rats. Frenzy and fear leap out from wide sockets, while my sister's vise grip on my hand remains white-knuckle strong.

Despite my muzzle, I manage, "Angela . . . ?" before she grabs the flashlight and puts it in her pocket. The tunnel returns to darkness.

"Twin for the win." Her whisper cracks.

"Shayna? Are you okay? Who's there?" Chang calls. Her flashlight shines on our two pairs of feet, and Angela recoils from me.

"You brought someone?"

"I had to. I didn't know anything about the catacombs. You're . . . you're alive!"

Chang sputters from the hall. "What?"

Angela grips my hand again. "We have to get out of here." She turns to the main path and begins speaking beautiful French to Chang, too fast for me to comprehend. The aria of her words is matched only by her perfect accent after three years here. Her shoulders straighten, and she waves a hand from her right hip, a stance I've seen her use in restaurants to get a dish taken off our check. My sister, the charming twin, even a building's length underground and weeks since her last bath. Angela chuckles, but Chang only nods. Angela makes another fluid gesture with her hand, then turns back to me in the dark.

"I told her this is a hide-and-seek game we play in different countries, and I was never missing. The police were confused. Get rid of her," she hisses. Dirt covers her blue hoodie and jeans. Only the tongues of her sneakers are still white.

"Gel, what exactly is going on? What happened?" I throw my arms around her, but she stiffens.

"Well, hello. Ça va? Que fais-tu ici?" Chang leans away from us, disappearing from the gap in the wall toward approaching footsteps. Shit. Jean-Luc? Mathieu? The police?

Angela pulls on my hand, scrambling to retreat farther into the darkness, but Chang hears her. Her face reappears through the uneven outline of the rock's opening. "Hey, Shayna, I don't think—" Someone extends a hand from around the corner to grab Chang's glasses. "Hey!" The person's fist closes around her neck, then tosses her backward with a loud thump.

"Chang!" I scream.

Silence. A figure steps into view. But it's not who I expect.

Seb stands there, wearing a sickening grin. Blood smears across his cheek. "Shayna, I must thank you. Without you, I never would have found Angela. Your bond truly is remarkable."

The feral urge to *Run! Run! Run!* rises somewhere within me. It reverberates in my heart, but terror plants my feet to the ground. He kicks through the wall, punches, and steps into the tunnel with us.

Seb. He played me all along. From the moment I landed, I've been doing the work for him.

Angela grabs my hand and turns to run, but Seb yanks me back, throwing me against a wall studded with stone. Pain explodes from my elbow in one sharp crack, and white flashes across my eyes. I slump to the ground, clutching my arm, and glimpse Angela tearing down the path with Seb on her heels. I could run, run now.

She gains distance in inches, thin and quick from her time in hiding, but then she trips and falls hard, swinging down like an ax. He's on her in two seconds. Howls rip from her throat as he drags her back, limping on her right leg.

Fever reignites across my skin, a terrible heat just like before. Seb's smile grows hazy. The gun he wields is a dull object rising with each sweeping movement as he gloats. Words I can't hear spill from his mouth as a loud ringing overwhelms my eardrums. I can't move. Numbness subdues both fight and flight instincts as he steps forward and drags us into the light.

Chapter 31

Hold still

Putain merde mais vas-y tu sais bien ce qui t'attend

Hold still you stupid bitch

A musty smell fills my nostrils, as though I'm in a library or a walk-in closet. Maybe back in high school. I breathe deep, eyes closed, listening for my surroundings. The absence of the familiar sound of running water is deafening.

My eyes snap open.

Thick wooden beams above reinforce the dirt ceiling—the only barriers between us and six stories of earth, waiting to bury us. Damp dust motes swirl around me.

"Shayna?" Angela whispers. "You okay?"

I moan in response from where I lie flat on the ground. All over my body throbs with ache, though the pain is mostly confined to my arm. Seb splinted my elbow, but it's now swollen to the size of a baseball.

"Mmm."

"Shayna," she tries again. "Seb left for more antiseptic from the hospital. We're alone." Angela speaks slowly, like the effort taxes her. The crushing verity of her words brings on new panic that constricts my chest and fat tears that sting. Angela was limping earlier, too; we're alone and both injured.

I roll to my side and struggle to an upright position. Zip ties bind my feet and hands in front of my body, and I note the plastic's sharp sensation, like it might slice through my skin at the right angle. "How long ago?" I ask, rubbing my wrists with opposite fingers.

"About five minutes," Angela says.

I lift my head and stifle a cry. Bones form a crisscrossing pattern from floor to ceiling on the wall opposite Angela and surround two complete skeletons side by side. The skeletons stand the exact same height, mirror images of each other.

"Did you forget where we were?" she asks.

I shake my head, recalling Angela's research. *A room filled with fibulae, a room devoted to soldiers, and a room full of twin bones.* The twin room. "Just disoriented."

Books, chemicals in industrial-size jugs, cords and cables looped in precise rings, and an illuminated construction lamp are piled in a corner, throwing shadows around the room. Only one wall contains a bone mosaic, while the other wall, behind Angela, appears to be constructed from bones stacked on top of one another. Behind me, overhead, hangs a rectangular board of felt nailed into the compacted dirt wall, covered in graph paper, newspaper articles, handwritten notes, and maps with places circled in red pen. A large, knee-high generator occupies a corner, beside a refrigerator, displaying dozens of vials and thin tubes visible from its glass door. When we first entered, I tried to reverse, scratched back into the corridor, but Seb caught me. He said he would always catch me.

"We have to get out of here." Angela struggles with her ties five feet away from me, her back against the wall of stacked bones. The bones clink together behind her jerking movements. "He'll be back soon—the hospital is in the next arrondissement."

My limbs are heavy. Exhausted from the adrenaline rush of terror bursting from every pore.

Six million unknowns is about to become six million and two.

"Shayna," Angela hisses. "Snap out of it!"

I can't see straight. My vision keeps making patterns in the bone mosaic, blurring the images together, then separating them. I know around a day and a half has passed since I came down here, because Seb mentioned he was waiting to go for supplies until the hospital staff switched over again. He plans to steal more, to steal equipment to test his theories and add to the inventory he already carted down here.

My plane home will depart in a few hours, without me. I'll be dropped from medical school and my life; my dreams of beginning again will be over. And Angela will still be classified as dead, so everything I've gone through in the last week was for nothing.

"Angela." My voice is like sandpaper working a block—despite Seb giving us water through a straw every few hours. "What happened to you?"

She inhales a ragged breath. "I tried to warn you. I even wrote it in our language. Typical, you wouldn't listen to me." Bitterness coats every word, like we time-traveled back to three years ago, right after our parents died. I'm so confused, seeing her for the first time under these insane circumstances, steps from life and literal death with Chang somewhere in the dark.

Chang. My heart tightens at the thought of my friend, no doubt dead by now, judging by the thump I heard when Seb threw her.

"I got your note," I say. "But it wasn't much to go on. Seb was . . . I needed a guide, and—Look, he fooled me. I thought he was your boyfriend, and I fell for it. I'm sorry." My words are staccato, sharp, not because I'm angry, but because I feel foolish. *I trusted someone when your note said not to. I failed us.* The thought makes my vision blur. The memory of Seb's lips on my skin that day in the park arouses new self-loathing.

Angela trembles. She bites the inside of her mouth, exaggerating the contours of her face. When Seb first tied us together and we walked into the light, I was shocked to see the hollow air of her once full cheeks—*lucky cheeks*, our Chinese grandmother used to call them, and our Scottish grandfather used to pinch them.

"I'm the one who's sorry," she whispers. "I got us into this mess. Seb and I went out, but I had no idea he wanted the both of us. I was devastated after Mom and Dad died, and I was so mad at you, even all this time later. If I hadn't cut you out, I wouldn't have been so willing to trust him."

I pause, allowing her words to fully pass between us—this is the closest we've ever come to talking about our family tragedy in person. "You don't have to say anything. These last three years have been hard for both of us. I'm disappointed in myself, too."

She snorts. "Wow. Perfect Shayna is *disappointed* in herself? Break out the champagne—we've got remorse."

Her anger is a slap, and I recoil, stunned. "What?"

"You don't get it," she says, emotion wrapping her words. "Seb was never my boyfriend; this is not an act of domestic violence. We went out on one date. Before he kept me here in the catacombs."

Angela draws her knees to her chest while I stare, dumbfounded. "I don't understand."

She focuses on the skeletons across from her. "I met him a month ago, but he'd been watching me for some time before. I thought he was a part of the internship, too. Agreeing to dinner was supposed to be for networking—I don't know. The next day, when the shooting happened at the Sorbonne, he found me in the library, hiding behind a shelf. Told me he would keep me safe. Instead he brought me here. He'd been waiting for the right time to make his move, I guess. I escaped when he went to the hospital where he works part-time."

Fear slinks down my chest, cold along my limbs. Goose bumps ignite the skin of my neck as I fill in the blanks between sentences. She was kidnapped. Beaten. Terrorized. I want to leave this space, disappear somewhere, to burrow away from her words and what she endured. The raw skin of my eyes burns with new wetness.

She clears her throat. "He knew you and I only had each other. He did his research, too."

"But why didn't you come and tell me all this? Why wait until we were trapped underground and I was followed? Why not go to the police?"

Angela grunts. "Seb took my passport. He told me he framed me for a friend's death, so if I did escape, I couldn't leave France or ask for help."

"Manu? The cops would have listened."

She pauses at the name, confirming my guess. "They wouldn't have. I tried to come to you the first day you arrived. Waited until I saw a light on in my apartment, but a homeless man tried to grab me, recognized me. Seb paid him, probably. Each day, the man waited out front, then followed you wherever you went, hoping to find me again. I knew as long as we weren't together, we would be safe, so I never approached you. I had to trust you would find me."

That scream the first night. Angela's scream. She was there just below the window. All that stood between us then was two flights of stairs and a mercenary. "I gave that homeless man my change."

"You chose this trip to be generous?"

Watching him miraculously heal from a limp when police arrived was bewildering; I thought it was the fever. She's right—he was watching me the whole time for Seb. "Then you left me a message under Nour's doormat, told me to go to the nightclub by hiding it in a to-do list. You wanted me to find Chang."

"Yes." We're each silent a moment, gathering our thoughts. "What day is it?" she asks.

"Not sure," I murmur. "Saturday or Sunday, July 29. I was supposed to fly out tonight." Past tense. Dirt has crept down the back side of my jeans, into my shirt, under my fingernails. Slowly invading every part of me. Burying me from the outside in. "How did you survive this last time?"

Angela meets my gaze, finally. "I got lucky. When he left to go to the hospital for something, the scissors were out, and I was able to cut myself free." A harsh edge sharpens each word she speaks. "I don't want to die in here. I can't. Not after escaping already. And not with you."

"What—?"

"Most of all," she resumes, her voice taking on a gravelly, thick quality. Her eyes become watery. "I don't want to die in here before I hear you say it."

I stop breathing. Her words linger, flat in the enclosed air. Every muscle in my body stiffens, fearful of what comes next.

Angela takes my silence for confirmation and nods. "Auntie Meredith told me, right after the funeral. I've known ever since that summer. You needed Mom and Dad to pick you up from somewhere because you drank too much. Again. On their way to rescue you, they were hit."

Cold shame roils across my body, unfurls in a cloud of anguish, and I don't even protest her words. The phantom taste of bourbon, my drink of choice then, along with the feel of the scratchy wool blanket I was sleeping on when the police officer called, stirs from my memory. Angela's easy summary is a punch to the gut, too reduced and too clinical, without the ensuing self-hatred that followed. More than anything I want to tell her she's wrong. But I can't.

It was a Friday, and I was on a date with some guy, drinking too much. I was neck-deep in oncology research that summer, trying to get an article published—to start medical school on the right foot—and, if I'm being honest, alcohol was a means of coping with stress long before that night. My mother always insisted, "Call if you can't drive home, honey. We'll come get you." My parents were nearing Genesee Avenue when they were struck by a delivery van whose driver had fallen asleep at the wheel after a long day of dropping off graduation wreaths. The force of the collision threw my parents over the elevated exit ramp from the highway and into the sloped valley below, where they died on impact. When they didn't show, I requested a rideshare to get back. Passed out on my couch for five hours, too out of it to navigate the stairs to my bedroom. The call from the police woke me.

Officer Rudolph asked if there was anyone she could phone to keep me company, but I shook my head. No one would want to come once they learned the truth: I was the catalyst to this night. By asking my parents to save me from myself yet again—as they had in the past from happy hours after exams, from wine tastings, from friends' birthday parties in Del Mar—I was the cause of their deaths. *Work hard, play hard* was the self-serving mantra I used to justify each binge—knowing they were always there for me, no matter the time of night or location.

"I blamed you for their deaths the last three years, after Auntie Mer told me," Angela admits, her cheeks wet. "And if I'm being honest, I still haven't forgiven you. I'm sorry, because that's awful, but it's true. The loss of them became the loss of all of you."

"All this time," I begin in a small voice, "I thought you were angry because I wouldn't sell the house."

"You could have. I meant it when I said I wanted it sold. Difficult memories are too much there, too concentrated."

"Don't you get it?" I shake my head. "I couldn't—not without you coming home. I needed us to say goodbye to them together, since you didn't come home for their funeral. I needed to tell you the truth in person."

"Ready for the hippie-dippie, Shayna? The thing is, I do get it." She gives a clipped laugh. "I *want* to forgive you. I want to move forward, because it's not your fault they died. You didn't know they would be hit. I just don't know how to."

"Angela." My voice breaks. Pleads. Strains from how much I need her to say it's all right, that she does forgive me, after three years of shouldering my unrelenting guilt alone. When I first saw her whiteboard message, the need rose so strongly, the sudden possibility of it gripped me to the point where I almost collapsed onto her floor. The cruelty of that hope slams back into me now. I can feel my heart hardening, because otherwise it would break.

A pebble lands on my arm. It's come loose from the dirt ceiling. This isn't happening.

I crane my head to my rear pants pocket. Seb shoved my hoodie into a yellow opera bag when he brought us here, just like the one I saw at the Leroux crime scene, but he didn't remove any other clothing. From my back pocket, the tip of something pokes out. The moose photograph. *Don't let anyone tell you you're unlovable*—undeserving of love, or otherwise. My mother's words ring in my thoughts, her creased, narrow chestnut eyes so concerned. I promised her I wouldn't.

Calm down. *Compter jusqu'à dix.* Start over.

"Angela, I'm sorry for . . . for everything. For Mom and Dad. For what you've gone through here alone, but we need to focus. After you cut yourself loose, where did you go?"

She swallows with a loud gulp. "Home. I used the spare key I hid in the lobby and grabbed some cash I kept in my apartment for emergencies, wrote the message on the whiteboard, hid the bookmark to my blog post for you to find, and the receipts. I knew you'd search everywhere and that Seb would contact you to lure you here." The rickety breath she takes swells her lungs, bolstering her words. "He told me he'd stolen a body from the hospital morgue, dumped it in the river, and everyone thought it was me."

The memory of rotting, waterlogged flesh fills my nostrils, and I gag picturing the thighs of that cadaver. But a quick glance at Angela's feet confirms her ankle does have the Gemini symbol, the symbol for twins, in black ink.

"After I escaped," she continues, "I started living in the catacombs, thinking—"

"That it would be the last place he'd look. Makes sense."

"I started thinking about what you would do in my situation, Shay. You're so precise about everything. But you can't logic him to death the way you normally would. He doesn't think in normal terms."

"No kidding. But why mention Jean-Luc in the updates folder I found? You had me convinced that he was the one who took you."

"I might be the better person to ask." Seb fills the doorway. He tosses a large canvas bag to the ground, items within banging together. "Since I wrote it."

We look at him—identical twins, the same petrified mien. A gust of cold air ruffles my long sleeves, searing my skin in goose bumps. How long has he been standing there? I try to catch Angela's eye, but she stares resolutely at the ceiling, our conversation paused. He strolls into the chamber.

"The party was *hyper chouette* last night! Sound familiar?" Smug victory stiffens his mouth.

I rack my brain for the exact wording of that email and remember the term *look-holes*. Yet another way I underestimated my sister; I assumed her English had dipped in those three years, that she might call peepholes "look-holes." The guilt returns, and I focus on calcified dirt until the lump in my throat dissolves.

Seb crosses to a corner. He flicks a switch on the generator, and the metal box whirs to life in a low growl. "Now that I've paid another visit to the hospital, we can move on to next steps."

Before I can react, he's on me, and I grab at a rock behind me a second too late. He whips out a syringe and yanks up my sleeve. Seb's face is reserved as he leans in close. "Shayna," he says, not unkindly. "It's time for blood work."

Chapter 32

Electrical cords explode from a thin, silver laptop, leading to various areas of the room. The wide laptop screen displays the entrance with the narrow hallway just out of view beyond; the lower-right-hand corner of the screen displays the fork in the path another fifty feet outside and closer to freedom, ready to transmit images of anyone coming to our rescue—or escaping. Following the line of sight, I spy the wireless camera wedged between studs overhead.

Seb arranges his supplies in a steel cabinet, talking over his shoulder. "I have everything necessary for the preliminary experiments—the anesthesia, antibacterial wipes, antiseptic."

"Please don't do this." I clear the rasp from my throat. "You can let us go."

He pauses tinkering with plastic bottles. "But I can't, Shayna," he says softly.

"You can." I press on, hearing the hesitation in his voice. "Let us go, and we'll give you a head start and everything before going to the police."

His head dips back as though examining the ceiling. Then he crosses to Angela, grabs the section of zip tie between her wrists, and drags her to the adjacent wall, beside the black pit of the entrance within the camera's scope. Taking a chain from the ground, he loops it through her linked arms, then secures it to a hook protruding from the wall with a metal lock. Pocketing the key, he turns to me.

"Please, Seb. You're . . . you're a good person. You don't have to do this," I cry as he crosses the fifteen feet to me in deliberate strides. He halts before me in a jerking motion, reminding me of that day on the Champs-Élysées when he caught me shopping for large-brimmed hats. Something in his face drops—lessens the unfeeling determination he's been wearing since he took us.

He surprises me by laughing. A blunted, empty sound that stops short. "Look at us, Shayna. Would you have imagined this, your first day here?"

I think back to Seb's morose expression, mirroring my own grief, in the lobby of Angela's apartment building. His deep-blue irises were red from crying, I had believed. "No, I wouldn't have. I thought you cared about us."

Something of that day's emotions returns to his face, pinching his eyebrows together. "The only thing I have cared for, for a long while, is finding a cure."

"For cancer?"

"For chemical weapons," Angela whispers, legs tucked underneath her, huddled against the wall.

Seb stares past me, over my head. "That is correct. My brother died from one. I watched him expire, unable to help. Only to watch."

Mustard gas, Valentin had said was the cause of death for Baptiste Bronn. I suck in a breath, then release it in a measured exhale—counting the seconds—not wanting to disturb whatever Seb seems to be reliving. "That's terrible."

Seb lowers his gaze to me. "Yes. Baptiste was taken from me. And I have been unable to truly rest since then."

"What do you mean?"

"When I came back to Paris, I saw him in crowds, or believed I did. At the grocery, the park, the catacombs. Realizing my eyes were betraying me was a devastation all over again. Men and women, everyone, fools and noncontributors to society, were a constant taunt that Baptiste was not alive. It was not fair. Why should they continue to live and not my brother? It was not right." His hands clench into fists at his sides, and I fight the urge to lean away from his tools of pain.

"What did you do?"

"I returned to the only thing I knew. To science, to search for a cure. At first, I tested existing theories to combat different forms of chemical warfare and disguised these tests as part of my hospital research. Then I realized, quickly, the field had become stagnant. Devoid of progress. Other studies, however—studies less palatable to some—showed parallels between the responses of human twins and those of test animals. Yet how could I find the resources to continue those studies?"

Angela and I exchange a glance, but neither of us breaks the spell by interrupting.

"One day, here in the tunnels, I met a man, a traveler passing through. He was homeless and eager for conversation from one who was unafraid and willing to engage with him, as I was. When he mentioned he was a twin, I knew my chance had come. I took him deep within the catacombs, into one of the many rooms, and performed my first experiments on a live subject, testing his blood, his muscle tissue, and taking these samples to the hospital lab before I had proper equipment moved here. I knew no one would come looking for him."

Cold fear spiders across my skin, hearing the preview of what's in store for us. I lick my lips and try to discreetly scan the room for a weapon. I'm not chained up yet, like Angela.

"I was clumsy, at first," Seb continues, nodding at this disappointment. "I gave too much anesthesia during procedures to make them more bearable, but I soon learned that progress will not allow for anything but precision." He purses his lips. As if he regrets withholding the one thing that could be considered a mercy.

"How many bodies did you need before becoming . . . practiced?" The cabinet of tools with its sharp and shiny objects is off in the corner, another twenty feet away and behind Seb. Out of reach.

"Too many. You'll recall studies show infant twins can sense when their sibling is in distress? At first, I focused on individual, fraternal twins, hoping to leverage this ability, before realizing—" He locks eyes with me. "I needed a complete set. From there, I theorized that twin abilities must be heightened among identical twins."

All those people. The four bodies before I arrived, and the three after. "You're the serial killer the police are looking for," I say on an exhale.

Seb straightens, stands up tall. "I will thank you not to trivialize my work, Shayna. Each contributor—the two homeless men, the carpenter, the woman I located through my access to records at the hospital, and the gypsy girl—took me another step toward finding a cure."

"Why did you kill Leroux? Was he a twin?" It seems years ago that I watched Valentin exit a building with scissors and thought he had taken something from the crime scene, like a serial killer would do. In hindsight, the pair of scissors was marked with masking tape, likely police property used to cut through Leroux's clothing or remove his zip ties.

A sob bursts from Angela; she didn't know, hiding underground, dashing out above for food and to leave me notes, that her internship director had been killed.

The pinched expression returns to Seb's face. "I didn't want to hurt Angela. She was different from the other experiment resources. You won't believe me, but it's not something anyone dreams of. No one dreams of this," he says, pointing first to me, then Angela. "I was concerned for Angela when she escaped, and I went to Leroux, believing he might know where she was. But he became suspicious. So he had to be dispatched."

I don't reply. I don't know how. I shouldn't feel this shock and terrible sadness that Seb's pragmatism would mean killing an acquaintance, possibly a friend. Even if he seems disturbed by his actions, too. Seb lost his brother to war—his only family, *his sanity*, he said—and somehow that means pursuing a cure at all costs. Maybe the tightening of my stomach, my chest, has more to do with finally seeing him for who he is. Who he was all along.

Weeping willow, my ass.

"What about Manu?" I say, trying to solidify the details still out of focus. "She disappeared two days before Angela but only turned up last week, deposited back in her apartment."

Seb shrugs, his candor revived. "In every experiment a control and a variable are needed. Without both, the experiment is flawed. Before it became clear identical twins held the key, I believed I needed her brother to advance my theories. Without him, my findings were assuredly inconclusive."

I picture the French heartthrob in the photo, his cheek pressed so lovingly to Manu's. Not her boyfriend, after all. "Manu was a fraternal twin."

"She blamed me for Christophe moving away to Belgium," Angela says, breaking her silence. She stares down at her dirt-covered sneakers. "For months she followed me around, pleading with me to speak to him, get back together with him, stealing my metro tickets so I'd need her to drive me home and let her talk."

"Finding adult twins without any family or people to ask after them was difficult," Seb continues, speaking more to himself now. He crosses to the cabinets along the wall of skulls, cutting off Angela's lament. "Imagine my surprise when I learned Manu was friends with another twin, an identical twin, working underground as an intern, and whom I recognized from down below. I only needed to follow Angela to learn where she lived, her interests, even her internship schedule. Once I saw her leaving Manu's apartment, and that's when I took the gypsy. I soon realized she would not serve my needs without her brother, but I kept her to serve as insurance. When Angela escaped, Manu became my leverage; Angela could not approach the police or the American embassy to obtain a new passport if she was the chief murder suspect, after being seen leaving Manu's apartment the day Manu disappeared. The only thing left was to ensure Manu's death appeared personal, emotional, as an angry friend might do it—with a shot to the heart."

Anger swells within me, remembering the tidy front room. Her neat, stacked magazines. The pink photo frames. "You're sick."

Seb turns from steel drawers with a glare. "Luckily, medicine cures all sickness, Shayna. The greater good calls for my research, despite those who would impede it. The Nazis used these catacombs during World War II, yes?" He watches me, lapping up my angst as I paw through my memory, desperate for something to stop this.

"The best of them was Josef Molinare," he continues. "A visionary. Physician of the Third Reich, banished to Brazil by the Allies for his extraordinary research. His experiments on twins gave me the idea."

Seb's hero: not just a textbook serial killer with unchecked impulses, but a sadistic tormentor.

I weigh my options for avoiding the same fate as Molinare's victims, but I'm in zip ties, with an injured sister chained across from me. The only option is to keep Seb talking. "Did you learn about Molinare before or after you were dishonorably discharged?"

His smile falls. Seb peers at me as though seeing me for the first time.

"What did you do?" My words are breathless. "Kidnap Afghan twins?"

He needs us. He didn't need Chang. He wants us alive. Fully functioning.

"Mourning," he says, his eyes sharp. "I was grieving my dead brother and the horrifying way in which he died. I was so emotional, I struck the officer who tried to remove Baptiste from the tent, to ready his body for transport back to France."

We lock eyes.

Valentin's phantom voice fills my ears—*Have you been watching the news?*

No, I've been busy mourning, I snapped in his office.

Understanding mingles with disgust before I can dash the thought: I would have done the same.

He searches for something in a cardboard box. A book, maybe. A fresh femur. "After I was discharged, I made good use of my time. Studies show twin rats can withstand exposure to nerve agents and doses of ricin longer than single births. Twin human fetuses recognize each other as nonparasitic organisms in the womb. This ability to differentiate between good and bad foreign agents must have further utility." His voice grows quiet, thoughtful. "What is it that makes the two of you together stronger than the one of you alone? Is it your blood? Your muscle tissue? Your cellular composition? I've tested each of these in my other subjects, and none has shown the strength to withstand chemical agents—none as I believe identical twin blood will. If I can prove that—" He breaks off and turns from the shelf, a cable trailing from his fist, his voice rising again. "If other scientists had had the courage Molinare did, the willingness to push boundaries, then Baptiste might not have had to die."

The fervor that lights his eyes sparks a flicker of recognition in me. We were in Angela's apartment, my second day here. Seb was trying to convince me of some extrasensory ability twins possess.

"What you're looking for isn't plausible," I say now. "Some extrasensory thing, if it exists, doesn't translate to cellular—"

His backhand connects with my cheek, slamming my head to the other side. Ringing fills my ear canal, like a gong struck inside my skull, then deepens to buzzing. An image from the Champs-Élysées fills my thoughts: Seb crushing a fly against his bare skin. No flinch. No wince. No spark of empathy.

Seb's mouth pulls into a frown. "Do not dismiss me, Shayna. I will find a cure, whatever it takes."

Angela continues playing deaf and dumb as Seb raises a type of syringe pump with a heavy cylindrical base—a small motor with a long cord trailing to his feet.

"Are you ready?"

"For what?" My voice is wispy, beaten.

"For your first tattoo." Seb tightens the ink cartridge on the tiny motor. "Did you know the local traffickers like to brand their product? Once I dispose of your bodies, the police will observe these tattoos—and the gunshots I'll administer to your heads—and conclude you were victims of human trafficking gone awry."

A notch, then a tug on the cable, and the machine clicks on. The whirring motor abruptly shrieks with all the ambience of a dentist's office, only infinitely more terrifying, because we're in a cave from God knows how many centuries ago filled with enough medical gear for a field unit in Kabul. I inch backward, my hands and feet bound, planting my back against the wall, trapped. My toes point, waiting for the first puncture, as Seb looms closer and grips my left ankle. My teeth clench in the interim, grinding tighter, my molars scraping, looking for purchase, some resistance, until finally the tattoo gun is at my feet.

He leans in. "Do not move."

The needles stab the skin of my ankle, just above the knotty bone, the lateral malleolus, and along the fibula. Pain radiates outward like a sound wave across my nerves, propelling the awful sensation through each layer of muscle and bone. Their rhythm jars like a jackhammer until I find an almost easy tempo to it that allows me to ignore the screams coming from my mouth.

"Hold still, Shayna!" Seb drops the gun and clamps a hand on my calf. "I cannot tattoo a dead body. I learned that with the hospital cadaver I left in the Seine," he growls. The whirr of the machine begins again while I steal a glance at Seb's table of tools. Angela's quiet stress radiates, and I try to withdraw to somewhere inside me, too.

You can't logic him to death.

I was wrong. I've been wrong for so long that it felt right. Angela's belief that we are connected via some ethereal twin plane and my obstinate belief in the opposite—in science, logic, and myself—probably grew out of reactions to one another. To how society pitted us against each other, insisted that we were antithetical, and we, foolishly, fed into the idea with our behaviors. I played the favorite with our parents, secretly loving it, insistent that mine was the only way, instead of realizing it was merely half the picture. We have always needed each other to be our best. To push each other out of our comfort zones and help the other be more than what she is—from ganging up as kids to get our favorite food for dinner, to my eighth-grade presentation that Angela completed while pretending to be me. I think of Angela's unsent emails and the way in which she strove for the middle ground between our defaults—for balance—here in Paris. But it wasn't enough for her. And moving on to medical school wouldn't have been enough for me. I am most wholly myself when I'm with her; she is my first friend, my ephemeral enemy, and the only person in the world who would do anything for me, just like I'd do for her. We are better together.

When Seb finishes he stops to admire his work. "Voilà. A perfect Gemini symbol, despite your antics. The curved bars were difficult, but I have had good practice recently."

"I think your brother would be proud," I reply.

Seb raises his eyes to mine. Angela shifts across from us. Nervous energy vibrates in the air. My flesh throbs, but I focus on my game of What Would Angela Do. She always knew to give people what they want, to intuit what they desire.

Seb lays the tattoo gun down. He studies me. "How magnanimous."

"I mean it. I came all the way from San Diego for Angela. I understand what it's like to do anything for your sibling." *Sometimes you have to go along to get along, Shayna.* Angela's words from her email pulse in my head. Play by his rules. Give him what he wants. "You loved your brother. If my sister were dying in a desert from some poisonous gas, I would be thanking you for finding a cure."

Dark eyes narrow to slits. "Baptiste was always afraid of me when we were children. But I loved him; you're right." He comes closer. "Medicine is the only way out for any of us, Shayna. I hope you see that. And you will contribute to the field. Just not as the doctor you intended."

He wheels a steel table from the corner to the middle of the room. He begins counting his instruments: three scalpels, a pair of surgical scissors, a retractor, a dermatome, clamps, two syringes, a spray bottle of antiseptic, a coiled tube, and a roll of paper towels.

Think, think, think. Weltering pity ratchets my throat. What does Seb want? It's Jean-Luc's words that provide the answer: *psychopaths— those are the ones who sneak up on you.* All of Seb's tears over Angela were an act. He lacks empathy. He's arrogant and rational to a fault. What I say has to be true in some respect, and also flattering. I clear my throat. "Seb?"

He pauses his tally with a huff. "Yes?"

"Do you remember that afternoon on the park bench? I didn't say anything then, but I need you to know something. That day I denied my feelings for you out of some loyalty to my sister—misplaced loyalty. Because she's only ever brought emotional upheaval into my life. But with you, Seb . . ." I meet his gaze. Dark blue stares back, bloodshot and round with cautious curiosity. "With you, I met my intellectual equal. And I threw it all away for a sister who moved six thousand miles from me. I was wrong to walk a path that diverged from you, from anyone I truly connected with. I guess it's all in the past now. But I had to say it."

Instead of excitement or a smile, the show of affection I wanted, he doesn't blink.

The curiosity recedes. Tentative appreciation hardens into dark fury that clouds his face and flares his nostrils. He grabs me by the shoulders, dropping his gun and kicking the wheeled table behind him. "Have you heard nothing I have said? *Misplaced loyalty?* Loyalty to your sister is the *only* thing you should feel in this world." His grip tightens, bruising me, and he shakes me like a child. "You should thank the heavens every day that she is still alive. That you were given this gift of being a twin, and a bond deeper than anything!"

He shakes me again, and my head bangs against rock. Stars crack across my vision, and I see Angela move in fits and starts as though she too feels the pain tearing across my skull.

"You will never know what you are missing until it is too late!" he roars with emotion.

Angela's leg continues to flail as clarity returns to my eyes. The table, the one holding Seb's supplies, has been pushed backward during his lunge forward—into Angela's reach.

"What if she's not worth the sacrifice?" I press on, giving Angela the best shot I can. "What if—"

Angela stretches for the aluminum tray. Her chains clang, and Seb turns at the noise, but I cry out, "Baptiste will never know! He'll never know how devoted you are in his death, how much you loved him, just like my sister will never understand me."

Seb slams me into the dirt, looming over me. Red, bloodshot eyes plead in outrage, and his lips pull back over his teeth. "Do you not see? The missing brother in my life has been my greatest ghost. I would make any sacrifice for him, even in his death. You have no idea the loss of a sibling, a missing sister from your life—"

Quickly, Angela withdraws the scalpel from the tray. She sits back and slices the plastic that binds her ankles in a swift upward motion. Placing the scalpel between her heels, she rubs the zip tie of her wrists back and forth, then shifts and presses the blade beneath her knee, sliding her wrists up and down until the plastic snaps. She stands.

"Misplaced loyalty," Seb says again, spitting the words, tears filling his eyes. "Shows how little you—"

Angela doesn't hesitate. She carves the scalpel through the air and stabs Seb's lower spine, again and again. Blood spurts as he releases an animal scream. He arches backward, then falls off me, his body contracting wildly, his hands scrabbling at the wound.

Angela slices through the ties binding my ankles and wrists, then whirls back to where Seb hunches over in the corner. I get to my feet, blood oozing from my new tattoo, entranced by the scene. Wrapping an arm around Seb, Angela rams the scalpel into his back again, tearing a soprano scream from his chest.

"How does it feel, Seb? Does it hurt? Do *you* like that?" Angela twists the blade deeper. *"Do you?"* Her voice is shrill, reaching a fevered pitch.

I shift my weight back and forth, waiting for the cue to run. Adrenaline pounds through my limbs. "Angela, we should go—let's go!"

"I will find you," Seb growls. "I have your passport—you cannot leave."

Angela and Seb are wrestling—dancing, almost—and as they move to the doorway, Seb gasps as Angela does something else from behind. Their hands dip into each of his pockets, but he whips out a passport—Angela's passport, I assume. Shocked, she releases him and tries to grab it, but he yanks it backward.

She leaps toward him, and, in one swift movement, he rips the passport in two. A wicked smile upturns his cheeks. He whispers something in French, too low, too fast for me, and she launches at him and stabs him in the chest.

"Angela!" I scream; she yanks her fist back, withdrawing the scalpel, and Seb's hands clap to his sternum, his face gone pale. She arches, then swipes the scalpel across his throat like it's warm butter, his insides dripping then gushing onto his white shirt, a Jackson Pollock canvas brought to life. Tree-trunk arms forget his chest and fly up, trying to hold the blood inside. Red eyes turn to mine, begging, pleading, and the seconds seem to tick by like hours until his body finally buckles to the ground.

I stand frozen. Shallow breaths rack Angela's frame while her face crumples at the carnage seeping across the dirt floor. A moan of chilled air carries into the bunker, freezing the sweat across my skin; the salty smell of the beach rises from somewhere in my memory.

Angela snaps to. She crosses to me—eyes wide, her stride deliberate, mechanical. Meeting my stunned expression for the first time since she cut herself free, she is all business.

"Now, where are those antibacterial wipes Seb mentioned?"

Chapter 33

Angela is alive. Seb is dead. We are safe. Repeat.

I stumble along behind my sister, my new internal mantra on a loop. Thinking it a dozen times somehow doesn't equate to believing yet. Dribbling water nearby directs our path in the dark. We're still underground and near the Seine, which means we're near an exit. My legs feel weak despite only having to walk fifteen minutes to get back to the official path. My arms continue to throb from Seb's crushing grip. Angela adjusts to the darkness like she never left, whereas, even with the key-ring flashlight, I fall twice on the uneven dirt path.

"You okay, Shay?"

"Yeah. Where was that manhole you mentioned?"

"Over here."

We continue forward and find crisscrossing bones wedged together, forming two narrow walls. I should be used to the sight by now, but I startle all the same. Angela plunges forward.

While Angela quickly began rummaging around for supplies—a bandage for me, food and water for us both—I continued to stand still, staring at Seb's body for another five minutes. *Angela is alive. Seb is dead. We are safe.* We found pamphlets for the Notre Dame crypts, dozens of printed emails from Angela's inbox, and surgery textbooks in Seb's steel cabinet, along with several handguns. We found a bowl of house keys and identity cards, one of which belonged to Clément Gress, the body found in a dumpster. Seb's first victim. When Angela shoved my clothes at me and said, "We have to move," I obeyed without conscious thought. Flashbacks to my sister's expression when she brought the scalpel to Seb's throat were still playing in my mind.

A domed hub extends in four different directions, four tunnels. A series of iron rungs leads up to the surface.

Angela turns to me. "All right, this is our exit. I don't want to run into anyone else down here."

"After all that—is there anyone worse?"

She dips her chin. "Depends. Did you find my bordels note?"

Mathieu. And the large scratch across his chest, from Angela, at the speakeasy brothel. "I did. I thought maybe Mathieu was working with Jean-Luc and they were involved in human trafficking down here."

She laughs, but her eyes remain tight. "I don't know about this Jean-Luc, but Mathieu was. The brothel couldn't survive without trafficking victims—although some women choose to be there. They think it's better than on the streets. Mathieu got a little . . . aggressive the last time I saw him, when I was researching the different catacombs entrances. The clue I left—I was hoping you would see the manhole in the cubed entryway and stop before going inside. He didn't hurt you, did he?"

I shake my head. "I'm just glad you're okay. And I'm beyond ready to leave this place."

"Same." She places a foot on the first ladder rung, and that's when the tiny voice inside me that's been anticipating this moment raises its hand.

"Shouldn't we go to the police before flying out?" I ask. "We have time. Maybe we should tell them about the brothel, all of this." I wave a hand around us. "There's no guarantee we can even get on the same flight." If the women in the brothel are victims of trafficking, I want to ensure they get help. But the desire isn't wholly based in selflessness; we killed someone. Despite it being done in extreme self-defense, Seb is dead.

Angela shakes her head, then drops back down. "The police already know about the brothel. Mathieu said some of them are patrons, and it's only the Pollyanna cops they worry about. I need to get out of here. I can't stay in this country one second longer. Besides, I killed Seb. I did the actual act, and the police must think I'm involved in Manu's murder, given my history with her—just like Seb wanted. It looks like a pattern. I can't risk it." She comes to my side where I continue to stand in the middle of the hub.

Imagine me, reluctant to leave underground.

"Shay, I don't know if you ever liked being a twin." She waves off my protests. "But I think you like being a sister. Do this for me, please. Trust me, as your sister. Leaving is the best solution for you and for me. It's time to go." She lifts her hands, palms up. The yellow track lighting is nonexistent here, but the flashlight shows that blood stains her palms. The pair of us will never make it through the airport. Identical twins, filthy and bloody—we'll have all eyes on us from the moment we hobble through the doors of Charles de Gaulle.

I take her hands and cringe at their slippery feel. "Angela, I love being your sister and your twin, always have. Even if I showed it in different ways. I'm sorry I failed you over the last few years, after Mom and Dad died, and the last week. But that changes now. You're taking the plane ticket and my passport. I'll stay behind to make sure the police know everything they need, and to tell them you did what you did in self-defense. I choose you this time, Gel."

Angela's face goes slack. "Sh—Shayna, no," she stammers. "No, we're going together. I can't leave you."

Maybe Nour will visit me in jail. Or Valentin will sneak me crois-sants. "I'll be fine. It can't take more than a week to sort through everything. I'll be back home before you're unpacked." I dig into my messenger bag for my passport and hand it to her.

"We're going together." She pushes it back. "I can't take that."

"It's our best shot. There's no way we can both get out on one pass-port, and any kind of damage to a passport invalidates it—yours won't work. You've served enough time down here."

She hesitates, examining my resolve, probably gauging whether I'll crack. "I don't know what to say. It's been so long that I've felt . . . a lot of things. Abandoned, disregarded. I guess, jealous." She pauses to tuck a ratty strand of hair back into the fray. "I was wrong. It was shortsighted to hold on to that for so long. It's no secret I've always had issues with Mom and Dad, but . . . I would spend another night here to get them back."

I stare at my sister, not knowing how to reply. "They . . . they loved us. They loved you."

"They loved you more, though."

I shake my head. "They weren't perfect. No one is. We just had more in common for a lot of our lives. I'm absolutely guilty of exploiting that at times, and making you feel . . . I don't know. The odd lady out."

A smile pinches Angela's face at the self-description she often used. Deep breath. "I'm so sorry. It's my fault that they—"

"Hey, don't." She shakes her head. "Let's not do this now."

"No—I've been waiting three years to say this face-to-face. Upright," I add, recalling our conversation on the ground of the twin bones room. My voice falters. Tears well in my eyes, blurring Angela's already dim features. "It's my fault that Mom and Dad died. If I hadn't asked them to come get me . . . they'd still be alive. It's been eating away at me, and I understand if you can't ever forgive me. But I need to say it. I'm sorry."

Tears run down my sister's face. She's quiet a moment, and I feel the familiar ache in my chest, anticipating the ax of guilt to my bruised heart, exactly what I deserve. She fixes me with dark eyes. "Shayna. You are not responsible for their deaths."

I don't reply. My entire body tenses, too scared to break the moment.

She steps closer. "You couldn't have known what would happen. It's not your fault."

Silence swims between us as I begin to tremble. I let another moment pass, give her the time to add a *but* or to take back her words. She doesn't.

"Really?" I choke out.

She shakes her head. "It's not your fault, Shayna."

A sob escapes my clenched throat, and I lift two hands to my face. Her words of forgiveness are sweeter than anything I'd imagined or hoped for. I'd convinced myself they would never come. "It is my fault—no, it is. But . . . I'm working on moving forward from that."

Angela wipes her cheeks. "I'll help you."

She takes my hands, and for a moment I forget where we are. Warmth fills my chest seeing her this way again after so long—loving, kind, the Angela who can brighten a room by entering, the effusive sister and the balance to my good, my bad, and then some.

"Angela, what changed for you here? You seem so . . . happy."

She gives a bottled laugh. "I am. Or, I was. At first, being so far away was the answer. I no longer had to wonder whether you cared or Mom and Dad cared, by the way you included me in something or didn't. There was no ambiguity; there was nine hours of time difference. It made me really take stock of our interactions and see them better, not listen to the usual voice that questioned all that. I learned to trust more of what you were saying before they died. Then, after, I really was alone. And I said some things I shouldn't have. And I'm sorry for that.

The distance and isolation, then, forced me to dig deep, and discover some—"

"Stability from within?" I finish.

"Yeah . . . that's it."

We share a smile. "Twin thought processes and twin emotional issues, huh?"

Her soft laugh mingles with mine. "Funny how that goes."

I allow myself the first deep breath since we trudged out of the room. "Well. You've got a flight to catch."

"I have to admit," she says, "I don't quite understand the changes you've undergone, either, and I don't understand why you're sacrificing yourself like this for me. But thank you." She throws her arms around me with more strength than I would have guessed, had I not just witnessed the extent of it when faced with death.

"You're my sister, Gel," I say, simply. There's no better answer.

My fingerprints aren't on the scalpel, the murder weapon, and the surveillance video will show the truth: Angela killed Seb in self-defense, and Seb was the serial killer all along. I'll be released within days. I can do this for Angela after all these years of her feeling slighted. After she made the ultimate sacrifice—taking on the burden of Seb's death, and doing what I know in my heart I never could to ensure our escape and safety.

"Can I ask you something?" I release her from the hug and pull back. "Do you remember that day on the beach, when . . . when you tried to bury me in the sand?"

Her eyebrows pinch together. "You mean the day you almost died by jellyfish sting?"

"What?"

Angela steps back. "You got stung so badly you couldn't walk the two blocks to the house. You wouldn't let me leave you to go get help, so I washed your legs and arms with seawater. Used sand to remove the venom. You were burned everywhere, so I had to cover you in sand and scrape off the jelly stingers with a seashell."

Jellyfish. I've been terrified of jellyfish since I was a kid, when a huge bloom came into La Jolla Cove. The normally light-blue waterline was covered in translucent pink and purple mushroom tops for days. In my mind, I'd separated the bloom's arrival and the pain of the jellyfish sting from the trauma of my sister trying to suffocate me, standing above me with a soda can and pail empty of sand and a vacant expression; I remembered both events without realizing they were the same memory. Understanding clicks into place. Almost. "Why was I pinned? Beneath two massive branches?"

Angela shakes her head. "You were in so much pain, you couldn't lie still. You were scratching the stingers and spreading the venom. You were near delirious. You don't remember any of that? Mom bathed you in vinegar afterward."

We look at each other. My sister wasn't trying to harm me or acting out because I stole her doll that morning. She was trying to help me. Relief courses down my limbs. Through a watery gaze, I see Angela's reassuring, if confused, face. "The logs were there to hold you down. You were always stronger than you think."

She gives me another squeeze, then limps up the ladder rungs leading to the manhole cover. My passport juts from her back pocket. We agree we can't both be seen emerging when it's not yet dark. At the top of the rungs, she pushes, grunts against the cast iron, but it won't budge. Panic squeezes my heart, and I climb up beside her. We push together. After her two weeks of hiding from Seb and my exhaustion, it takes intense effort, but we manage to lift then push it to the side. She kisses my cheek, an arm slung around my neck. "Thank you, Shayna."

I pat her hand and feel the bones of her wrist. "See you soon." Her feet disappear above into the red-streaked sky, then she's gone.

Alone in the catacombs, I lean back against a rock wall for the agreed-upon five minutes to give her a proper head start. I wait for the pummeling fear to surge, to take my breath and clench my stomach. But it doesn't. The most frightening thing I could ever experience has already occurred—and the most euphoric. Even if I'm not certain what I would have done, I'm grounded in the knowledge that Angela did what she had to. She did it for us. And we'll choose each other from now on.

Chapter 34

Jean-Luc found me within minutes. The time that elapsed between Angela escaping above and Jean-Luc climbing into the tunnels below was barely enough time to say *Amélie*. I listened in a daze as he explained he was never actually employed by the American embassy; to the contrary, he was an officer with the United Nations unit investigating international trafficking.

I didn't understand at first—blamed my disorientation on dehydration, trauma, shock—but he kept going in slow, measured tones until I had no choice but to believe him. *My team suspected the catacombs were a possible point of transit for traffickers. When Sebastien Bronn was spotted exiting the catacombs from an unusual point of entry, we became interested in him; when he began spending time with Angela, a young woman, we added him to our watch list. I have stuck with you, Shayna, in the hopes of learning more about him and his ties to Paris's black market.*

My fingers were numb from the cold, but my heart surged with this knowledge. The newspaper headline in the lobby of Angela's building, the brothel madam believing I was police and almost kicking me out, the ticker along the cab's television screen. Jean-Luc wasn't stalking Angela or me to abduct us; he was working to stop human trafficking.

While Jean-Luc wasn't able to prevent Angela from being abducted, he had been following me all week, certain that Seb would try something. He lost me after the club Friday night, and it took him a few hours before he realized I went underground.

Babbling with relief at this point, I told him everything—Seb kidnapping us, his plans to find a cure for chemical attacks, his emulation of the human traffickers' mode of operation, Angela being alive—then stopped short. He asked where Angela was now.

Shadows surrounded us then but none as thick as the partition that dropped between us. With two hours left before ensuring Angela had a shot out of here, I only had half-truths to offer. Whatever we shared during the week together, it was as different people. Even as the memory of his arms around me, and the soft fabric of his shirt against my cheek, pulsed behind my eyelids.

I spoke to the void over his shoulder. "I'm not sure where she is."

Jean-Luc didn't blink. "Is that true?"

"Between the two of us, I think I have a better record of telling the truth. You've been lying to me this whole week."

He licked his lips. "Not the whole week, Shayna. I shared things with you I haven't shared with anyone else."

A depressed silence filled the already dank space. "Something still doesn't add up," I began. "Seb wasn't a trafficker. He was a sick man who thought he could find a cure for mustard gas. Why did he write a fake email pointing to you as Angela's attacker?"

Jean-Luc peered down the cavern I'd just crawled out from. "My guess is to drive you away from me. If he had people following you, I'll bet he knew you were spending time with me and that I was linked to the UN. Probably to throw off the authorities and yourself and make it as hard as he did to catch him."

Fatigue draped across me at that point. Seb had been single-minded to the end.

I asked to wait up above for the police and the UN officers Jean-Luc told me were coming. When they arrived, they ventured down two by two, like Noah's chosen investigators. The sun dipped behind large buildings across the square, the tip of the Eiffel Tower blazing farther beyond.

When their team emerged a good while later, Jean-Luc crouched before me and waved Seb's silver laptop. He had watched some of the surveillance footage of our captivity before we escaped and found video of each of Seb's other experiments. He asked me to share any information I might have on Angela's whereabouts, to get to the bottom of things and learn the whole truth—"Shayna, please." I repeated the same line—that Angela had disappeared, left me below, and I couldn't tell him where she was now. He spoke with an earnestness, a vulnerability, that reminded me of our time at Angela's apartment and the Deux Moulins restaurant. For a moment, the butterflies in my stomach fluttered their wings, waiting for the cue to commit to a full swell and build a storm of pleasant tension. The impulse to pick up back where we left off and before I read Seb's fake email—back when I thought I was the one with secrets—was there. Knowing I remained capable of those emotions, of that connection with a virtual stranger, was reassuring. Jean-Luc and I had almost crossed that line, from strangers to familiars—maybe lovers. But that time had passed. Aching filled my chest at the thought before cautious hope replaced it. The world was wide, and I might finally be ready to explore it again.

"What time is it?" I asked.

His shoulders dropped. "Ten twenty."

Relief bloomed in my chest, and I clutched the blanket I was given tighter around my shoulders. If Angela hadn't made it past customs, Jean-Luc would have known about it by then. Anything on that laptop would only substantiate that her actions were in self-defense. The police might have to hire a video specialist, but someone could check the eye color of the twin holding the scalpel. Mine have heterochromia—two different colors of green and brown. Staying behind proves that I chose Angela this time, our collective safety, what's best for both of us. And finally exonerates me in her eyes—both brown.

"Shayna?" a strong voice calls from the corridor of filing cabinets that leads out and into the lobby.

The comfort of the police holding cell took me by surprise. Its singular cushy bench might serve as a bed in a pinch, and a straight-backed, carved wooden chair in the corner could have been found in Delphine Rousseau's office. Nothing adorns the stone walls, but a stack of outdated magazines fills a woven basket at my feet. They've let me keep my own clothing for now, and I was thankful to retain the wool blanket I was given at the catacombs.

I raise my head and lurch backward; a petite woman, a ghost, stands at the metal bars, like some rendition of Jacob Marley with glasses. Asymmetrically cut black hair and the bedazzled jean jacket she wears can only identify her as one person.

"Chang? How are you—?"

"Oh, I'm alive, all right. Barely." She lowers her voice and beckons me closer. A sense of déjà vu washes over me as I cross the ten-foot space, just like the day I met her in the apartment building. She casts another glance at the lobby, then reaches through the bars to pat my arm. "How are you?"

"Chang!" Gleeful laughter tumbles from my mouth, a long trill that surprises us both, and I hug her small frame. My throat clamps shut, and I have to blink back new tears. "How is that possible? Seb killed you."

"That Sebastien was too transparent. Obsessed with the catacombs and those rooms since he was a kid. He used to tell me all his discoveries when we ran into each other in the tunnels." She muses on these things like it was a year instead of just hours ago he tried to kill us both. "After he took you girls, he came back for me. But I climbed into a series of pocket spaces he didn't know about and hid until I was sure he was gone. I passed out for a while—concussions will do that—and by the time I got out, it was Sunday afternoon." She rubs her shoulder, massaging between large costume rubies on her shoulder pads. "I called the police right away and told them your location. Did they get to you quickly?" The skin below her eyes is a purplish black, half-moons reflecting her own battle back to fresh air. A long red scratch covers her neck from ear to clavicle.

"Not quick enough," I reply. Chang nods like she already knows all the details I can't say in this setting. "I'm so sorry, Chang. About everything. Thank you. I . . . I had to find my sister." Aloud, the words sound hollow; they don't dull the fact that helping us almost cost this woman her life.

She smiles. "I understand. I'm glad the pair of you is okay. She is okay, isn't she?"

I nod, not quite trusting the police aren't listening to my answer.

"What about your flight?" Chang asks. "Did you miss it already?"

"By about twelve hours. Not sure when I'm going home now, but I'm hopeful in the next week. I . . . lost my passport, so I'll need the embassy to replace it before I can leave. The police are still reviewing the surveillance and checking to make sure my story holds up. They think Seb kidnapped Angela, took her underground, then went back above to purchase cigarettes from the tabac. The time frame is narrow, but it points to holes in his original alibi. I'm hoping for news tomorrow."

Chang takes my hand in hers. "That's a good plan. Once I learned you were here, I had to come and verify you were in one piece. You can take care of yourself now, Shayna—it's okay to. You know that, right?"

A small smile spreads across my chapped lips. "Yes, I know now."

"Good girl. Well, we certainly got the adrenaline rush I wanted, didn't we?" Chang smirks. She gives my hand a kiss. "Let's get going. No sense in staying close to the beehive."

"I'm . . . I can't go anywhere, Chang."

"Of course you can. I posted your bail."

"You posted fifteen thousand euros?"

Chang reaches through the bars of my cell and slides a hand under my chin. "You'll pay me back when you become a big-shot doctor. Or judge. Or deejay."

Tears stream down my face as the guard approaches from behind her. He unlocks my holding cell, and Chang wraps me in her arms.

I sign several forms with carbon copies attached, each one stating I'm in charge of all my faculties and will return when summoned. My translator, Jean-Luc, elucidates each clause, careful to explain the sentences I stumble over; he sails through the pages with all the levity he showed when I first found him at the café beside the Sorbonne.

After I was fingerprinted, both he and Valentin spoke to me together in my cell, and Jean-Luc stayed close by to write out his reports. The United Nations had been working with the police to curb trafficking, but Jean-Luc's assignment to monitor me was strictly need to know. As Valentin explained, he began reexamining Seb as a suspect, as more than the grieving boyfriend, when the morgue director saw us leave together on Monday, despite Valentin warning me to avoid strangers. Valentin had learned of Seb's dishonorable discharge, but it was only after he dug further and discovered Baptiste's death and Seb's personal interest in the catacombs that he became concerned. The note that Valentin slipped under Angela's door was meant to encourage me to stay put while the police tracked down Seb and brought him in for questioning.

Seb's pattern of tattooing his victims, of linking them forever to himself, was likely a form of possession, when everyone he'd loved had been taken from him. The Gemini symbol, chosen as his crest, would have alluded to his belief that twins were the key to scientific advancement. The act of tattooing his victims paid homage to his hero, Molinare.

Valentin pauses a phone call as Chang and I pass his glass-walled office. The measured nod he gives me is softened with a smile before he barks into the receiver in English, "I don't care if she is in a meeting, get me the American ambassador now!"

Steps from the main glass doors, fear and anticipation mingle in my chest, so close to freedom and all that it symbolizes—a new start despite recent weeks, months, years of self-destructive action. A new chapter, with Angela once I land stateside, on a more even plane and celebrating our duality, ignoring society's fascination with singular labels—the emotive twin, the angry twin. I've been waiting so long for someone to say it's okay to move forward—waiting to tell Angela about our parents' deaths in person and for her to forgive me, always seeking external validation, instead of forgiving myself—that I missed the option. As Chang said, I can take care of myself—it's okay to. Setting healthy boundaries and expectations is okay.

I slide inside the back seat of a black car commissioned by Chang, then watch as representatives of the press trail our path until we turn a corner out of sight. The route to the hotel room Chang booked is short, but it is filled with the only peace I've known since landing in Paris. Clear blue fills the sky when I exit the car. I stare straight up until my eyes burn. The crash of waves resonates in my eardrums, and this time, for the first time in years, the fear that always spooled through my core at the memory is silent.

Shouts in French rise from the hotel lobby as reporters stream out: *Miss Darby!* Le Monde News *would like a quote from you! Would you care to comment? What can you tell the world?* Frenzied voices blur the rest, but I already know what I'll reply. When I raise my face to the slanted afternoon light and the rows of media eager for a glimpse of my unwashed hair and streaked cheeks, my comment is simple: "Twin for the win."

Acknowledgments

I distinctly recall when I first saw mixed-race couples and their children presented on camera, in television commercials. I was in college, in the mid-2000s. I'd long ago accepted that standardized testing would never allow me to accurately describe my ethnicity by checking more than one bubble on the Scantron, so I was at once shocked and thrilled. Pretty great to be writing about them today.

Endless thanks to my literary agent, Jill Marr, who plucked me from a Twitter pitch party to get things started. I could not have journeyed this dazzling road without you, truly. Your spark, insight, and good humor have all been more than I hoped for. You are the very best.

Thank you to Megha Parekh, who believed in this book from the get-go and not only understood it but valued its unique set of characters. I am so appreciative of you as a guide and editor, to have your brains and vision in my corner; you knew exactly what my book needed to level up. To Caitlin Alexander, who lit my world on fire with her enviable judgment, thank you for reading and rereading, and rereading, still. I could not have asked for a better developmental editor to cut out subplots and make these sisters shine. To Sarah Shaw and the entire crew at Thomas & Mercer, thank you for making my dream a reality.

Special gratitude to Arielle Max Drisko, who convinced me that writing a full-length novel was possible—a thought I carried with me for two more years before I actually attempted the feat (despite many journals and rambling diary entries from childhood). Additional call-outs must be made to writer and editor Nicole Tone, for taking my story and nudging it along when my manuscript was still in its early form.

To my friends in France who puzzled at me when I first said I was writing a book ("—de . . . quoi?") and yet let me mine their histories a bit more, thank you for smiling and serving more Calvados. With express recognition to the city of Paris, the Paris catacombs, and the six million-plus souls that reside belowground, thank you for serving as inspiration for the setting of this story, and giving me some of the best experiences of my life. A bientôt, j'espère!

This book couldn't have been written without the expertise of Dr. Erin Healy, my genius friend and generous resource, even as I asked question after question regarding things clearly not scientifically possible. I appreciate you. Any error in this book regarding the practice of medicine, the subject of science as a whole or otherwise, is my fault alone (or that of my short-lived biology major).

To my writing friends and critique partners who read this story in its first, intermediate, and final iterations—Heather Lettere, Elaine Roth, Raimey Gallant, and Cathy Holst—thank you for the quick reads and gut checks. In unique ways, you each kept me going with your camaraderie, talent, and incisive commentary. Thank you a thousand times over.

To my in-laws, your support of this whole writing thing, since day one, has been striking and thoughtful. I completely lucked out with you all.

To my family, spanning the length of California, who have always been supportive, if not entirely sure what to make of the creative itch I've had since middle school, thank you for being part of my story, for forming the first pages of my life with your love, good food, and group photos (turned photo collages, turned never-ending photo albums). Big families are the best.

To my thoughtful, artistic, and brilliant friends all over who asked for updates, my parents, and, in particular, my mother, who always offers to read, my wonderful brothers, Thomas, Andrew, and Ben, and my incredible sisters who inspire me every day, Kimberly and Liana, I am so grateful for each of you.

Finally, to Kevin. Thank you for allowing me to turn a kitchen table into a writing office, for the home-cooked meals, for your unfailing belief in me and this book, for being my first reader and favorite dance partner. I promise, one day I'll learn how to follow. #PC

About the Author

Photo © 2019 Jana Foo Photography

Originally from Sacramento, Elle Marr explored the urban wilderness of Southern California before spending three wine-and-cheese-filled years in France. There she earned a master's degree from the Sorbonne University in Paris. Now she lives and writes outside Portland, Oregon, with her husband and one very demanding feline. When she's not busy writing her next novel, she's most likely thinking about it. Connect with her online at www.ellemarr.com, or on Facebook, Twitter, or Instagram.